NIGHT RULES

NIGHT RULES

A SEAN WYNN THRILLER

KEITH J. WEBER

ISBN (ebook): 979-8-9898229-0-4

ISBN (print): 979-8-9898229-1-1

Cover design by GetCovers.com

To Patrice, with love and gratitude.

AUTHOR'S NOTE

NIGHT RULES involves mature themes and contains depictions of sexual violence. While the events of *NIGHT RULES* are fictional, sadly, sexual violence and trafficking are not. If you or someone you know needs assistance, please contact the National Sexual Assault Hotline at 1-800-656-4673 or the National Human Trafficking Hotline at 1-888-373-7888. You may also visit their websites at **https://www.rainn.org** or **https://humantraffickinghotline.org.**

For more Sean Wynn thrillers, including a free short story, visit
www.keithjweber.com

PROLOGUE

Friday, 3:41 p.m.

Heavy rain slapped like firecrackers against the windshield, blurring the landscape beyond. Despite the wipers furious pounding, Ann could barely make out the lonely stretch of two-lane Wyoming highway. Slowing, she flipped on her headlights to pierce the darkening gloom. If she couldn't see the approaching cars, at least maybe they'd see her.

The problem was, there hadn't been any cars. Not for the last twenty minutes. Not since an old red Jeep raced past her coming out of the small town of Douglas.

Maybe they know something I don't, she thought. *Probably trying to outrun a damn tornado. Stupid cell phone's useless. No service in half this god-forsaken state.*

She tapped the AM radio icon on the dashboard touchscreen, scanning for a local weather report. A gnawing sense of isolation grew in the pit of her stomach. Even the white van that had been behind her since leaving the convenience store was no longer visible in the rearview mirror.

Maybe I should pull over and wait this thing out.

The decision was made for her when the faint flash of red tail-lights leaked through the rainy veil. Lightning ripped the sky, revealing the old red Jeep with its hazard lights flashing, parked diagonally across the road, blocking both lanes. Ann slowed further, feeling both relief and sympathy at the sight of two men out in the deluge. One knelt near the rear of the Jeep with a tire iron in his hand, the other held an umbrella in a futile attempt to block the rain.

Crappy time for a flat.

The kneeling man rose as she pulled to a stop and hustled through the downpour toward Ann's car. The second man dropped the umbrella and followed a few steps behind.

Probably need someone to call a tow truck.

Ann cracked her window as the man approached, ready to ask how she could help, then recoiled in horror as he raised the tire iron in a backhand swing and smashed it against the glass, shattering the window.

She screamed, but it was already too late. A hand punched through the broken glass, her left shoulder exploding as if by lightning. Her muscles convulsed, paralyzed as the electricity surged through her body. Bright flashes sparked across her vision as the current continued, excruciating and unrelenting, until darkness consumed the rain.

CHAPTER 1

Sunday

THE WIND TORE at Sean Wynn's face, causing tears to leak from behind his sunglasses. He leaned to the left, allowing his eight-hundred-pound Harley Davidson to drift across the double yellow lines as the memories flashed through his mind.

The restaurant. The tinkling of dishes and silverware. The quiet murmur of conversation.

Nicole. Her eyes bright, her smile beaming, leaning toward him across the table.

The sudden gunshots. People running, screaming.

The blood. So much blood.

The frantic blast of a semi truck's airhorn startled Wynn out of his stupor, shattering his resolve. He swerved the bike back into his own lane as the eighteen-wheeler thundered past. The blast of compressed air in front of the big rig's grill alternately pushing Wynn away from the truck, then sucking him back toward the huge trailer's rear tires.

He struggled to keep the bike upright, then glanced in his side mirror. The trucker's arm extended out the window in a single-finger salute.

The voice popped unbidden into his head. *Can't even do that right. Coward.*

He shook the voice away. Like the nightmares, it'd be back.

He'd thought after two years, the images would ease up.

They hadn't.

If anything, they'd become more frequent. Plaguing his days as well as his nights. His parents and friends insisting it wasn't his fault; the choir of voices in his head singing, *you know damn well it was.*

A second glance in the mirror showed the truck already a half-mile away.

There'll be another.

But deep down he knew he couldn't do it. Not to his parents. Or Nicole. Her memory, anyway.

He bowed his back, pulling his shoulders forward while pushing his abdomen back, stretching the muscles across his shoulder blades. *The infraspinatus,* if he remembered correctly. Just one of the many chronic aches and pains exacerbated by endless hours on two wheels.

Normally, his morning kata, a combination of martial arts and yoga recommended by one of his military doctors, eased the stiffness. It was the one routine, ingrained after eight years in the Marines, he'd been able to maintain.

Mostly.

But this morning he'd cut his workout short, the tiny closet the hotel called a gym being overrun by a women's college soccer team.

At thirty-six, they hadn't even noticed him.

Not that he didn't prefer it that way.

Not just with women, but people in general. There was a reason his blue jeans, a black t-shirt and leather jacket had become his standard daily apparel. At six-one and a hundred ninety pounds, there were often bigger guys in the room, but regular workouts in the decade since leaving the Corps had kept him in impressive shape.

Normally, he wore his hair short and sported a trim goatee, but since Nicole's death, he seldom bothered with shaving or haircuts, leaving his dark hair long, his straggly beard sprinkled with the first hints of gray. Add sunglasses and an extra inch-and-a-half in height from his heavy riding boots, and most people gave him a fairly wide berth.

Just the way he liked it.

The abbreviated workout had, however, allowed for an early start. He'd left the small mountain town southwest of Denver a little before seven. The sun, already well into the clear blue Colorado sky, illuminated the snow-tinged summits of the Rockies. The temperature, even now in the low-sixties, promised a beautiful day for a ride. If he pushed it, he could easily make it to Sturgis in less than eight hours. But on the bike, with the constant ache in his back, he'd take his time, maybe make a few stops along the way.

But not yet.

He merged onto Interstate 25 slicing through the middle of Denver, his pipes rumbling out a low, boiling rhythm that shattered the Sunday morning silence.

Someplace smaller. Maybe stop for gas in Cheyenne.

———

Above the roar of the interstate, Jessica Davies hit the snooze button for the fourth time. Grimacing, she rolled over and looked up at the ceiling.

Not spinning.

That was good.

She turned her head toward the sunlight streaming through the window and the bright blue sky beyond, but instantly regretted it, closing her eyes to ward off the scathing ache that pierced her head.

Despite her friends' insistence that closing down the bar was the only way to prove her thirtieth birthday didn't make her old, she'd convinced them to call it an evening shortly after midnight. Earlier than they wanted, but plenty late for her, considering the long drive she had ahead of her today. Besides, one thing was clear; she couldn't party like she used to.

It was a six-hour drive from Denver to her sister's place in Rapid City. Thankfully, during the first full week of August, the weather, other than the occasional Wyoming thunderstorm, wouldn't be an issue. She'd be there sometime this afternoon regardless.

Jessica made her way to the bathroom, then out to the kitchen to set the coffee going. Scrounging for a bottle of Advil in a drawer next to the refrigerator, she tipped two into her hand, grabbed a bottle of water from the fridge, and washed them down. Back in the bathroom, she stepped into the shower and breathed deep to let the steam fill her lungs. She let the water run long, hoping the steam would detoxify her pores, help rid her body of the evening's excess.

Eventually, she turned the water off and wrapped herself in an oversized bath towel. Grabbing another, she dried her dark hair as she went back to the kitchen and poured the coffee. Normally doctored with various creams and sweeteners, this morning she craved the bitterness of pure black.

She opened the curtains to the small balcony of her one-bedroom apartment, this time savoring the warmth as the sun shone through. It was mornings like this that made her appreciate living alone. No explanations necessary. No bullshit to worry about. The breakup with her last boyfriend had been a disaster. As a result, she hadn't been serious with anyone for a couple of years, not counting the occasional overnight guest.

Taking a seat at the table, Jessica grabbed a piece of fruit and finished her coffee, then dressed in blue jeans and a white V-neck. She pulled her suitcase into the hallway and took the elevator down to the garage, then towed her bag across the dim, musty space to her black Subaru Outback. She threw her bag in the back, hopped in, and checked the time.

9:03 a.m.

Only an hour later than she had planned.

No big deal.

Two hundred fifty miles north, in a two-story farmhouse set into the side of a small, wooded bluff, the residents were beginning to stir. Normally home to three men, its occupancy had swelled to seven as it was expected to be a busy week.

And really, what other options did they have? There wasn't much else around. Access to the home came by way of a mile-long dirt driveway before finally reaching pavement, which itself wasn't much more than a secondary county road. It was still more than three miles to the nearest neighbor, and eight miles to the closest highway.

Thirty yards north of the main house sat a large, trailside-style barn, typical of any working ranch.

On the outside, at least.

But inside, it rivaled the finest auto shop in the state. Large double doors on either end accessed a center aisle around which a dozen, fully outfitted work bays lined one wall and half of the other. Two large walls with a heavy steel door cordoned off the final quarter of the interior space.

Several cars and pickup trucks were parked within, some sparkling clean and ready to go, while others sat in various states of dismemberment and repair.

The third and final building on the property was a horse shed. Sizable by most standards, but small compared to the barn. At least a half-dozen horses, along with all the gear and hay needed to care for them, could be accommodated. Curiously, there were no horses on the property.

And while the house and barns could all use a fresh coat of paint and the yard had long gone to weed, the setting itself was rather picturesque. Like an oasis in the surrounding grassland, the entire homestead sat inside almost two thousand acres of sparse forest occurring naturally along the bluffs of an ancient river. A river that over eons had eroded the earth into a miles-wide delta between its valley walls but was now barely a trickle several miles away. The exposed rocks and pine trees along the side and top of the bluff gave the ranch a mountain-living feel and an extra level of privacy, despite being surrounded by millions of acres of wide-open prairie.

Inside the main house, a grizzled man in his mid-sixties was the first to make his way to the kitchen. At five feet ten inches and two hundred ten pounds, he was neither overly heavy nor overly slim, but time and gravity had clearly won the battle in dragging the bulk of his once-powerful body mass from his shoulders to his waist. A two-day growth of facial hair surrounded the cigarette that protruded from his lips, which clamped down on his most distinguishing feature, a mouthful of crooked teeth.

Having grown up in and around Albuquerque, Tomas was a product of the state's 1960s-era foster system. The result of an abusive white father and partially Latina mother, he was surrendered to the system when he was eight years old. Listed as Caucasian, his hair, skin, and eyes were just a shade enough darker to produce nervous glances between prospective parents.

At sixteen he'd had enough of foster homes, rotating parents, and ever-changing rules, so he ran. With no money and no job, he took to stealing from convenience stores to eat, moving around the city and suburbs to remain anonymous and unseen.

Until he stole from a store protected by a local gang.

Cornered and outnumbered, Tomas was beaten and left for dead, blood pouring from his mouth where he'd been hit with a baseball bat. Over the years he'd had the chance to get his teeth fixed, but chose to leave them as is, a reminder to himself and others that he was a survivor, not to be fucked with.

Using a pot from the stove, Tomas filled the coffee maker with water and scooped a large cup of grounds into the filter. Shoving it all into place, he hit the power button and sat at the Formica-covered kitchen table to wait.

Moments later, a younger man in his mid-twenties ambled into the kitchen and was about to pour himself a cup, when he spotted an empty mug sitting on the counter. He stopped, looked over his shoulder at Tomas, then awkwardly backed away.

"Sorry," he muttered as he leaned against the opposite counter, looking down at the floor.

A long, uncomfortable minute later, a third man, stepped into the kitchen. Quickly assessing the situation, he mumbled a quick "G' morning," and settled against the counter next to the younger man.

A few minutes later, a small click from the coffee maker broke the silence. Tomas heaved himself up from the kitchen table, took the mug off the counter, filled it, and returned to his chair. The two younger men lined up to fill their mugs, then joined Tomas at the table.

Within minutes they were joined by four more men, all ranging from their mid-twenties to mid-forties. Two came from inside the house, two from a door that led outside. The first to arrive took the last chair at the table, leaving the remaining three to stand or lean against the kitchen counters.

When they had all settled in, Tomas looked around the room, making eye contact with one of the two who had come from outside. "Any trouble?"

The man shook his head. "All quiet."

Tomas nodded. "Okay. We've got three being delivered today that we'll take up north tomorrow, meaning we need one more pickup today. That'll give us a full house tonight. Do we all know what to do?"

The men nodded.

"Good. Then let's get to it."

CHAPTER 2

WYNN CRUISED NORTH on I-25, the bike purring contentedly beneath him. The wind, cool when he descended the mountains earlier, felt comfortable as he approached the Wyoming border.

Traffic had been light when he left Denver but picked up as the morning grew long. In no hurry, he stuck to the right lane and reeled in the asphalt at a steady seventy-eight miles per hour. Various cars, trucks, and SUVS sped past, most pushing eighty or above.

The low, distinct rumble of Harley pipes swelled against the wind. A glance in his mirror revealed a swarm of bikers approaching from behind.

As they passed, Wynn dropped his left hand toward the road, two fingers extended in a universal greeting among bikers; a way of saying, "Stay safe, Brother." Many returned the gesture as they went around, the message in stark contrast to their club colors, displayed prominently on their black leather vests; a grey ace of spades with a knife blade jutting from the center, trailing red blood.

Classy.

Familiar with most of the large motorcycle clubs, Wynn didn't recognize the logo.

True badasses, or weekend warriors?

Virtually all of them sported tattoos spreading down their arms or snaking up their necks, but that no longer meant much of anything. More telling was the eighty-mile-per-hour wind that stretched the rider's jeans, revealing the bulging outline of a handgun strapped to many of their ankles. He had no doubt that several others, like himself, chose to carry their weapons inside their vests or jackets.

Wynn estimated forty riders. Their destination, he assumed, was like his, the Sturgis Motorcycle Rally, arguably the largest and most iconic gathering of motorcycle enthusiasts in the world. For more than eighty years a half-million cyclists from around the world have converged on this small, South Dakota town for a week of racing, exhibitions, concerts, and general drunken debauchery. Last year had been Wynn's first. While more reserved than most, he'd enjoyed the feeling of being an anonymous part of something larger.

He'd also hoped it would take his mind off Nicole, that night at the restaurant and the random stray bullet that changed his life forever.

Random. Now there's a funny word.

Before Nicole's death, he hadn't believed in random. Or coincidence. In Afghanistan, he'd learned that fractions of a second, spur-of-the-moment decisions, or the speed of a man's reflexes can mean the difference between life and death. Never had it come down to dumb luck. There was always a reason, always something to point to.

Except with Nicole.

He'd run it through his mind a thousand times, but a reason still eluded him.

Tortured him.

It was one of the reasons he'd bought the Harley. To escape. Not just down the road, but in the hypnotic rhythm *of* the road.

Rolling hills mostly barren from the late summer sun marked the transition from the mountains of Colorado to the plains of Wyoming. A huge herd of buffalo grazed peacefully on what little grass remained, unfazed by the roar of engines from the highway. A few miles further on, signs for motels, food, and most importantly, gas, appeared along the side of the road. He eased back on the throttle and took the next exit.

Two truck stop gas stations, one on either side of the crossroad, sat at the top of the ramp. The closer teemed with the same group of bikers that had passed him earlier. Deciding to refer to them as "Aces," he pulled onto the crossroad and headed to the other station.

Wynn pulled up to a pump, swiped his card, and filled the tank. At forty-three miles to the gallon and a six-gallon tank, he had a comfortable range of two hundred twenty miles. He could possibly stretch it to two-fifty, but after that, there was a good chance he'd be walking. Knowing the sometimes vast distances between towns in rural Wyoming, he tended to fill his tank often.

Across the road, the Aces were forming up, the stragglers still at the pumps while the leaders were saddled up and ready to roll. Wanting to leave some space between himself and the Aces, Wynn strolled into the convenience store and bought a bottle of water.

A thunder-like rumble greeted him as he came out. One-by-one the Aces pulled onto the crossroad, slid down the entrance ramp, and flowed onto the interstate as if tied together by some invisible Slinky.

Taking his time, Wynn drank half the bottle, then placed the remainder in his saddlebag. He launched the maps app on his phone and checked the two routes north. One was shorter but littered with road construction.

No thanks.

He committed the longer route to memory, then put his phone away, fired up the bike, and eased onto the crossroad. As the rumble of the Aces faded in the distance, he accelerated down the entrance ramp, somehow feeling like a lonely little boy tagging along after his big brother and friends had gone out for the night.

———

Sixty miles south, Jessica was making good time. With the city behind her, she set the cruise control at eighty and let it ride. Pressing the hands-free button on her steering wheel, she asked Siri to call her sister in Rapid City.

After two rings, the phone dinged with an incoming text message, then the call went to voicemail. While she listened to her sister's voice apologize for not being able to get to the phone, she quickly glanced at the text. It was from her sister, one of those automatic, *"Can I call you later?"* replies.

Must be on another call.

The tone to leave a message beeped.

"Hey Tami, it's me. Just calling to let you know I got started a little later than expected. Should be there around three o'clock. I'll try calling you later with an update, but you know how sketchy the coverage is through Wyoming. Love you. See you later."

Jessica disconnected the call and hit the Bluetooth feature on her radio, soon tapping her fingers in time with her favorite tunes.

———

Up at the ranch, a red Jeep Cherokee, its paint dulled by dust and age, pulled out of the large barn and rolled down the dirt driveway. It was followed by a white Chevy panel van, *All Season Plumbing* painted in thick block letters along both sides. A driver and passenger could be seen in the front of both vehicles, but little else.

When they reached the county road the Jeep turned north, into a vast expanse of nothingness that stretched for over eighty miles. The van paused, then turned south toward the tiny outpost town of Elderville some eight miles away. With nothing more than a post office and gas station, Elderville depended on its slightly larger sister city of Linert, ten miles to the east.

Inside the van, the younger of the two men, a fair-skinned, dark-haired, twenty-something with a prominent nose, sat slumped in the passenger seat. "Tomas was in a hell of a mood this morning."

"Yeah," the driver said. "He gets that way on pickup days." John was older, in his mid-forties and slim, with short gray hair.

"What's he got to worry about?" Brandon asked. "We're the ones risking our asses out here."

"You don't think he worries about that?"

"Yeah, I suppose. But I still don't like it."

John rolled his eyes. "Listen. As long as your little stunner does its job, we'll be fine. You get the voltage fixed on that thing?"

"The voltage wasn't the problem. It was the amperage."

"Whatever. I don't want to be hauling *your* ass off the road next time."

"I'm touched." Brandon's voice dripped with sarcasm. "I didn't know you cared."

"I don't. I just don't want to have to explain to Tomas that we failed because of a fucking homemade Taser."

"Technically, it's a stun gun."

"Again, whatever. As long as it works."

"It'll work."

"Good." John pressed the gas. "Then let's go hunting."

CHAPTER 3

NINETY MINUTES AFTER leaving Cheyenne, two days of riding, restless nights and the monotony of the Wyoming grasslands caught up to Wynn. A few miles ahead the routes diverged, Interstate 25 continued north to Douglas, while the route he needed, Highway 18, split off to the east toward Linert.

Wynn slowed as he sailed up the exit ramp, the bright sunlight gleaming off the Harley's chrome tailpipes. He turned onto the highway, then a hundred yards later, into the asphalt oval that circled the Prairie Junction rest area.

One thing he could say for Wyoming, they knew how to make rest stops. As long and manicured as an NFL football field, the restroom facilities occupied one end, while a wide, curving sidewalk wound through clusters of trees and picnic shelters, allowing ample space for weary travelers to stretch their tired legs. The one-way road circled the park in a clockwise direction, with diagonal parking spaces flanking inward along either side.

He followed the road past a half-dozen cars parked along the east side, then rounded the empty picnic shelters at the far end and eventually pulled into a spot mid-way up the west side. He shut down the bike and stretched his stiff limbs. Yawning as he went, Wynn strolled along the sidewalk into the restroom.

Returning a few minutes later, Wynn guzzled the rest of the water he'd bought in Cheyenne, then pulled his duffle out of a saddlebag and followed the sidewalk to a tree near the far end of the park. Using the duffle as a pillow, he sat down in the shade of a maple tree and leaned back, half-sitting, half-lying against its trunk. Behind his dark sunglasses, he closed his eyes. While real sleep wasn't going to happen, he often found just a few minutes of shut eye to be highly rejuvenating.

Although his eyes were closed, Wynn kept his ears open. The purr of engines, the crunching of tires, and the slamming of doors all signaled various cars coming and going. Over the next ten minutes, three cars entered the rest area as two more left.

The fourth vehicle to enter, however, sounded different. The breath of its engine louder, the crunching of tires slower. While the other vehicles had all stopped along the east side, this one made its way around, just like Wynn had, and parked close by, on the west. When the crunching stopped and the engine shut down, he waited for the sound of a door opening, but none came.

Curious, Wynn opened one eye. A white Chevy van sat twenty yards away, in the spot furthest from the facilities. A sign on its side read *All Season Plumbing,* and a young guy, maybe in his mid-twenties, was visible through the passenger window.

On their lunch break between jobs. Wynn closed his eyes.

Over the next ten minutes, several more cars came and went, but once again, an unexpected noise broke the pattern; the creak of a rusty car door opening nearby, then banging shut. Wynn cracked his eye. The passenger of the plumbing van was walking toward the facilities.

Finished his lunch. Using the restroom.

A few minutes later, the passenger returned and exchanged a few words with the driver. More doors opened and closed, and now the driver, at least fifteen years older, walked toward the facilities.

Journeyman and apprentice, not wanting to leave the van unattended. Don't want any tools stolen.

When the driver returned, he came around to the passenger side as the window lowered. Although they were relatively close, Wynn couldn't hear the conversation, their voices low and muffled.

———

"Anything?" John asked when he walked around to Brandon's passenger window.

"Not yet." Brandon looked past John's shoulder at the sleeping biker. He'd been there when they arrived and appeared to be dead to the world. Brandon turned the other way to look out the driver's side window, at the Harley Street Glide, a few spaces away.

"Nice bike, though," he said. "Wonder if we could kick his ass, grab the keys and take it."

John laughed. "Shit, kid, I'd like to see you try. He'd kill you."

Brandon was about to protest when John reached through the window and tapped his chest, pointing across the way to where a young woman was making her way to the restroom.

———

Wynn heard the two plumbers laugh and saw them glance in his direction.

Have your fun, boys.

But then the laughter stopped as the driver pointed across the park. Moving only his eyes, Wynn followed their gaze in time to see a young woman enter the restroom.

Hounds.

When he looked back, the two plumbers were still watching the building's door.

Intently.

Something had changed. The men were quiet and focused. Staring.

Minutes later the driver nodded toward the facilities. Across the way, the same young woman came out of the restroom and walked back to her car, a relatively new, silver Hyundai Elantra.

She was alone.

With his eyes on the plumbers, Wynn tracked the movement of the woman's car by the sound of its tires on the pavement, the crunching growing louder as the Elantra approached and rounded the end where Wynn lay, then faded as the car passed and continued away.

The plumbers now openly watched the Elantra as it approached the exit. The young passenger sat up straight in his seat while the driver had taken two steps toward the front of the van, leaning forward on his toes. Wynn watched as the car sat waiting at the crossroad. There was no blinker to indicate whether it would turn left to the interstate, or right, toward Linert.

It turned left.

The young guy leaned back while the driver noticeably deflated and lowered onto his heels. He walked around the front of the van and the driver's door creaked open, then slammed shut, but then nothing. The engine didn't start. The van didn't move.

Wynn alternated between closing his eyes and watching the occupants in the van. Although now that the driver had returned to his seat, he could only see the young passenger. The sun was behind Wynn and shone directly through the window, giving him a pretty good, albeit profile, view. Dark hair covered the passenger's ears and swept into his eyes, while a prominent nose stood out beneath his sunglasses. As more cars came and went, he could see the passenger checking each vehicle, but quickly losing interest.

They're waiting for something.

———

Jessica had been on the road three and a half hours when she pulled her Outback into Prairie Junction. She parked and scanned the area. A couple of other cars sat nearby, while a white van and a Harley were parked across the way. Near the far end of the park, a man lie propped against a tree, his blue jeans, boots, and black leather jacket immediately pegging him as the biker.

Having grown up in Rapid City, less than a half-hour from Sturgis, she'd experienced her share of bikers. Most were great guys, always willing to lend a hand. But as an emergency room nurse, she'd also seen the carnage the few bad ones could bring. Best to know which kind you were dealing with right away. The problem was that it was often impossible to tell until it was too late.

She watched for a quick moment, and when he didn't move, she unbuckled her seat belt and stepped out. Standing between the open door and driver's seat, she turned toward the car, pushed up on her tiptoes, and stretched her arms overhead, long and luxuriously, twisting from side to side. The sun felt good on her back, the final remnants of this morning's hangover dissipating into the breeze. Settling back on her heels and closing the door, she beeped the car lock and made her way to the facilities.

———

"What have we got here?" Brandon watched as the slim brunette stretched her arms overhead. Her hair fell to the middle of her back.

"Shut up," John replied.

They watched as the woman strolled into the restroom. When the door closed, Brandon glanced at the car. No one else was visible inside.

"Quick," John said. "Go check it out. Make sure there's no baby or dog or boyfriend."

Brandon jumped out of the van and strode toward the Subaru. With his view inside hampered by the tinted windows, he stopped directly in front of the car and knelt to tie his shoe, getting a good look through the clear windshield. He stood and walked over to a trash can, faked throwing something in, then hustled back to the van, getting in just as the brunette came out of the restroom.

"Anything?" John asked.

"Nope. All clear."

"Plates?"

"Colorado."

"That's good," John said quietly, never taking his eyes from the woman.

———

Two new cars were in the lot when Jessica returned. A couple about her age walked toward her, and a family with young children spilled from a Toyota SUV. She maneuvered around the sudden onslaught of bodies and quickly slid back inside her Outback. Pulling out her phone, she sent a short text to her sister.

Leaving Prairie Junction. See you in a bit.

She dropped the phone onto the passenger seat and started the engine. Pausing, she glanced again at the sleeping biker. He hadn't moved. Safe enough.

Pulling the transmission into reverse, she checked the rearview camera and slowly backed out, the tires crunching softly on the asphalt.

———

John and Brandon watched as the Subaru slid backward out of its parking spot and circled around the oval drive. They lost sight of it momentarily as it disappeared behind the restroom building but picked it up again as it left the oval. They collectively held their breath as the Subaru approached the crossroad and stopped to let an eastbound vehicle cruise by.

"Turn right, turn right," Brandon mumbled under his breath.

It did.

"Let's do it," John said.

———

The scratchy whine of the van's starter, followed by its loud breath of exhaust pulled Wynn from his languor. Tires crunched as the van backed out, then squealed softly as it accelerated toward the exit. Wynn sat up as the van approached the crossroad where the Subaru had been a moment before, then watched as it turned to follow.

By itself, the fact that the van had gone the same direction meant nothing. There were only two options, left or right. They had to go one way or the other. But this was odd. For forty-five minutes the two guys acted as if they were waiting for someone. Or something.

Wynn had thought it might've been the woman in the Elantra, but she left without any interaction at all. When the young guy walked over to the Subaru, Wynn thought maybe that's who they were waiting for. That he would talk to her.

But he didn't. They hadn't spoken.

Was it coincidence then, that when she left, it was suddenly time for them to leave, too?

No way.

A tingling sensation he'd developed in the corps—his buddies called it his spidey-sense—gnawed in the pit of his stomach. It had only let him down once before. With Nicole.

No way that's happening again.

Wynn picked up his duffle and walked back to the bike, mounted up, and slowly accelerated away. He idled through the last quarter of the oval, eventually approaching the crossroad, where he stopped to let another car speed past.

He turned right.

CHAPTER 4

JOHN STAYED A half-mile behind the Subaru, planning to close the distance when they got closer to Linert. He was confident that's where she was going because, well, there just wasn't anywhere else.

"Should I give Andy a heads up?" Brandon asked.

"Yeah."

Brandon pulled a small burner phone from his pocket. They all had one. He found the contact and punched the number. "Hey. It's me. I think we've got something."

He listened for a moment, then said, "We're thirty minutes from Linert. She's in a black Subaru Outback with Colorado plates. Get everyone ready. We'll let you know when she leaves town."

———

Two cars separated Wynn from the van, which was a good thing on the one hand, bad on the other. On the plus side, it helped camouflage him. He'd just spent forty-five minutes as the only person within twenty yards of these guys. Follow them for more than a turn or two and they'd notice.

On the minus side, he was limited by the speed of the cars

between them, and neither was going to win a race anytime soon. As the miles rolled on, the distances between the cars stretched out such that Wynn eventually lost sight of the van, catching only sporadic glimpses on the long, open straightaways. The woman in the black Subaru was long gone.

The slower pace gave Wynn a chance to think about what he'd seen. What was it, really? A couple of guys checking out the ladies.

Happens the world over, for as long as man's been around. The most natural thing ever.

Nicole would've hated it, but she'd have understood.

So, what was it about these guys that got his spider-sense tingling? They paid equal attention to the woman in the Elantra but didn't follow her. Was she going the wrong direction? If so, that meant they had a reason to go east. The most likely explanation being that's where the next job was. They were plumbers, after all, moving from job to job. Usually on tight timeframes. Not wanting to make customers wait through four-hour appointment windows.

But if they were on a tight timeframe, why drive all the way out to Prairie Junction and waste almost an hour on a leisurely lunch? Made no sense.

So then, were they truly plumbers? The sign on the van said so, but why wasn't there a phone number? And didn't most plumbers wear company shirts, with their names embroidered, usually on an oval name tag, above the left breast pocket? Make themselves easily identifiable? These days you had to be careful about who you let into your home. He'd gotten a good look at both these guys. Blue jeans and t-shirts. Sloppy looking. Not the dress of someone to whom you'd happily open your door. Not the image you'd want your company to project.

But this was Wyoming. Maybe people here didn't care.

Wynn sped past a road sign. Highway 27, one mile ahead. A crossroad at a two-mailbox town called Elderville. If there was a place where either the Subaru or the van could turn off and get out of sight before getting to Linert, this was it.

He turned his right wrist ever so slightly and the Street Glide responded, its pipes thundering as the bike accelerated. He glanced in his mirror for vehicles behind and checked for oncoming traffic. Seeing none, he leaned left, sweeping into the opposite lane, and roared past the first car. He swept back into his own lane as a pickup towing a large trailer appeared on the crossroad and made its way toward the intersection. Wrong vehicle, wrong direction. Nothing else.

Past the junction, a second sign indicated ten miles to Linert. The second car, a blue Honda CR-V, was a mile ahead, the van nowhere in sight.

Growing more anxious and certain of what he'd seen, Wynn glanced at his speedometer. Ninety miles per hour. It would take almost three minutes to catch the CR-V; seven minutes to reach Linert. He twisted the throttle further.

———

Eight miles ahead, Jessica pulled into the outskirts of Linert. She passed a campground on her right, a pasture passing for a golf course on her left, and a long open space before entering a mostly residential neighborhood. The road gradually curved to the right before coming to the first of only two stoplights in the entire town.

It was red. Of course.

When the light changed, she turned left and proceeded several blocks north. On the corner of Third and Main she pulled into a combination gas station and convenience store called the Fresh Start. She smiled slightly at the familiar picture of a cartoon chicken plastered to the side of the building. Over the years she'd stopped here often. It wasn't huge, but it had gas, food, and bathrooms, the three essentials required by every traveler making the long trek through the state.

She eased up to a pump, filled her tank, then went inside, unaware of the white van driving by.

———

John and Brandon parked across the street on Third. Having kept a safe distance, they'd followed the woman into town. When she pulled over, they'd continued past and circled the block. A four-story brick building on their right provided cover. It prevented them from actually seeing the Subaru as it sat at the pump, but they had a clear view of the intersection, including every car that passed through. They'd know when she left.

———

Oncoming traffic prevented Wynn from passing the CR-V, forcing him to creep frustratingly slowly to a stoplight in the middle of town.

Decision time. To his right, the road led south to another small town some fifty miles away. Four blocks straight ahead was a visible dead end, and to his left, eighty miles and beyond, lay the towns of Newbury, Deadwood, and eventually, Sturgis. Figuring that was the brunette's most likely direction, he turned left.

Wynn cruised slowly up Main Street, scanning both sides, searching for the van or Subaru. The first two blocks consisted of boarded-up businesses or small, single-family homes. A chain sandwich shop sat on the right, but there was no white van or black Subaru in the lot. The next few blocks were much the same, with homes on one side and a library, bank, and supermarket on the other.

Unlikely destinations.

He was finally rewarded at the end of the fifth block. On the right-hand side, beneath the green awning of a Sinclair gas station, sat the black Subaru. No sign of the slim brunette, but there was also a convenience store. She was probably in there.

Wynn pulled up to the only open pump, directly behind the Subaru. He shut down his engine, dismounted, then swiped his card and inserted the nozzle into the tank, all while casually scanning the area for the white van. A midsize RV parked at the next island partially blocked his view of Main Street, but he'd checked that area as he pulled in. The white van was nowhere in sight.

He turned his attention back to the filling tank as the brunette came out of the store. She glanced in his direction, briefly making eye contact.

"Nice bike," she said as she walked around the rear of her car.

"Thanks."

She stopped before getting in. "Going to Sturgis?"

"That's the plan."

"Maybe I'll see you."

She slid behind the wheel, pulled away from the pump, and turned onto Third Street before making a quick right to head out of town. She was fine. No white van in sight.

Nothing to worry about.

———

Across Main, John and Brandon sat silently as the Subaru turned through the intersection. Brandon flipped open the phone and redialed the last number.

"She's coming. A black Subaru Outback. Brunette driver, alone. Just leaving Linert, going north on 85. We're on."

———

Twelve miles north, Andy, the fourth man who'd come down for coffee at the ranch that morning, sat behind the wheel of the dusty red Jeep Cherokee along with Nathan, another of the housemates. They were parked along the side of a gravel road, atop a small rise, watching traffic move back and forth along the highway. Andy held a phone to his ear, listening.

He lowered the phone and tapped the red "end" button. "We're on," he said to Nathan.

He pulled up another number from the phone's memory and hit the green "send" button. After four rings it was picked up as a voice said simply, "Yeah?"

"It's on. Fifteen minutes."

———

Wynn relaxed after the Subaru disappeared up the road.

My imagination running wild again.

He finished topping off the gas and was returning the nozzle to the pump when the RV pulled away from the next island, revealing the west side of the intersection.

The white van was turning north.

CHAPTER 5

JESSICA SET HER own pace for the first ten minutes as she traveled north out of Linert, eventually catching up to an old, red Jeep Cherokee. It increased speed just enough to prevent her from passing, so she settled in behind it.

Her rearview mirror showed several cars and a few motorcycles stacking up behind her, the closest being a white van about a hundred feet back.

On the road ahead, a tightly packed stream of vehicles came toward her in the opposite lane.

Crap. She knew what that meant.

Road construction. The highway would be reduced to one lane with flaggers stacking up traffic from one direction while a line of vehicles was let loose from the other. When the first line of cars cleared the work zone, the opposite side would be released. Alternating back and forth all day. Depending on how long the construction zone was and which side's turn it was, the delay could be as little as a few minutes or as much as a half-hour. She sighed heavily.

Wynn took less than a minute to get back on the road, but in the meantime, four other cars had gotten between himself and the van. Any lingering illusion that it might be a coincidence was now fully swept away. He'd been able to pass one car in his attempt to keep the van in sight, but oncoming traffic prevented him from getting any closer. Fortunately, they'd all kept a pretty good pace until the whole procession, led by the black Subaru, bunched up behind a slower moving Jeep Cherokee.

A few minutes later, the entire group slowed further as they passed a temporary sign announcing *Road Construction Ahead*. Within a quarter-mile, the procession finally came to a halt. Wynn eased the Street Glide to the left, close to the double yellow line. From there he could see past the low sedan and two pickup trucks between he and the van. But the van itself, large and boxy, allowed only a partial view of the Subaru.

He craned his neck to the left, looking forward. Forty yards and six cars ahead, a flagman stood in the middle of the road, holding a red stop sign atop a six-foot pole. Not seeing any cars approaching from the opposite direction and with a comfortable eye on both the van and the Subaru, he shut down the engine and settled in to wait.

———

Jessica sat behind the old red Jeep. She put the transmission in park but kept the engine going to run the air conditioner. She grabbed her phone to check messages. A single reception bar blinked in the corner of the screen, then disappeared.

Middle of nowhere.

Tossing the phone back on the seat she looked around. Wide-open prairies of sun-dried grass swept away on either side, eventually blending into low-rise bluffs more than a mile away. Ahead, a row of orange cones blocked the northbound lane and stretched away down the center of the highway. Bulldozers and excavators, dump trucks and graders, all moved about in the distance. Closer, a half-dozen support vehicles sat parked along the berm to her right with several men in hard hats milling about.

Directly in front of the Jeep, the flagger leaned on his pole, slowly rotating the sign back and forth. Bored. He straightened up and put a small radio to his ear, then spoke into it. Clipping the radio to his belt, he turned and looked to the north, where a long row of vehicles gradually made its way toward them. When they finally cleared, the flagger turned his sign to "slow" and motioned the Jeep into the left lane. Jessica put the car into gear, eased her foot off the brake, and followed. Out of habit, she nodded a quick "thank you," to the flagger as she passed.

———

Wynn hit the ignition as the last of the southbound cars swept past, then watched the Jeep and Subaru ease around the orange cones and begin moving away. The sedan in front of Wynn inched forward but then stopped short.

Ahead, the white van followed the Subaru, but the flagger had turned his sign to "stop," and stepped in front of the next vehicle in line, a black pickup.

What now?

The flagger talked into his radio. He listened and talked some more, then clipped it to his belt and walked over to the black truck, now first in line. The driver lowered his window and listened as the flagger said something. The guy pointed ahead and raised his arms in frustration. The flagger shrugged and stepped back, then went back to his position, not allowing any more cars to pass. Wynn revved his engine and was about to zip around the three cars and the flagger, when a semi-truck pulling a large dump trailer pulled out of the ditch behind the van, blocking the entire road.

———

The construction zone stretched for more than a mile as Jessica followed the Jeep at a modest twenty miles-per-hour. When they finally broke clear, the Jeep blasted down the highway, quickly opening a sizable lead. Jessica pushed down on the gas until the speedometer touched seventy-three, then engaged the cruise control. The white van stayed close behind.

She continued steadily for a few minutes until the Jeep reappeared on the downslope of a small rise, stopped at an odd angle in the middle of the road, blocking both lanes. She tapped the brake to disengage the cruise control then braked harder as she approached. The Jeep's front doors hung open and a man lie face down on the asphalt. A second man knelt over the first as Jessica slowed to a stop thirty feet away.

Her medical training kicked in. Jessica slammed the transmission into park and jumped out of the car. She glanced over her shoulder as the white van pulled to a stop, then turned back and hustled to the men in front.

"What happened?"

The kneeling man looked up. "I don't know! We were cruising along, and he just slumped over the wheel!"

Jessica sensed that someone, maybe more than one, had rushed from the van. They approached from behind. Without warning, her lower back exploded with thousands of fiery pins. Every muscle in her body stiffened as electricity radiated through her limbs. Bright flashes filled her vision only to be followed by an ever-deepening shadow as the current continued. She felt herself begin to fall, but was overtaken by darkness before hitting the ground.

———

Brandon kept the stunner jammed against the girl's back. They'd learned that short blasts weren't enough. If they wanted her down, it had to be held for several seconds.

Stepping in front, John caught the brunette as she fell, quickly lowering her to the ground. He grabbed her wrists and used a plastic zip-tie to secure them over her stomach. Brandon pocketed the stunner and used another zip-tie to bind her ankles. John tapped her pockets and reached in to retrieve the Subaru's key fob. He tossed it to Nathan who jumped into the Subaru and started it up.

By now, Andy was already off the ground and sliding behind the wheel of the Jeep. The door was still open and swung wildly as he took off down the road.

Brandon and John hoisted the girl by the legs and shoulders and carried her to the van. Tossing her through the side door onto the hard floor, Brandon crawled in beside her and slammed the door shut. He pushed her back until her head was lying next to a metal ring bolted to the floor. Using a third zip-tie, he raised her wrists above her head and secured them to the ring, pinning her to the floor. John sprinted around the front of the van, jumped into the driver's seat, and quickly sped away in pursuit of the Jeep. Nathan, in the Subaru, followed close behind.

The entire stop lasted less than thirty seconds.

CHAPTER 6

WYNN HOPED THAT when the semi-truck cleared the road, the flagger would allow them to go, but it didn't happen. For three long minutes, a backhoe rolled back and forth, filling the semi-trailer with dirt and chunks of asphalt while Wynn felt his blood pressure rise. When the truck finally lumbered away, the flagger spoke into his radio, then glanced up the road. He turned back to the black pickup that was first in line and held up a single index finger. One minute.

The driver returned a single-finger response.

Wynn shook his head. Despite his frustration, he almost felt sorry for the flagger. In his mid-twenties, the guy was skinny, of average height, had long, curly blond hair that stuck out beneath a yellow hard hat, and a scraggly beard that was sure to impress no one. His arms and face were reddened by the sun. Wynn hoped they rotated jobs every so often. Doing nothing but standing in the hot sun day after day had to be at least someone's definition of hell.

As the minutes ticked by, Wynn continuously ran the calculations in his head. Assuming the Subaru drove eighty miles per hour, he would have to do better than ninety just to pick up two-tenths of a mile each minute. It would take five minutes to close by a single mile. Almost a half-hour to close five miles. He'd have to push it.

Two minutes later, a relatively short procession of southbound cars cleared the work zone. The flagger turned his sign to "slow" and the pickup eased into the left lane. As his rear bumper came even with the flagger, the driver blasted his engine, leaving a thick cloud of black exhaust. The flagger coughed and moved out of the fog, his shouts at the pickup lost in the roar of engines. The haze was still thick as Wynn rode through.

Easing into the left lane, Wynn bounced along the dirt-spattered pavement for over a mile before a second flagman motioned him back into the northbound lane. He hugged the double yellow line as the three vehicles in front of him passed the row of southbound cars, already lining up for their turn through the one-lane section. When he was clear, he twisted the throttle full on, pulled the clutch, and used his left foot to lift the Harley into a higher gear.

The bike responded instantly as he leaned to the left, swinging gracefully into the opposite lane and roaring past the sedan. With the Street Glide's speedometer creeping close to one hundred, he stayed in the left lane as he reeled in and passed the two pickups. Leaning right, he swung back into the northbound lane and pressed on into the open road ahead.

Having come this way a year ago, Wynn knew that somewhere ahead, maybe twenty-five miles at the most, the route split. Highway 85 would continue north to Newbury, while Highway 18 would head east toward South Dakota. If he didn't catch the Subaru before the routes split, he'd have no way of knowing which way she went.

Wynn pushed on, straining to look around each turn, anticipating every rise that would allow him to see further up the highway. He glanced left and right, scanning for any side roads they might have taken, but there was only open prairie. His eyes began to water from the wind swirling behind his sunglasses, but still he pressed on. He passed a sign that indicated sixteen miles to the route split. At a hundred miles per hour, he had nine minutes.

———

After grabbing the girl, it had taken only three minutes to disappear. They had gone north less than two miles before coming to a dirt road heading off to the west. "Road" in this case, was a generous term. From the highway, it looked more like a driveway providing access to a farmer's field, complete with a barbed-wire gate that blocked access.

But Andy had been here before. Many times, in fact. He'd spent years driving and mentally mapping every patch of pavement, gravel road, and dirt path for a hundred square miles. He knew that this road received such little traffic that the ground was still solid, and grass would be growing over the surface so as not to kick up a revealing rooster tail of dust as they passed.

He also knew that this road dropped over a small hill a half-mile away, perfect for concealment. Further on, two miles across the field on the other side, was another equally unassuming gate, leading to another dirt road, through another empty field, and eventually to a paved county road that would take them south to the ranch.

With all this in mind, Andy turned the Jeep into the driveway. He pulled to the side and jumped out to unhook the gate. Dragging it clear, he let the van and Subaru roll through before hustling back to his car. He drove through the opening and stopped again to close the gate, before finally following the Subaru up the grass-covered road.

On the far side of the rise, Andy slowed to pick up Nathan, who had parked the Subaru in a patch of tall grass hidden below the hill. Better to leave it here out of sight than to drive it back to the ranch. As few and far between as the neighbors were, they were used to seeing the Jeep and the van on these roads. A Subaru with Colorado plates, not so much.

Taking a casual pace, Andy drove the Jeep off in the same direction John had taken the van moments before. The goal was to put a little distance between the two so they wouldn't appear to be traveling together, yet remain close enough to be able to come to their assistance if needed.

He rolled down the window, listening for sirens or any hint of trouble. Instead, the sound of a Harley's tailpipes roared in the distance, screaming down the highway.

———

Sixteen miles after passing the sign, a cluster of trees surrounding a small, tan building indicated the Mule Creek Junction rest area, where the routes split. Wynn scanned the road ahead, seeing no sign of any vehicles on the road in front of him, nor on the split route to the east.

He hadn't caught them.

Odds of doing so now slipped by fifty percent.

Slowing, Wynn pulled into the rest area, looking for, but certainly not expecting to find either the van or the Subaru. Like Prairie Junction, the Mule Creek rest area consisted of a one-way asphalt drive circling a squat, brick building with trees and picnic shelters scattered throughout.

As he rounded the last corner, Wynn had a choice to make, straight on Highway 85 to Newbury and a more direct route to Sturgis, or right on Highway 18, looping around the southern Black Hills to Rapid City. Which route would she take? Fifty-fifty chance.

Then he remembered. *Maybe I'll see you,* she had said.

He wheeled back around to the entrance, glanced to his left to check for oncoming traffic, then roared onto the northbound highway. Newbury lie thirty-four miles ahead. At his previous pace, he could make it in twenty-one minutes.

———

Jessica was jarred awake as her body bounced on a hard steel floor. Urgent, muffled voices came out of the fog.

"Dude! Take it easy! You're going to kill us back here."

"Shut up," said a second male voice. The jarring didn't ease.

Jessica bounced to the right. Sharp pain bit into her wrists as she attempted to move her hands. Trying to clear her mind, she gradually became aware that her arms were extended above her head. She moaned dully. The harder she tried to pull her arms down, the sharper the pain became. Gaining clarity, and with the sudden realization that her hands were tied, Jessica's dull moan strengthened to a full-throated, terrified scream.

"Hit her again!" a voice yelled.

Once again, agony exploded from beneath her ribs like the sting of a thousand volts. Her muscles convulsed as bright flashes filled her vision, and darkness encroached around the edges. She tried to fight it, tried to keep her senses, but the assault continued as her world shrunk until there was nothing left but pain.

CHAPTER 7

WYNN CONTINUED HIS torrid pace north up the highway, taking only a couple of minutes to catch the first of three vehicles ahead. It wasn't a van. Or a Subaru. Therefore unimportant. Checking for oncoming traffic, he repeated the passing maneuver once, twice, then a third time, his speedometer exceeding one-ten as he rocketed past a semi-truck.

With each passing mile, a gnawing suspicion that he'd chosen the wrong route grew stronger. He planned to push hard until he reached Newbury, which according to a road sign, was only eight miles ahead. If he didn't catch them by then, he wouldn't catch them at all.

As he raced down the highway, a line of cars approached in the opposite lane. It wasn't until he sped past that he realized the third car in the group was a Wheaton County Sheriff's cruiser. Glancing in the mirror, the cruiser's brake lights flared, and the lights on top flashed red and blue.

Shit. With just a few miles to Newbury, he hated the idea of giving up the chase, even on the slim chance that the van or Subaru might be right ahead. It would take the cop at least a few seconds to turn around and two or three minutes to catch up, hopefully giving

Wynn enough time to make it to town. At that point, he could pretend he hadn't seen the cop.

Seek forgiveness instead of permission.

He pressed on.

Two minutes later, the road swung gradually to the right, down a slight hill toward the small town of Newbury. There was nothing on the road ahead. The Subaru was gone.

Wynn checked the mirror. The cruiser was now less than a half-mile behind, closing fast.

Maybe he can get out an APB.

Finding a wide section of shoulder, Wynn pulled to the side. He shut down the engine and stepped off the bike as the cruiser ground to a stop ten yards behind, the blaring siren dying away, its tires stirring a cloud of dust as they skid in the dirt.

Wynn stood without moving as the officer inside jumped out and drew his weapon. Using the car door as a shield, the officer pointed his revolver at Wynn from the "V" shape that formed between the car and its open door.

"On the ground, asshole!" the officer screamed.

Wynn paused. *Pissed him off real good.*

"On the ground, now!"

"Okay, okay." Wynn raised his hands. He slowly lowered one knee to the ground, then the other, keeping his hands in the air. "I need to report..."

"Shut up!" the officer yelled. "All the way down. On your face. Hands behind your back."

Wynn did as he was told. He'd seen country cops before. High school tough guys who wanted to legitimize their bullying. He was getting a bad feeling about this.

The officer kept his weapon drawn as he came around the open car door. He knelt next to Wynn and used one hand to pull a pair of handcuffs from his belt.

"Officer, I apologize if I was speeding but I need to report a suspected abduction in progress."

"Shut up. Are you carrying?" He snapped a cuff onto Wynn's left wrist.

"Officer, a kidnapping!"

"Bullshit! I said are you carrying?" He cuffed the other wrist, securing Wynn's hands behind his back, then holstered his weapon.

"Yeah, I am. Inside left pocket. Permit's in my wallet."

The cop grabbed him by the elbow and lifted him to his feet. He pushed Wynn back to the cruiser, slammed the driver's door shut, and spun him around so Wynn's back was to the car, giving Wynn his first good look at the cop.

The guy was maybe an inch shorter than Wynn, about six feet tall, but with his boots, Wynn stood a couple inches taller. The guy was a little younger, maybe early thirties. He was relatively thin, probably a hundred seventy-five pounds, dressed in forest green pants, a khaki uniform shirt, matching green tie, and a Dudley-Do-Right campaign hat. Wynn had to wonder if the guy took the time to put the hat on before drawing his gun a few moments ago, or if he wore it all the time in the car? He smiled ever-so-slightly as he wondered which was worse.

A brass name tag pinned above his left shirt pocket read *E. Crower.* Underneath the hat, tiny blond hairs stuck out next to his ears, indicating a tight crew cut. Dark aviator sunglasses hid his eyes, but Wynn didn't need to see those. The cop's beet-red face was enough to tell him the guy was pissed.

A radio microphone was attached to his left shoulder, with the spiral cord stretching down to his waist where he wore the requisite police duty belt, complete with a handgun, radio, Taser, pepper spray, and flashlight. There was also a spot for handcuffs, but that pouch was empty. They were on Wynn's wrists.

"Let's see what we've got here." Crower patted down Wynn's jacket. Reaching inside, he pulled out Wynn's Glock 19 and held it out to the side. "You got a permit for this?"

"Like I said," Wynn replied, "in my wallet."

"Take two steps to your left," Crower ordered.

Wynn did so, moving down the side of the car toward the trunk. Crower released the magazine from the Glock and checked the chamber to make sure it was empty. He opened the driver's door, leaned in, and placed the Glock and magazine on the front passenger seat.

The semi-truck Wynn had passed earlier roared past, throwing up dust and small pebbles into Wynn's face. Wynn looked past Crower toward his bike, which shuddered in the passing wind, but remained upright.

Straightening up, Crower stepped back in front of Wynn. "Where's your wallet?"

"Inside right pocket."

Crower reached in again and pulled out Wynn's wallet. He opened it. "Where's the permit?"

"Behind the driver's license."

Crower took out both the permit and the license. "Sean Wynn. Ventura, California."

Wynn nodded.

"I guess I don't need to ask what you're doing out this way."

Wynn paused. Knew he shouldn't say it but couldn't help himself. "Are you really going to dick around with me while there's a serious crime in progress?"

"You'd love that, wouldn't you? Send me off on a wild goose chase while you skip away scot-free. That'd be a great story for your friends, wouldn't it? Too bad for you we're not all country bumpkins out here."

Wynn shook his head and looked past Crower to the field on the other side of the highway.

"Fuckers think you own the place."

Wynn sighed. "Officer Crower, I apologize. I know I was speeding, but—"

"Shut the fuck up! You'll talk when I tell you to, otherwise keep your mouth shut."

Wynn stared into Crower's sunglasses, seeing only his own image reflecting back but knowing Crower's eyes were locked on his, daring him to say something.

Wynn eventually dropped his eyes, slowly shaking his head.

"That's better," Crower said. "Get in the car."

Grabbing Wynn by the left arm, Crower pulled him away from the rear door. Opening it, he put a hand on Wynn's head and forced it down, guiding Wynn into the back seat of the cruiser. With Wynn inside, Crower slammed the door shut and climbed in the front.

Inside the cruiser, Crower replaced the permit, then tossed Wynn's wallet onto the passenger seat next to his gun. He reached up to his left shoulder and pressed the transmit button on the microphone. "Hey, Sam, you there?"

Wynn was surprised to hear a woman's voice come back.

"Yeah, I'm here. What do you have?"

"I need you to run a name for me, see if there's anything out there."

"Sure. What's the name?"

"Sean Wynn. Spelled S-E-A-N, W-Y-N-N. Ventura, California. I'll wait."

Wynn looked around the inside of the car. Not old, but not new either. The vinyl seats in the back were holding up reasonably well, but there was a distinct underlying odor. Organic. Probably vomit. Maybe blood. Possibly a mixture of both. And worse. He tried not to think about it.

In front of him, a crosshatch of eighth-inch metal wires created a cage barrier between the back seat and the front. Crower sat on the bench seat in front of him, his Dudley-Do-Right hat barely missing the cage when he turned his head.

I guess that answers that question.

"Ed?" The woman's voice came over the radio.

Crower leaned his head left and reached up to trigger the microphone. "Yeah?"

"Got nothing. He's clean."

Crower paused. "Not anymore. I'm bringing him in. Evading an officer leading to a high-speed chase. Send a tow truck for the bike."

Wynn and the voice on the radio spoke at the same time.

"Seriously?" said the voice on the radio.

"Shit! C'mon Crower. I'm trying to tell you..."

"Shut the fuck up!" Crower screamed.

Pausing to calm himself, Crower thumbed the microphone. "Yes Sam, I'm serious. Just send the truck."

There was a slight pause, then the woman's voice said, "On its way," and clicked off.

Crower sank back in his seat and took a deep breath. "Okay, hotshot. What's your story?"

So Wynn told him. Complete with how he was lying under a tree, minding his own business. How the van arrived and how he watched its occupants react to the various people they saw. How the van followed the Subaru. Twice. How he got stopped at the road construction zone north of Linert, and finally why he was speeding, as he tried to catch them.

When Wynn finished, Crower paused.

"That's it?" he asked.

Wynn waited.

"No physical altercation? No assault? No 'I saw them grab her and throw her in a van'?"

Wynn closed his eyes and shook his head.

"Bullshit," Crower said. "I expected better."

"Listen, officer. It may not sound like much, but I know what I saw."

"You know what I see? An entitled fucking biker wannabe." Without another word, Crower opened his door and got out, then leaned against the front fender, waiting for the tow truck.

Wynn glanced at the clock on the dash. It was 2:58 p.m.

CHAPTER 8

W YNN WAITED A half-hour for the tow truck to show up, all the while watching the cars he'd passed earlier speed past him now. He imagined the slight smiles on the driver's faces as they saw him sitting in the back of the cruiser. He didn't blame them. It was human nature. There's just something satisfying about seeing someone who broke the rules get caught.

Thankfully, Crower had lowered his window to allow some fresh air to flow, but it was still hot. Wynn noticed Crower himself chose to spend the wait outside, leaning on the hood and filling out paperwork.

Eventually, an old Ford pickup pulling a small trailer eased to the side of the road in front of the Harley. As the driver got out, Crower immediately began barking at him. Apparently, his mood hadn't gotten any better.

The driver, to Wynn's amusement, basically ignored Crower as he flipped down a ramp from the trailer and checked the bike for the keys. Seeing them, the tow driver said something to Crower and walked back to the cruiser.

He stuck his head in the open driver's window and said, "Hey man, I can either ride it up the ramp or push it, but that's a heavy bitch. If you want me to push it, I can't promise it won't tip, but that's not on me if you don't want me riding it. What do you want me to do?"

Wynn knew why he was asking and instantly liked the guy. He knew the Rules of the Road: Never sit on someone else's bike without permission.

"You ride?" Wynn asked.

"Fat Bob, twenty years."

"Ride it," Wynn told him.

The tow driver straightened up, tapped the inside of the door, and gave a thumbs up. He walked back to the bike, threw a leg over the seat, and slowly rode it up the ramp. Using ratchet straps, he began securing the bike to the trailer.

At least this guy knows what he's doing.

Finishing up, the driver exchanged a few words with Crower, then climbed into the old Ford and pulled onto the highway, hauling the bike away.

It was only a mile or so into Newbury, but Crower seemed to relish his prize, cruising slowly as if the streets were crowded for a July 4th parade, and he was the Grand Marshall.

Within minutes, they arrived at a large brown brick building set on a corner lot with a short, curved driveway leading to a double-wide garage. Crower thumbed his radio as they approached. "Sam, can you open door one, please."

A moment later the garage door began to rise. Crower waited until it was clear then eased inside, the door immediately closing behind them. The space grew dark as the panels lowered, the only light provided by four small windows and a few dim bulbs.

Ahead, a second door exited to the other side street, the layout finally making sense. Cruisers would come in one side, close the entrance behind them, take their prisoners inside, then pull through the opposite end without ever backing up. Great for ensuring hardened criminals had no chance of escape. And for preventing prying eyes from getting a front-row view when their neighbors were brought in on various drunken infractions.

Crower shut down the engine, then grabbed a clear plastic evidence bag where he placed Wynn's wallet, gun, magazine, and ID. He pulled Wynn out of the cruiser and led him across the garage to a steel door with a small, rectangular window.

Stepping through, Wynn entered a brightly lit lobby where two young men were handcuffed to chairs in a small waiting area. One had his hand wrapped in a bloody bandage, while the other sported a bright purple bruise on his left cheek. Along the back wall, a large window looked in on what Wynn assumed was a supervisor's office. It was dark inside.

That figures. Late on a Sunday afternoon. Nobody'll be in there 'til tomorrow.

Next to the office, a long hallway led off the lobby with multiple, evenly spaced doors on either side.

Jail cells.

The left side of the lobby was dominated by a deputy work area. A chest-high half wall curved from back to front, with four cut-out receiving stations reminding Wynn of a teller line at a bank. A lone, female deputy occupied the second station while two other deputies sat at desks against the far wall. The woman stopped typing and looked toward Wynn.

"So, this is him?" she said to Crower. The same voice as was on the radio. Sam.

"Yup," said Crower. "Speeding, evading, and resisting. Mr. Wynn here hit the trifecta."

"Okay. Bring him over."

As Crower led Wynn over to where she sat, he noticed the floor behind the half wall had been raised two steps to allow the deputies behind the counter to sit while remaining eye-to-eye as they processed detainees. Crower stepped up close to Wynn and said, "Now, I'm going to uncuff you, then re-cuff you here." He nodded to a steel eyelet on the counter. "You're not going to do anything stupid, are you?"

"I'm not the one being stupid here," Wynn replied.

Sam dropped her eyes, hiding a slight smile.

Crower leaned in close and whispered, "Keep talking, asshole. I got you for the night, but I can keep you all week if I want."

"Cool it," she said to cut him off. "You got the paper and belongings?"

"Right here." Crower set the clipboard and evidence bag on the counter. He then uncuffed Wynn's hands from behind him and re-cuffed them to the counter.

When he was finished, she said to Crower, "Why don't you go move your car and get a cup of coffee. Let me talk to Mr. Wynn here."

"Whatever you say." Crower turned and left through the same door they'd just entered.

Sam let out a heavy breath. "Well, you certainly pissed him off. You want to tell me your side?"

"Not really," Wynn replied, still watching the door Crower had left from. "You won't believe me."

"Try me."

Wynn turned back to face the deputy. It was the first time he'd gotten a good look at her. Not what he expected. It was hard to tell her height as she was sitting on a raised platform, but he guessed around five-foot-six, maybe a hundred twenty pounds. Mid-thirties and holding up well. Really well. She had auburn hair pulled back in a loose bun, with a few stray strands framing her lightly freckled face. Her dark eyes sparkled. The brass name tag above her left uniform pocket read *S. Miller*.

"Pretty simple," Wynn said. "I saw a couple of guys in a van checking out women who were traveling alone at the rest stop at Prairie Junction. It looked like they selected a target and started following her, so I followed them. We got separated at a construction zone north of Linert. I was speeding trying to catch up."

"But you didn't?" Miller asked.

"Obviously. My guess is they turned off at Mule Creek Junction."

"Why didn't you go that way?"

"I spoke with her briefly at a gas station in Linert. She asked if I was going to Sturgis. When I said yes, she said maybe she'd see me there. Figured this was the most direct route."

"You spoke with her?"

"Just a couple of words as I was filling my tank and she got in her car."

"You didn't say anything about the van?"

"It was gone. At that point I figured it was just my imagination. Didn't want to freak her out."

"Hmm. Tell me about the van," Miller said.

"It was a white Chevy panel van. Older model. Had the words 'All Season Plumbing' painted on the side."

"Did you get a plate?"

Wynn silently cursed himself. "When they were close enough at Prairie Junction, I wasn't that suspicious. By the time I became convinced they were up to something I never got close."

"Don't beat yourself up. If they really did it the plates were probably stolen or fake anyway."

"So you believe me?"

Miller paused. Looked him in the eye as if struggling with an internal debate. Finally, she said, "We've had two other missing persons reports, women, in the last week. Both within two hundred miles. One can happen. Two might be bad luck. But three?"

Wynn nodded.

"What kind of car was the lady driving?" Miller asked.

"A black Subaru."

Miller turned to her computer and started typing. She paused. Wynn saw her eyes scan the screen. She typed some more and scanned some more.

"Well," she sighed heavily. "We've got nothing new on a missing person or a missing Subaru. No kidnappings or abductions."

"It just happened a couple of hours ago."

Miller paused again, then turned away from Wynn to the two deputies sitting against the far wall. "Hey, Balls. Got a sec?"

One of the deputies from the back got up and came over. Miller continued, "Can you put out a BOLO on a black Subaru while I process Crower's guy here?

"Sure," Balls said, "What else you got?"

Miller turned back to Wynn. "Can you describe the car or the woman?"

Wynn described both, then Balls went back to his desk to put out a "Be on the lookout" notice to other agencies and departments in the area.

"We appreciate your help, Mr. Wynn," Miller said. "Unfortunately, that doesn't dismiss the charges against you. You've explained the speeding, but what about the evasion charge?"

"Didn't happen," Wynn lied. "I was concentrating on the road in front of me, not behind. If I didn't pull over fast enough it was because I didn't see him."

"You didn't hear his siren?"

"You ever ridden a Harley at eighty miles an hour? You don't hear much of anything."

"Crower says you were doing at least a hundred."

Wynn shrugged. "I'm not confirming that, but if so, that would make it even harder."

She raised her eyebrows, conceding the point. "What about resisting?"

"Didn't happen," Wynn said again. "I cooperated completely once I saw him and pulled over."

"Alright. But I've still got to detain you. I'm going to come around and uncuff you. Put you down in one of those chairs." Miller got up from her station and walked toward the back where she tapped another deputy on the shoulder. "A little help?"

As the deputy followed, Miller grabbed a possessions bag, then walked down a couple of steps and around the curved half wall toward Wynn. She stopped in front of him while the other deputy walked around and stood behind.

He's the muscle.

She set the bag on the counter and unlocked the cuffs. "Empty your pockets, put it all in the bag. Phone, jewelry, sunglasses, it all goes in there."

Wynn did as he was told. No choice really.

She sealed the bag, then directed him to a chair away from the other two detainees. He sat down as she re-cuffed his left wrist to an eyelet on the bulky frame. When he was secured, the other deputy walked back to his desk.

"We'll only do one if you promise to be good," Miller said.

Wynn nodded.

Miller grabbed the possessions bag from the counter and walked back around the curved wall. Wynn saw her place it next to the evidence bag that already contained his wallet and gun. She came back a few minutes later with a small tablet computer; had him press his thumb and all four fingers against the tablet's screen. They repeated the process with his left hand. New fingerprint technology. At least new since the last time Wynn had been printed.

"What about my bike?" Wynn asked.

"Impounded," she said. "You'll get it tomorrow. Assuming Crower cools off by then."

She returned to her station.

The clock on the wall read 4:23 p.m.

CHAPTER 9

HEARING WAS THE first sense to come back online as Jessica slowly became aware of faint voices, distant and muffled. She opened her eyes and felt her lashes brush against a blindfold, the darkness becoming only slightly less so. She tried moving her arms, but they were still tied securely above her head. She tried to scream, but a cloth was bound tightly across her mouth. Panicking, she began to squirm and twist her body, trying to free her hands.

A strong hand clamped down over her mouth. She froze.

"Shh." A man's voice came out of the darkness. "It's all right. We're not going to hurt you." The voice, while attempting to be soothing, sent a chill down Jessica's spine. It continued, "We just need you to be still and quiet, otherwise, I'll have to stick you again, so be still, okay?"

Jessica paused, then with renewed terror she bucked and squirmed and screamed and tried to free her hands, until a third jolt of electricity pierced her body. This time it was brief. A quick zap, but it stung like hell. Her muscles contracted, involuntarily, until the stun gun was removed, leaving behind an intense tingling sensation that lingered for some time before slowly fading. Only when the tingling dissipated could she again control her movements.

Now, after the third shock, Jessica's whole body ached. She could feel the hard steel beneath her but could see nothing. The gag in her mouth made it hard to breathe. She rolled her head to the side and then froze as the voice came again. Close.

"Let's try this again. We need you to be still and quiet. If you do that, we won't hurt you. I promise. But if you scream, I'll have to keep sticking you. Understand?"

Jessica remained still.

"Understand?" the voice asked, a little louder, more intense.

Jessica nodded.

"Good girl. We'll be getting out in a little bit."

Jessica sensed the man move away, possibly crawling into the front seat. The vehicle gently rocked and swayed. The road felt smooth, paved.

She heard the voice quietly say, "She's a little older."

A second male voice, rougher and deeper, responded. "So?"

"Just saying. Don't want to have to do this again."

"She'll do fine."

Jessica's mind raced as she pieced together what was happening. She was obviously being kidnapped, but neither she nor her family had any money. Which left only one reason.

God help me.

Eventually, she felt the vehicle slow, then turn onto a bumpy dirt road. She bounced across the metal floor, slamming her head against the hard steel. She pushed her hips against the side wall and tried to use her feet to brace herself, but with her ankles tied, it was impossible to gain any leverage as the van continued to bounce and jolt along.

Once again, the voice came from right beside her.

"Hey. I need you to listen up. We're going to be stopping soon, understand?"

Jessica remained still.

"Understand?" he asked again, more urgently.

Jessica nodded.

"See, this is going to be a problem. The people we're going to see won't ask twice. When they ask you a question, you need to respond right away. Understand?"

Jessica nodded.

"Good. That's good. Now when we stop, we'll untie you, but then we're going to walk quietly to where I tell you. Do that and you won't get hurt. If you try to yell or scream or run, we'll zap you again. And after that, it'll get serious, got it?

Jessica hesitated, wondering how much more serious it could get, and then nodded quickly.

A few moments later, the vehicle stopped. The passenger door opened, then slammed shut. The van moved forward again and eased up onto a smooth surface and rolled a few feet before finally stopping. The engine shut down.

The side panel door slid open and rough hands grabbed onto her arms and legs. Her ankle restraints were cut, and her wrists, still tied together, were freed from above her head. She lowered her arms to ease the pain in her shoulders as the hands slid her across the steel floor. Her feet fell from the van as she was pulled to a sitting position, then more hands grabbed onto each arm as she was pulled to her feet and led no more than fifteen steps away.

"Remember," the voice whispered as they shuffled forward. "He won't ask twice."

Smooth straps were placed around each wrist and her arms jerked above her head. When the rough hands released their grip, her knees buckled. Her arms wrenched in their sockets as she was held off the floor, her feet dragging across the concrete. Summoning all her strength, Jessica pulled herself up, regained her feet, and leaned into her aching arms that were once again bound high above her head.

Without warning, a powerful jet of cold water slapped her in the face, causing her breath to catch. She spun her head away as the stream assaulted every inch of her body, soaking her clothing and sticking it to her skin, before eventually going back to her face. She swung her head back and forth, gasping for air. When the water stopped, a powerful hand grabbed the hair at the back of her head and pulled down, forcing her face up. Another hand tore the blindfold off.

It took a moment for her eyes to adjust to the brightness of the sudden light. When they finally focused, she saw only the grizzled face of an old man. When he spoke, she was immediately hit by the foul smell of cigarettes and the sight of twisted teeth. "Understand one thing," he said. "Your life is over. You're mine. You'll do what I say, when I say it. Do you understand?"

Jessica screamed through the gag still in her mouth.

The powerful hand released the back of her head, and the old man took several steps backward as he locked eyes with Jessica. She saw a slight smile appear at the edges of his crooked mouth as his eyes shifted to a spot behind her. He gave a small nod.

She heard a brief whoosh of air before her back exploded with an excruciating blaze from the thick leather strap that landed just below her shoulder blades. Her legs buckled, her arms stretching tight as they held the weight of her collapsing body. She couldn't think, couldn't scream, couldn't even breathe as the air was sucked from her lungs. She struggled to comprehend what was happening, her brain overwhelmed by the piercing pain that overrode all other thoughts.

Suddenly her head was roughly yanked back again as the foul breath returned. "I will say this only one more time. You, are mine. Your life, is over. You will do what I say, when I say it. Do you understand?"

She nodded quickly, eager to end the pain. "Yes, yes." She struggled to breathe the words through the gag as tears streamed down her face.

He shoved her head roughly forward and stepped away as a second explosion ripped across her back.

———

Brandon winced as the second stroke fell. He'd tried to warn her, but Tomas was probably going to give her at least two anyway. He was grateful she stopped resisting. At least that way she wouldn't get any more. Too many lashes and she wouldn't be able to move at all for what he had planned later.

He stood with the entire crew inside the large barn waiting for Tomas to give the signal. Several cars, including the white van and red Jeep, were parked in the eight work bays lining the left side of the shop, while the skeletal remains of an unidentifiable sedan sat in the first bay on the right. Further back, where the two solid walls cordoned off the back quarter of the shop, the heavy steel door remained locked.

The seven men stood in a wide semi-circle around the girl, barely conscious as she hung from her wrists. Carlos, a skinny, twenty-something with dark skin and black hair, held the rope that kept the girl upright. Nathan, in his mid-thirties and only slightly smaller than an NFL linebacker, had driven the Subaru after they'd taken the girl and was now holding the water hose. Tony, another twenty-something, held the leather strap. Brandon thought he enjoyed that job a little too much. And finally, on either side of Brandon were John and Andy, both in their early forties. John had been with Brandon in the van, while Andy had driven the Jeep.

They were all waiting on instructions from Tomas, who gave a small wave of his hand. Carlos let out the rope as Brandon and Andy stepped forward and lowered her to the floor. Brandon removed the leather straps from around her wrists and gently tapped her face.

"Hey, hey. You with me?" he asked.

She moaned softly.

Brandon and Andy each took an arm and lifted the girl to her feet, then half-carried, half-dragged her toward the steel door. John went ahead and pulled a key off a hook next to the door, which he unlocked, then held open as Brandon and Andy took the girl in.

The door opened to a small eight-by-ten-foot mudroom with a washer and dryer immediately in front of them, and a door on either side. The door on the left was open to what resembled a small studio apartment. A couch and chair sat against the opposite wall facing a television next to the door. Further back, a galley kitchen lined the outer walls around a table and two chairs.

To the right was a solid wood interior door. John went up to it, pounded his fist three times, then yelled, "Back off!" as he unlocked and opened it.

Inside was a fifteen-by-twenty-foot room with a concrete floor and painted brick walls. Canister lights dotted the ceiling. A bathroom was tucked behind the mudroom, its door open to the left.

Pushed up against the walls were four sets of bunkbeds, eight beds in all. Five women, three Latina, all in their early twenties, and two Caucasian, one in her early twenties and one in her thirties, sat huddled on the lower bunks. The three Latinas had been dropped off earlier today while Brandon was out. He didn't know their names. The older lady, a sandy-haired blonde named Ann, had been picked up in a rainstorm on Friday, while the younger blonde, Hailey, had been picked up yesterday in Nebraska.

Brandon and Andy hauled the new girl into the room and laid her down on the hard, concrete floor. The sandy-haired blonde, Ann, glared at him. He smiled and winked at her, then silently turned and left.

John closed and locked the door, then gathered with the others in the main barn.

"Where'd you leave the car?" Tomas asked.

"Out of sight in a field near Waterberg Road," Nathan replied.

"What kind?"

"Subaru."

"Did she have a phone?"

"It was in the car," Nathan said. "There was no signal in that area, so I removed the battery, smashed it, and tossed it in the field."

"Her name?"

"Jessica Davies."

Tomas nodded. "Okay, good. You and Tony get back up there

before dark. Get the car moved close to the main road. Don't want people seeing headlights in a field after dark, sure way to get noticed. When it gets dark, bring it in and start tearing it apart. People don't see a lot of Subaru's around here."

Turning to Brandon, Andy, and Carlos, Tomas continued, "Tomorrow, you three will make the delivery up north."

CHAPTER 10

WYNN SAT HANDCUFFED to the seat for over an hour before Crower returned to the sheriff's office a little before 6:00 p.m.

The waiting room was empty except for Wynn, the other detainees either released or taken to their cells. A door at the end of the hallway opened, then footsteps reverberated on the tile as Crower came down the hall. He was still wearing his sunglasses, but even so, Wynn could feel his eyes watching him.

What a douche.

Crower took the two steps up to the raised platform where the deputy workstations were located, said a quick hello to the two other deputies, then came around to where Miller was seated at her computer. "Come up with anything else on my boy there?"

"Nope," Miller replied. "Ran his name and prints through all the databases, FBI, NCIC, NICS, all of them. He's clean. You sure you want to keep him? I mean, he admits to the speeding but says he didn't hear your siren; pulled over as soon as he saw you. Tough to prove a negative. Same with the resisting. Says it didn't happen."

"It happened all right," said Crower. "We're keeping him. Just to teach him a lesson if nothing else.

"Smitty's not gonna like it."

"Fuck Smitty. And fuck you, too. I said we're keeping him so just shut up and get him processed, alright?" Crower stomped away. "I'm going back out on patrol. Call me if you need something."

Crower sulked to the far end of the raised platform, down the steps, and around the half-wall, keeping his eyes straight forward, not acknowledging Wynn at all. He went out the door into the garage, his hollow footsteps cut off when the door banged shut.

"All right, Mr. Wynn," Miller called over the counter. "Time to get you settled in. Anyone you want to call before we do this?"

"No calls, but I would ask a favor."

"What's that?"

"Check the wires for a missing person's bulletin again. See if anyone's responded to that BOLO."

"Already ahead of you," Miller said. "I've been checking every twenty minutes. So far nothing."

"Humor me. Do it again."

Miller paused and looked at him, then turned back to her computer. She clicked the mouse a few times and then typed for a moment. She scanned the screen, then shook her head. "Nope. Nothing. Let's hope you're wrong."

Wynn nodded. "Let's hope."

Miller sighed and got up from her workstation. She gave a quick nod to one of the other deputies who followed her down the steps and over to Wynn.

"Let's be clear about this," Miller said. "You are not under arrest. But per deputy Crower's report, you are being detained overnight on suspicion of speeding, evading a deputy sheriff, and resisting arrest. Too late to get your bike out of impound anyway. The sheriff will be in first thing in the morning, and we'll get you cleared up and out of here. Deputy Harris will see to it you get something to eat tonight, as will the guys in the morning. If you change your mind about that phone call, let him know. Any questions?"

Wynn shook his head once.

"The silent type. My favorite." She released the cuff from the seat. The other end stayed on Wynn's wrist. "Stand up. Let's go."

Wynn stood, glanced at Deputy Harris then followed Miller past the dark office and down the hallway that led off from the lobby. Miller stopped at the third door on the left, pressed a code into a keypad, then opened the door and ushered Wynn inside.

"Take a seat on the cot and remove your belt and boots, please," Miller instructed.

Wynn rolled his eyes. "Really?"

Miller shrugged. "Wouldn't want you getting distraught and hurting yourself."

He sighed. *Tried that earlier. Couldn't do it then, either.*

He opened his jacket and lifted his shirt to show he wasn't wearing a belt, then sat down and removed his boots. Harris removed the cuff from his wrist, grabbed his boots, and walked out.

Miller stepped out and closed the door. "Have a good night, Mr. Wynn."

Wynn looked around the cell. He hated to admit it, but he'd probably paid for worse hotel rooms. It was small, eight feet by ten feet, but it was clean. Sparkling, really. The floor was polished concrete and the walls were the same not-quite-white painted cinderblock as the waiting area. A long fluorescent light fixture sat flush with the ceiling. A single cot was pushed against one wall while a stainless-steel combination commode and sink sat along the back. The steel door had a small window and a slot for passing food.

Wynn took off his jacket, sat down on the cot, and swiveled his feet up. He lay back, looking up at the ceiling. Once again, his mind ran through what he'd seen. All the pieces fit. Except one. How'd they grab her? How would they get her to stop in an isolated area without being seen? Were they going to follow until a random opportunity presented itself? What if that opportunity never came? Would they just give up? Not likely.

He was missing something.

Ann sat in the dark, waiting.

He would come. She was sure of it.

The new girl mumbled and groaned on the bunk to her left, just as Ann had two nights ago, when she was alone.

He had come for her then, when she was too injured to resist. Even so, she'd put up a fight. Forced him to use the stun gun. He'd gotten what he wanted, but it hadn't been easy.

Unlike last night, after Hailey had been brought in. Ann heard the deadbolt slide back, followed by the click as the latch turned. He came straight for her. Thinking he was going to attack her again, Ann fought hard. But he stunned her, tied her hands to the bed, then forced her to watch while he raped Hailey.

Not tonight.

She sat for two hours, then three, watching the door. Listening intently. Holding the three-inch bolt she'd loosened from the bed frame.

The new girl moaned. Hailey whimpered. The three Latina girls breathed softly. Every so often, the oldest of the three sat up, saw her waiting, and shook her head.

No help there.

She waited.

Click.

Ann sprang to her feet, silently dashing across the room and pressing herself against the wall next to the door as the deadbolt slid back. The knob turned, and the door cracked open.

At first, all she could see was his hand, then his arm, then his forehead, pale and matted with greasy hair.

Ann held her fist high, the bolt protruding like a knife. She leapt forward, slashing down, crashing her fist on top of his head. The man cried out as Ann felt the warm stickiness of his blood splash onto her arm.

He pushed into the room and grabbed her by the throat, then

spun her to the floor while she hammered away at his head. Now wet with blood, the bolt slipped from her grasp as she scratched and clawed, trying to push him off.

A dark shape joined the fight, jumping on top of the guy, trying to pull him off. The long black hair meant it was one of the Latina girls, but Ann had no idea which one. Light suddenly spilled in from the open doorway and a fourth shape joined in. Larger and darker. Angrier.

The stunner crackled and the girl fell away. Ann was still on the ground as the first guy was pulled off, swinging his arms and kicking furiously, landing a solid shot to her ribs that expelled the air from her lungs.

She gasped and rolled, curling her arms and legs to ward off the attack she was sure to come, but never did.

"What the fuck are you doing?" The voice was male, but not him. The second guy.

"The bitch cut me!"

"If Tomas catches you, or these girls are damaged, he'll fucking kill you."

The guy didn't say anything, just loomed over Ann. He breathed heavily, silhouetted by the light from outside the door.

"Let's get out of here."

The two guys backed out of the door and closed it. The deadbolt slid back into place.

Ann sat up. The older Latina girl lay sprawled next to her. Ann helped her up and back to her bunk, rubbing her arm to restore feeling.

"*Gracias,*" Ann said as the girl lay back.

Ann let the girl rest, then scanned the floor for the bolt. She found it, picked it up, and tucked it into her pocket.

CHAPTER 11

Monday

Wynn woke around what he guessed was 6:00 the next morning, although with no clock or windows, it was hard to tell. His dreams alternated between the new and the familiar. The new ones centered around the brunette in the Subaru, while the familiar continuously replayed his last night with Nicole.

Deputy Harris had kept Miller's promise of providing something to eat. He banged on Wynn's cell door after an hour or so with a tray full of chicken-fried steak, mashed potatoes, and gravy. There was even a piece of cake for dessert. It looked and tasted like it had come from a local diner, which Wynn was grateful for. Better than the microwave crap he'd been expecting.

He was beginning to feel the dull pang of hunger already this morning, but more than anything craved a strong cup of coffee. Since that wasn't an option, he stripped to his boxers and spent the next forty-five minutes going through his kata, the one thing that had been constant the past few years. Space was tight, but there was enough. When finished, he cleaned up as best he could in the small sink, got dressed, and sat down on the cot to wait.

Roughly thirty minutes later, an electronic click sounded from the door. It opened, revealing Miller on the other side. She was dressed casually, in civilian clothes. Blue jeans and a black pullover. She looked good, but she did not look happy.

"Come on," she said as she handed him his boots. "We're gonna go see the sheriff."

"Okay." He sat down to put them on. "I didn't expect to see you this morning."

"I didn't expect to be here. But I couldn't get that story of yours out of my head, so I came in early to check the wires."

"Tell me."

"Jessica Davies. Lives in Denver. Turned thirty, two days ago. Drives a black Subaru. Was on her way to Rapid City yesterday to spend the week with her sister, but never made it. The sister reported her missing at about seven o'clock last night, but it didn't make the wires until ten. Still nothing on our BOLO but the sheriff wants to talk about it."

Wynn finished lacing up his boots and followed Miller up the hallway into the office that sat off the waiting area. A heavyset man in his mid-fifties with short grey hair sat behind a desk, dressed in the same khaki shirt as all the other deputies, minus the necktie and the Dudley-Do-Right hat.

"Sheriff Smith," Miller said by way of introduction, "This is Sean Wynn. Mr. Wynn, Sheriff Smith."

Wynn nodded, but neither man offered their hand.

Smith paused, apparently sizing Wynn up, then said, "Sam here tells me you might have some information regarding this missing person's report."

Wynn shrugged. "Maybe. It depends."

"On what?"

"These bullshit charges that kept me here all night."

"Yeah. About those," Smith said slowly. "Sam says you admit to the speeding, under extenuating circumstances, but deny the evading and resisting, correct?"

"That's right."

"Okay. I'm willing to make all the charges disappear, including the impound fees on your bike, in exchange for a little cooperation. Fair enough?"

"How much is a little cooperation?"

"Just tell me what you saw."

Wynn nodded. "Fair enough."

"Okay, then." Smith leaned back and laced his fingers across his stomach. "Let's hear it."

Wynn told the story again while Smith listened intently, without interrupting, all the way through the point when he saw the white van pull out from the side street across from the gas station. At that point, Smith leaned forward. "Which gas station?"

Wynn paused a moment, searching his memory. "The Fresh Start. Right on the main drag."

"About what time was this?"

"One fifteen, maybe one-thirty. "

"That works," said Miller. "The report says the sister received a text message from her about twelve-forty, saying she was leaving Prairie Junction."

Smith turned to Miller, "Call the sheriff's office down in Linert. Have them send someone over to the Fresh Start to see if they've got video of the pumps and streets around there. We need to look at everything between one and two o'clock yesterday."

Turning back to Wynn, he said, "Tell me more about the van."

Wynn shrugged. "Typical white Chevy panel van. Hard to tell exactly how old, but not new. It'd been around." Wynn paused, again searching his memory. "All Season Plumbing. It had a sign on the side that said All Season Plumbing."

"Anything else?"

Wynn shook his head.

Smith turned back to Miller, "Go."

Miller got up and left the room to make the phone call.

"All right," Smith said. "So, you saw the van pull out from a side street to follow her. Then what?"

"I followed them. But I lost them at a road construction zone about fifteen miles north of Linert. They were let through in the group in front of me. By the time I got through they were gone. I tried to catch up but that's when Crower pulled me over. You know the rest."

Smith nodded. "If she was going to see her sister in Rapid City, she would've turned off at Mule Creek Junction. Why didn't you go that way?"

"When I was behind her at the gas station, we exchanged a few words. She said maybe she'd see me in Sturgis. Figured 85 was the most direct route."

Smith nodded again. "Okay. You said you saw those guys at Prairie Junction, right? What'd they look like?"

Wynn spent the next twenty minutes giving Smith a description of the two men he'd seen and answered the rest of his questions. Miller came back as they were finishing up.

"So?" Smith asked.

"They've got tape," she said. "It's digital, but they don't want to release it. They're saying if the abduction took place in their county, they want to hang on to and control all the potential evidence. They said we're welcome to come down and look at it, but they won't send it over."

Smith leaned back in his chair and sighed. After a moment, he said, "Mr. Wynn, I know we've imposed heavily on you already, but I'd love to have you confirm if there's anything on that tape that'll help us. Would you be willing to run down to Linert with Sam here to take a look?"

"Two conditions. First, stop with the mister stuff. Just call me Wynn."

Smith smiled. "All right. And the second?"

Wynn turned to Miller. "Can we get some coffee along the way?"

———

Jessica woke physically broken, her entire body stiff from the residue of the stun gun. Her back still smoldered like hot coals that reignited to an excruciating fire with each tiny motion or breath. She lay on her side, on a bottom bunk near the door, breathing shallow to minimize the pain.

The room was dark, lit only by a rectangle of light that spilled from a bathroom door left halfway open. There were no windows; no way to tell if it was day or night. No way to tell what time it was. The sound of sleepy breathing drifted across the room, along with the occasional whimper.

There'd been a commotion last night. Screaming, yelling, and scuffling. She'd been so out of it she wasn't even sure what happened. All was quiet now.

Across the room, two figures shared a lower bunk, their feet near the bathroom door. A third figure, female, lay in the bunk above them. Two more huddled bodies occupied the other two lower bunks that spanned the wall between. The other upper beds were empty.

She remembered most of what happened, being pulled out of the van and strung up by her arms. She remembered the man with the bad teeth and cigarette breath, and what he said.

Your life is over. You're mine.

More than anything she remembered the pain. How her back seemed to explode each time the lash fell. She remembered being dumped on a cold concrete floor, gentle hands helping her onto the bed where she now lay. Seeing the five other girls in the room left no doubt as to what was happening. And try as she might to resist, she feared that eventually, she might do anything to avoid the pain.

CHAPTER 12

MILLER LED WYNN out of the office. "Second window," she said, pointing to her workstation. Wynn walked around the front of the curved half wall while Miller took the two steps to the raised platform and came around the other side.

"Let's get you released first, then we'll head out," she said.

She sat down at her computer, signed in, and quickly pulled up a few documents, then made some notations. While they were printing, she took a set of keys off her desk, unlocked a drawer beneath the counter, then placed both the evidence and property bags in front of Wynn. Grabbing the forms off the printer she turned back to him and said, "This one dismisses all the charges and this one acknowledges we've returned your property."

Wynn opened the property bag first and took out his cell phone. It looked none the worse for wear. He turned it on. No messages. No texts. Thirty-eight percent battery remaining. "You got an iPhone charger in your car?" he asked.

"Yep. No problem."

Wynn put his sunglasses on top of his head and emptied the rest of the bag. There wasn't much in there. "Where are my bike keys?"

"They're at the impound yard. We'll get those when we get back."

He took his wallet from the evidence bag, opening it to make sure his ID was still there. It was. As were his credit cards and cash. He closed it and slipped it into his back pocket. He reached in and pulled out his gun.

"Hey," said Miller. "Would you mind not loading that until we get outside? Cops get nervous seeing guns in any non-uniformed hands."

Wynn nodded. He checked the chamber to make sure it was empty, then put the gun in his inside jacket pocket and placed the magazine in an outside pocket. He picked up a pen and signed the forms.

"We good?" he asked.

"We're good." Miller took the forms and placed them on top of a pile on the corner of her desk. "Have a seat," she said, nodding to the waiting area. "I'll be just a minute."

Wynn stepped back and settled into a chair as Miller went back to the desk area where two new deputies sat. She exchanged a few words Wynn couldn't hear, then grabbed a set of car keys off a rack on the wall and turned down the hallway past the cells, eventually disappearing through a door at the end of the hall.

Moments later, the door from the drive-through garage opened and Crower strolled in. He stopped short when he saw Wynn sitting in the waiting area, unsecured and unattended.

"What the fuck?" he said loudly as he looked around. He went to one of the windows and called out to the guys in back, "What's my perp doing out here?"

"Smitty dismissed," one of the guys replied. "Sammy's finishing him up."

"Fuck!" Crower said under his breath, yet still loud enough for Wynn to hear. He followed Crower's gaze across the lobby to Smith's office. The lights were on, but with the blinds closed, it was impossible to see if Sheriff Smith was in there. Crower stormed back to the office, knocked once, and entered. The door closed behind him.

Wynn could hear their voices as Crower and Smith yelled, but couldn't make out exactly what was being said. That was okay. He knew the gist of it. Within minutes, Crower came out of the office and made his way across the lobby to the garage door. As he passed Wynn, he slowed just a second, a slight hesitation as if he was going to say something, then changed his mind. He quickly pulled open the door and left.

Sheriff Smith had appeared at the doorway of his office and watched. When Crower was gone, he walked slowly up to Wynn.

"Since Crower's too chickenshit to say it, I'll say it again. We apologize for the inconvenience and appreciate your cooperation. I hope his BS doesn't reflect too badly on the department."

As he was speaking, Miller came out of the door at the end of the hallway behind Smith and walked toward them. She had changed into her uniform shirt but was still wearing the blue jeans. Her duty belt, with her gun, Taser, and all the accouterments, hung from her hips. She looked good.

"I'll get over it," Wynn replied.

Smith nodded, then noticed Miller join them.

"We ready?" she asked.

"He's all yours," Smith said.

"Alright. Let's do it."

Wynn followed Miller past the cell where he'd spent the night to a door at the end of the corridor. She punched a code into the keypad and went through, holding it open for Wynn. On the other side, the whole look and feel of the building changed. Instead of the harsh white concrete blocks that made up the prisoner processing area, the main area was nicely appointed with warm tones, paneled walls, and new carpet.

Managing the public image.

Miller took an immediate right and exited through a set of glass double doors. Wynn followed as they went down a short sidewalk to a small parking lot full of vehicles. Miller approached a taupe-colored Ford Explorer and opened the driver's door.

"We'll take the Crown Vic over there," she said, nodding further along. "I just want to grab that phone charger for you."

Wynn nodded, then followed Miller as she strode over to another Wheaton County Sheriff cruiser. He wondered if it was the same one Crower had driven him in yesterday. Same white paint. Same two-tone stripe down the side. Same insignia on the doors.

Miller unlocked the cruiser with a key fob and got in the driver's side. Wynn took off his jacket and opened the back door.

"You can ride up front," Miller offered.

Wynn smiled and held up his jacket. "Damn right," he said. "This is for my jacket."

"Oh, yeah." Her face flushed with embarrassment.

He tossed the jacket onto the back seat and got in the front. He sniffed cautiously. Not the same cruiser. No smell. Or to be more precise, a faint but pleasant scent. Perfume.

Miller handed him the charger. He thanked her, plugged in his phone, and set it on the floor by his feet, the white cord running down the side of the console.

"We don't have a lot of choices for drive-through breakfast, but there's a place on our way out of town that's pretty decent," Miller said.

"As long as they have coffee, I won't be picky about the rest."

Miller maneuvered the Crown Vic out of the lot, and they were soon passing the same streets Wynn had come in on yesterday. She pulled into an off-brand hamburger joint and ordered two breakfast sandwiches and two large coffees.

"The sandwiches are for you," she said, "but I get one of the coffees." She pulled around the building, paid, and soon they were on their way, heading south on Highway 85 in the opposite direction Wynn had come less than twenty-four hours before.

While Wynn ate his breakfast, she said, "I want to thank you for being so cooperative about all this. I wouldn't have blamed you if you'd told us to f-off and gotten the hell out of here."

Nicky would've insisted I help. He shrugged but said nothing.

"So, why are you helping us?"

Wynn swallowed and took a sip of coffee. "Let's get something straight. I'm not helping you, and I'm sure as hell not helping that dick, Crower. I'm helping the lady, Jessica, because it's the right thing to do. She seemed like a nice person, but regardless, no one deserves something like this happening to them. If I can help, I will. It's what decent people do."

Miller drove in silence while Wynn finished his meal. When he was done, he crumpled the wrappers and napkins and stuffed them inside the paper bag, then placed it at his feet.

Feeling bad that he may have been too hard on her, he asked, "So, Deputy Miller, I heard the sheriff and Crower call you Sam. Is that short for something?"

"Samantha. But everyone calls me Sam. And since I'm now calling you Wynn, feel free if you want."

"Fair enough."

"So, Wynn," she said, "I assume you were coming out for the rally?"

"Yep."

"Are you meeting anyone there? I was surprised you didn't make a phone call last night."

"Nope. Going solo this year."

"Where are you staying? Wasn't someone expecting you?"

"A motel near Sturgis. I've got it for eight nights. I'll check in tonight."

"Hmm. You know, a lot of these places will cancel your reservation if you don't arrive when scheduled. Then they can keep your deposit and re-rent the room. And this week in Sturgis they'll get a pretty penny for it. You should call and make sure it's still there for you tonight."

Deciding it was a good idea, Wynn picked up his phone, searched his email for the confirmation, then dialed the number.

"Put it on speaker," Miller said.

He glanced sideways at her. "Why?"

She rolled her eyes. "Just do it."

He did. It rang three times before a gruff male voice picked up. "Boulder Canyon Motel Inn."

Wynn paused, expecting something more. When nothing came, he said, "Hi. My name's Sean Wynn. I was supposed to check in yesterday but got delayed. I was calling to make sure you still had my reservation when I arrive later today."

"Okay. Let me check."

Wynn could hear the clicking of a keyboard over the phone. There was a longer-than-expected pause before the guy came back on.

"I'm sorry, but according to our cancellation policy when you didn't check in as expected and we didn't hear from you, we canceled your reservation."

"Can you reinstate it? I'll be there tonight."

"I'm sorry," he said in a fake apologetic tone, "but we've already re-booked the room."

Miller spoke up. "Excuse me, sir, I didn't catch your name."

"Randy."

"Randy, are you the manager?"

"I own this place."

"Okay Randy," Miller said, her voice growing stronger. "My name is Deputy Samantha Miller, with the Wheaton, Wyoming County Sheriff's office. Badge number 87648. Mr. Wynn here has, at great inconvenience to himself, been helping us with a very serious investigation. I would hate to inconvenience him any further.

"Now Randy, listen to this next part carefully. We enjoy a friendly, helpful relationship with your local Meade County Sheriff's office there in Sturgis. When they have information about a possible crime occurring at an establishment, say a hotel, in our county, they call us. And vice versa. In this situation, if Mr. Wynn were staying at your motel, we'd know we have that base covered, and we'd have no need to call the Meade County Sheriff. If Mr. Wynn is not staying in your motel, we may need constant surveillance of your establishment over the next week or more. You could really help us out if you could reinstate his reservation. Understand?"

Randy cleared his throat, his voice faltering. "Yes ma'am, I understand. Tell you what. We'll have to move some things around, but we'll make sure we have a room available and ready when Mr. Wynn arrives."

"That'd be great." Miller smiled at Wynn.

"My pleasure," Randy said. "And Mr. Wynn? We look forward to welcoming you soon."

"Thank you." Wynn disconnected the call.

He smiled as he looked over at Miller. "That was impressive."

"What's the use in having a badge if you can't throw your weight around a little every once in a while?" she asked.

"As long as you don't become like Crower."

"Please. Give me a little credit."

"For sure," he said. "Thanks. For the call, and the tip. I'd have been screwed."

"No problem. It's our fault you got canceled in the first place." She paused. "So why are you going to Sturgis alone? If you're hoping to get lucky, I've got to tell you, most of those biker chicks are pretty rough."

"Yeah." He laughed softly. "I was there last year, saw it all. I don't know, I just liked it. For the most part, it's instant camaraderie. Ask a guy what kind of bike he rides, and you've got a friend for an hour. Last year I met all kinds of people, heard all kinds of stories. Saw all kinds of different lifestyles." He paused. "Who knows," he said quietly, "I might find one I want to emulate someday."

Miller looked at him. After a moment she asked, "What's your story, Wynn? You don't strike me as a typical biker."

"Why not?"

"Because typical bikers don't use the word emulate." She laughed.

He smiled. She had a point. "What do you want to know?"

"The typical. Where'd you grow up, go to school? When did you start riding? That kind of thing."

"I grew up in Colorado Springs. The whole city is dominated by the military, so that was pretty ingrained. My dad was a Lieutenant-Colonel in the Air Force so when I graduated high school, I joined the Marines."

"Marines? Why not the Air Force?"

Wynn hesitated, unsure how much he wanted to reveal. "I was a senior in high school when September 11th happened. I probably would've enlisted anyway, but that sealed the deal. My dad was at the Pentagon that day. He survived but was pretty badly burned. And the thing is, ninety-nine percent of those Air Force guys never get close to the action. It's the Marines they call for the tough jobs. Those are the guys who get up close and personal. At that time, after seeing what happened to my dad, it was personal. I wanted to get close."

"Wow. Well first, thanks for your service. How long were you in?"

"Eight years."

"Hmm. You also don't strike me as a typical jarhead. What'd you do?"

"Classified. I can't talk about it," he teased.

"Bullshit! What'd you do?"

"Seriously. I was MARSOC. Marine Forces Special Operations Command. It was new at the time. Not quite the same as the Navy SEALS or Army Rangers, but in that vein. We did a lot of counter-terrorism stuff."

"Stuff?"

"Like I said, I can't talk about it."

"All right," Miller said, half-disappointedly. "Then what? After eight years you're maybe twenty-six? What'd you do then?"

So he told her. Most of it anyway. Not all of it. He told her how he went to college, studied computer systems, got a job, quit, started his own company, sold it, and here he was. "Taking my time to figure out what I want to do next," he said.

"Wow," said Miller. "I never believed that old slogan, but you really did do more before you were thirty than most people do in their entire lives."

"Thirty-five," Wynn corrected. "And that's an army slogan."

"Whatever. That's still impressive. Any time for a personal life? Wife? Girlfriend?"

"Married once. Not anymore." He didn't elaborate.

Miller didn't push it.

"What about you?" Wynn wanted to change the subject. "What's your story?"

"Oh, you know. Small town girl goes to the big city to find fame and fortune. Gets chewed up and spit out, then returns home."

"There's got to be more to it. Talk."

"I grew up in Rapid City. Like you, typical middle-class upbringing. At the time, I wanted to be a lawyer, so I went to college at U.W. in Laramie, but became more interested in catching the bad guys than in prosecuting them. Thought I'd be some great, hotshot detective. Graduated, got a job with the police department in Lincoln, Nebraska. Met a guy and married him before I realized what kind of a loser he was. Divorced him but he kept stalking me. And not just him, his brothers, sisters, parents. The whole damn family was nuts. Kept running into them everywhere, even in places they had no business being. Finally had enough so I started looking for jobs closer to home. Newbury sheriff's deputy was the first thing that came up. Been here six years now."

"No kids?"

"Nope. Got lucky on that one. Corrected the mistake with the husband before compounding it with kids. Don't get me wrong, I'd love to have kids, but that clock is winding down fast. And Newbury's a small pond to be fishing for Mr. Right."

"Hmm," Wynn acknowledged. He looked up and saw they were already approaching the route split at Mule Creek Junction. They'd covered those thirty-four miles fast. "Pull in here."

Miller hit the blinker, slowed, and turned into the rest area. Wynn recognized the squat tan brick building at one end of the oval. He saw the picnic shelters surrounded by manicured lawns, the walkways that connected them all. *Fifty-fifty if she even made it this far.*

"Park over there," Wynn said as he pointed to a spot on the right. "Away from the main area."

Miller pulled to a stop where indicated. Wynn got out and walked back to the first of the parking spots that circled the rest area. He ambled slowly, not on the sidewalk but through the parking area itself, head down, eyes sweeping back and forth.

Miller joined him. "You're thinking this is where they grabbed her?"

"It's possible. She stopped at Prairie Junction."

"And if so, we're looking for scuff marks, tire tracks, lost buttons. Anything that might indicate a scuffle."

"You got it," he replied. "Anything that looks out of the ordinary or seems out of place."

Miller took up a position between Wynn and the sidewalk as they slowly walked the entire circumference of the rest area, then the pathways leading into and away from the restroom itself. They saw a lot of the ordinary. Mostly fast food and snack wrappers, but nothing that seemed out of place. Nothing to indicate anything unusual had happened at all.

They also saw a lot of people.

"Is this place always this busy?" Wynn asked.

"Not always, but it's the only thing for twenty-five miles in any direction. It gets used, for sure," Miller replied.

They split up and searched the outer parking areas, Wynn taking one side of the oval, Miller the other. When finished, they met back at the cruiser.

"That was a bust," Miller said.

"Not completely," Wynn countered. "At least now we know there's a good chance it didn't happen here. Not only from the fact that we didn't find anything, but also based on how busy this place is. And it likely would have been busier yesterday, on a weekend. Even if they happened to get lucky and corner her here alone, they wouldn't have risked grabbing her in case someone pulled in."

"Agreed. On to Linert?"

"On to Linert," he said.

CHAPTER 13

MILLER AND WYNN drove the next ten minutes in silence, each consumed with their own thoughts as mile after mile of prairie grass streamed by. Wynn continued to gnaw on the one piece of the puzzle that had bothered him last night; how had they gotten her to stop in an area where they were sure they wouldn't be seen? The abduction had to have taken place along the same stretch of highway they were now on, but neither the road nor the prairie were giving up their clues.

Cruising through a long curve, Miller slowed and pulled to the side.

"What's up?" Wynn asked.

"Want to check something out." Miller glanced over her shoulder, confirming the road was clear, then pulled a U-turn. She backtracked a hundred yards and turned into a dirt driveway on the west side of the road. A barbed-wire gate cordoned off the field beyond.

"Look at that," Miller said.

On the other side of the gate, the dirt drive was overgrown with dry vegetation. Two perfectly parallel paths, the width of a car's tires, had been trampled in the grass.

"You think that's them?" Wynn asked.

"Looks fresh enough." She nodded ahead. "Go open the gate. Let's see where they go."

Wynn climbed out. The gate itself was nothing more than four strands of barbed wire attached to four, three-inch-diameter wooden posts. Two loops of plain wire held the gate to the end post. Wynn pushed on the gate, creating a bit of slack in the wire loop, which he then flipped over the gate post. The gate went limp. He pulled it out of the way, allowing Miller to drive through.

"Close it," Miller said. "No need to broadcast that someone is here."

Wynn closed the gate, then hopped back in the cruiser.

"Let's see where this thing goes," Miller said.

They followed the tracks up a bumpy path to the top of a small rise before dropping down the other side. The two parallel paths split into four tracks at the bottom of the embankment. Miller stopped.

"Two cars," she said.

"At least."

They got out and walked ahead. Miller pulled out her phone and took pictures. Wynn crouched down, examined the trampled grass. Much of the younger, greener stuff had already bounced back, giving no indication it had ever been harmed. It was the older, browner stalks that remained bent or broken, indicating someone had come this way.

"Over here," Miller said.

Wynn joined her at the widest point between the four tracks, where two cars could have sat side-by-side. On the diverging track, four impressions pressed into the vegetation, damaging the green grasses as well as the brown.

"They parked it here," Miller said. "Dollars to donuts says the distances between those impressions will match a Subaru Outback perfectly."

"No argument here." Wynn glanced back in the direction of the highway, hidden behind the rise. "Wouldn't have taken them two minutes to get out of sight. So, where is it?"

"They came back last night. In the dark."

"To take it where?"

Miller nodded ahead, to where the four tracks merged back into two. "Let's find out."

They got back into the patrol car and drove on, bouncing two miles over bumpy roads. Tall grasses scraped the sides of the cruiser. They passed through another gate, and another field, and eventually to a paved county road.

"Damn," Miller said. "Was hoping this might actually lead us someplace."

"Would've been too easy," Wynn said.

"Which way?"

"Your state. You know it better than me."

Miller paused. "South will take us to Elderville and then to the interstate. Could go anywhere from there. North will eventually hook back up with 85 to Newbury."

"South, then?"

"I don't know. Our chances of finding something either direction seem slim at best. Once they made it this far, they wouldn't stop until they got to wherever it is they were going. Since we have no idea where that is, I'm thinking our best move might be to go back to 85; see if we can find the actual abduction point. Maybe we could find something there."

"Makes sense."

Miller paused, as if struggling with an internal debate. Finally she nodded. "Yeah." She pulled out onto the county road and turned around.

Thirty minutes later, they were back on 85, heading south toward Linert. They drove slow, kept the their eyes peeled, looked for anything out of the ordinary either on the road, the shoulders, or in the ditches. They found nothing.

Eventually, a dozen or so tightly bunched cars in the oncoming lane indicated they were approaching the one-lane construction zone. Miller slowed as brake lights flared ahead.

By chance, they'd timed it pretty well. The last of the northbound cars cleared the work zone as they pulled to a stop behind a long line of vehicles. He couldn't see the flagger ahead, but Wynn could imagine him turning his sign from "stop" to "slow" and stepping out of the way to let the southbound cars go.

One by one, the brake lights of the cars in front of them dimmed, and they slowly rolled past the flagger. Miller had her left hand on top of the steering wheel and gave a weak wave with two fingers as they drove past.

Wynn twisted in his seat and looked at the flagger as the guy stepped into the southbound lane behind them. The guy flipped his sign back to "stop" for the oncoming cars that were still more than a mile behind.

Wynn hadn't paid much attention to the construction zone itself when he came through yesterday. Today, he watched with more interest as dozens of men went about their work. Some used large asphalt cutters to slice through the road, while others operated backhoes to tear out the old pavement.

Still more workers drove front-end loaders that picked up the rubble and deposited it into large dump trucks that hauled it away. At each stage, groups of three to six men, with shovels, pickaxes, and rakes, stood by to assist.

This is a big operation. Lots of manpower.

At the south end of the construction zone, the same skinny, blond-haired flagger watched them as they passed.

Someone's definition of hell.

Miller interrupted his thoughts. "Is this where you last saw them?"

"Yeah. They were the second and third cars in line. I was four back." Wynn turned in his seat and counted the cars that were stacked up, waiting to go north. Eleven.

"So, what? There must've been a space between the cars somewhere that made a natural break to stop you?"

"No. A big dirt hauler pulled across the road after the van went through. The guy stopped a pickup three cars in front of me."

"Huh."

"The dude in the pickup wasn't happy," Wynn said, recalling the driver's frustrated body language.

Looking past Miller to the east, a path had been worn through the grass on the side of the road. It went down from the shoulder, through the ditch, and up a small berm to a field where several uneven rows of cars, trucks, and SUVs sat parked.

Staging area, Wynn thought. *This must be where they all meet up in the morning before heading out to the worksite. Park their personal cars here and take the company trucks and equipment wherever they need to go.*

He'd noticed it yesterday, but had been so consumed with the van and Subaru he hadn't paid attention. In addition to the cars and trucks, there were a half-dozen pieces of heavy machinery along with several large, semi-trailer box containers. Further away, a huge white gas tank stood elevated on spindly braces high in the air. Beyond that, massive piles of sand and gravel created miniature hills and valleys on the otherwise flat plain.

It was indeed a big operation. Wynn estimated at least forty or fifty cars in the field. He turned to look at the road behind them and watched as the long string of cars crossed over the yellow line and proceeded away north in the southbound lane. The scraggly blond flagger stepped back onto the road and turned his sign to "Stop."

———

Sometime later Jessica woke again to a sudden burst of light. Blinking, she looked around to see the other women still in their bunks, also waking. The lights had been turned on from outside. A young Latina woman, fully dressed, dropped from the top bunk across the room and quickly shuffled into the bathroom and closed the door.

"That means breakfast is coming," a voice said.

To Jessica's right, in the lower bunk closest to her, a woman she guessed to be about her age sat with her back against the wall, knees pulled up defensively, covered by a blanket. She had fair skin, blue eyes, and sandy-blond hair cut to right above her shoulders. Her neck held familiar red patterns and her left cheek was puffy and discolored. Jessica had seen those kinds of bruises before.

"What?" Jessica asked as she sat up, her back re-igniting with each movement.

"The lights. It means they want us up. The last two mornings though there was only me and her." She indicated a blond-haired Caucasian girl in the next bunk over. "They brought us breakfast shortly after the lights came on. But these three," she indicated the three Latina girls, "were brought in maybe an hour before you yesterday, so I don't know what they're going to do with so many of us. How are you feeling?"

"My back hurts like a bitch," Jessica replied. "Where are we?"

"Who knows?" the woman said. "I've been here three days, she's been here two. Haven't been outside of this room since. Give it a couple of days. It'll get better."

"What?" Jessica asked.

"Your back. Give it a couple of days. They did the same thing to all of us. The girls over there don't speak much English but after you were brought in, we were able to piece together that they were taken at least two weeks ago, then brought here yesterday. The marks on their backs have pretty much healed. Hers and mine," she again indicated the girl on the next bunk, "are still pretty fresh. Where'd they get you?"

The first girl came out of the bathroom and a second Latina girl went in. The first one sat down on the edge of the lower bunk with her hands in her lap, looking down.

"I'm sorry, what?" Jessica asked again.

"Jesus, girl, wake up," the woman said urgently. "If you want to know where we are, maybe we can piece it together based on where they grabbed us. Where'd they get you?"

"Between Linert and Newbury. Wyoming," she said.

"That's on the east side of the state, right?" the woman asked.

"Yeah, it's the main route between Denver and Rapid City."

"Hmm. They got me between Douglas and Gillette, a little west of where they got you. They took her somewhere in Nebraska, to the east." The other blonde girl was beginning to get up. "I'm guessing they kidnapped those three in Mexico. Do you remember about what time they grabbed you or how long it took to get here?"

"Umm...Early afternoon, maybe. Didn't seem like it took real long to get here but I was pretty dazed for most of it," Jessica said.

The second Latina girl came out of the bathroom and sat on the bottom bunk next to the first, while the third took her turn. Neither spoke. They just sat with their hands in their laps, looking down.

"Hailey said the same thing, but she was taken in the morning. Thought it took a few hours to get here."

"Who?" Jessica asked.

"Hailey," the woman said, pointing to the girl in the next bunk who was now sitting up and stretching. "I'm sorry. That's Hailey, I'm Ann. That's Cristina and Lucy," she said, pointing to the two girls sitting on the bunk, "Graciela's in the bathroom."

"I'm Jessica. Can't say it's nice to meet you."

"You either," said Ann. "I'm not an expert, but I'm thinking we can't be more than a couple of hundred miles from Casper or Douglas. They're the only semi-sizeable towns within two or three hours of where we were all taken."

"Okay, but that could stretch from what..." Jessica was trying to think. "Rapid City to Cheyenne? Valentine to...what's west of Casper?"

"Not much of anything. Not 'til you reach Boise," Ann said quietly.

They both watched as Graciela came out of the bathroom and sat down next to the other two. Ann went over and crouched in front of her. They whispered a few words, then Ann squeezed her shoulder and came back and sat down.

"What's that all about?" Jessica asked.

"Had a little scuffle with one of those assholes last night. Graciela tried to help out. She got tased."

That explains the commotion, Jessica thought. "What is that thing? I've seen what Tasers do. They don't sting like that."

Ann shrugged. "A stun gun?"

"Not like any I've ever seen."

Ann shrugged again.

Jessica looked at the three Latina girls. All in a row. Hands in their laps. Heads down. "You said they've been held a couple of weeks?"

"Uh-huh."

"Shit."

CHAPTER 14

BRANDON WORE A baseball cap to hold his hair in place over the ugly open cut on his forehead. It hurt, but a hell of a lot less than what Tomas would inflict if he found out what he'd done.

Just got to avoid him for an hour or so. We'll be on our way up north and he'll never know.

"How's it look?" Brandon asked. He and Carlos spent their nights in the bunkhouse inside the barn, in the room opposite where the women were held.

Carlos examined his face. "Same as always. Like shit."

"Fuck off."

"Shit man, she scratched you up pretty good. It's obvious. You can't hide it with a hat."

"I'm gonna stay here," Brandon said. "Tell Tomas I'm getting the van ready."

"We did that last night."

"Tell him I'm finishing up."

After getting their instructions from Tomas the previous evening, Brandon and Carlos had prepped a second van for the trip north. Unlike the white Chevy, this was a burgundy Plymouth Grand Voyager with a broad wood panel stripe from grill to tail.

Whereas the Chevy looked like a work van, this one portrayed a classic passenger vehicle, with large, tinted windows all the way around. Brandon and Carlos had spent the evening installing thick cloth shades inside the rear windows and adding extra tinting to block the view of curious eyes.

"He wants us all in the kitchen every morning," Carlos said. "You know that."

"No shit! Just tell him I'm getting the van ready."

Carlos shook his head and left.

Brandon went out to the shop, opened the van's hood, checked the oil and fluids, adjusted the tire pressure. Anything that would help them leave as soon as Andy and Carlos were ready.

A half-hour later, Carlos returned, along with everyone else. Brandon pulled his cap low and climbed into the rear of the van, pretending to adjust the shades as Tomas approached.

"Is everything ready?" Tomas asked.

"Looking good," Brandon replied. "Just wanted to double-check a few things."

"What else have you done?"

"We added some extra tinting, that kind of thing."

"Show me."

"Hey, Carlos! Show Tomas what we did last night."

"No. I want you to show me."

"I've just got a couple of minutes left to finish up. It'll be faster if Carlos shows you."

"Get out of the van. Now." Tomas's tone left no room for debate.

Brandon pulled his cap low and kept his chin down as he climbed out of the van and immediately walked around the back of the vehicle. "If you come around here..."

"Stop."

Brandon stopped with his back to Tomas. Tomas walked slowly around until he faced Brandon head-on, then reached up and removed Brandon's cap, revealing the open wound.

"What happened?"

"A wrench slipped. Got me pretty good."

Tomas nodded his head slowly. He reached up as if to brush Brandon's hair out of the way. Instead, he grabbed Brandon's head and yanked him forward while at the same time lowering his chin and head-butting Brandon square in the nose. Bones crunched as the nose broke, sending blood spraying. He then brought his knee up, hard into Brandon's groin, doubling him over.

Brandon collapsed to the floor, gasping for air.

Tomas crouched beside him. "Was it a slip like that?"

Brandon rolled and gasped, unable to speak.

Tomas stood and raised his voice for everyone to hear. "If any of you touch those girls again, you'll pray I don't slip."

———

Both Hailey and Ann struggled to walk as each took their turn in the bathroom, clearly still aching from their own lashings. Ann moved a bit better than Hailey, but she'd had an extra day to heal.

When it was Jessica's turn, the simple acts of scooting forward, standing, and walking, came with renewed agony. When she finally got to the bathroom, she turned her back to the mirror, lifted her shirt and twisted as best she could against the pain to see the damage. Two bright, scarlet stripes, each four inches wide, crossed her back. One below her shoulder blades, the other through the small of her back. There were also six bright burn marks, three pairs of two, where the stun gun – or whatever it was – had gotten her.

She suddenly realized her bra had been removed. She could see its outline in the welts on her back, meaning it had been done after she'd been beaten. By Ann and the other girls, she hoped.

When finished, Jessica crept gingerly back to her bunk. "What now?" she asked.

"We wait," Ann said.

Jessica slowly sat down and cautiously scooted back until she was pressed against the brick wall. She had to adjust her position every few minutes as the coolness of the bricks initially felt good. But the wall soon warmed, leaving only the pressure that caused more pain than the coolness relieved.

A little while later, Jessica heard movement outside. She was startled by a loud pounding on the door and an angry male voice yelling, "Back off!" The door opened and two men entered the room. The older was a skinny white guy with thin hair graying at the temples. Jessica guessed maybe in his mid-forties. The younger was Latino, in his mid-twenties.

The older guy entered first, then stepped to the side and stood against the wall between the bathroom and entrance doors. He held a gun in his right hand. The younger guy had a basket of microwavable breakfast sandwiches in one hand and a stack of paper cups in the other. He knelt and set them on the floor in the middle of the room.

"Breakfast is served," he said.

Then turning to the three Latina girls he said, "*Diez minutos.*"

One of the girls, Graciela, looked up at him, nodded, and quickly dropped her eyes.

He stood and walked out. The older man followed. The deadbolt slid back into place.

As soon as they left, the three Latina girls hurried forward and each took a sandwich. Ann took the paper cups into the bathroom and filled them with water, then gave one to each of the others. Hailey grabbed the remaining sandwiches, handed one to Jessica, and set another on Ann's bunk. They ate in silence.

Ten minutes later Jessica again heard movement outside the door. Once again, she heard the loud banging and the yell, "Back off!" The door opened and this time three men entered. The older guy from before took up his same position between the doors while a new guy, young and skinny, with an obviously broken nose, stepped forward and pointed a gun at Ann, Hailey, and Jessica.

"You three stay put," he said.

Jessica's stomach pitched. The voice was deeper and more nasally due to the tissues stuffed up his nose, but there was no doubt it belonged to the passenger in the van yesterday. The guy who had stung her with the stun gun at least twice. She looked closer. The guy wore a baseball cap and had scratches all over his face. His gaze locked on Ann. She stared right back.

The third guy was the young Latino. He walked over to the three Latina girls. "*Levantate!*"

They immediately stood. He approached the first one on the left and said something Jessica couldn't understand. The girl raised her hands, wrists together. The guy used a zip tie to bind them. He then turned her around and used a strip of black cloth to blindfold her, tying it tightly behind her head. Tears appeared in the eyes of the last girl as the man repeated the process twice more, but none of them made a sound.

When they were securely bound, each of the men took one of the girls by the arm and led them out of the room. Jessica heard the deadbolt slide back into place.

———

Ann stared at the door after he left. *The scratches on his face? The cut on his forehead? Yeah, I did that. But the broken nose? I don't remember hitting him there.* She wracked her brain, trying to remember exactly what happened. Exactly what was said.

If Tomas catches you, or these girls are damaged, he'll fucking kill you.

A brief spark of hope ignited inside.

They want us unharmed. And alive.

CHAPTER 15

Shortly after clearing the construction zone, Miller let off the gas as they rounded a broad turn and descended a long, low hill leading into Linert. The Norfolk County Sheriff's Office sat on a mostly residential street two and a half blocks from the Fresh Start. Miller pulled into a parking spot right outside.

The building itself was a tale of two eras. On the left stood a majestic, two-story brick building, painstakingly constructed from rich red blocks. Large arched windows were set into thick white frames. Four broad, white pillars topped by scroll-like volutes surrounded the main entrance and supported a wide second-story balcony with heavy white balusters. It was clearly built at a time when government was revered, its offices a source of civic pride, a reflection of the wealth and sophistication of its citizens. Wynn imagined the Fourth of July celebrations of years past. When crowds of people would picnic on the front lawn with fried chicken and potato salad, while local politicians stood on the balcony overhead, surrounded by red, white, and blue balloons, making promises of prosperity and opulence.

The right half of the building was a different story. Clearly built as an add-on many years later, it was a single-story, completely utili-tarian affair. Built from tan concrete blocks, it contained the bare minimum of windows and corners. Wynn imagined this half was built at a time when money was tight and the reverence for govern-ment long gone. The bond measure to finance it had probably failed several times before voters finally approved it, the need becoming overwhelming. But what they did approve was the absolute mini-mum. Every dollar went to creating useable square footage, with no consideration for design or aesthetics.

The sheriff's office was in the right half of the building.

"Who are we meeting?" Wynn asked.

"Sheriff Johnston," Miller replied. "I've met him a few times. He's okay. A little full of himself. Not nearly as bad as Crower but maybe leaning that way."

Wynn rolled his eyes. "Great."

A sidewalk led to a small glass foyer that was no larger than the width of the sidewalk, itself an add-on to the add-on. Probably an afterthought, built after the occupants had suffered through the building's first Wyoming winter.

Inside, a series of stanchions with retractable belts directed visi-tors to a reception counter where a middle-aged woman with short, dark hair was on the phone. She looked up, saw Miller's uniform, and held up a finger, silently requesting a moment longer.

While they waited, Wynn scanned the small office. It reminded him more of a bank lobby than a sheriff's department. A hallway on the right led past two glass offices along the back wall. The one on the left was dark, while a man of medium build in a sheriff's uniform was on the phone behind a desk in the other. Johnston, he presumed.

Four desks occupied the bullpen space between the offices and the reception counter. A male deputy, large and muscular, and one female deputy, small by comparison, sat behind two of the desks.

The woman in front of them hung up the phone. Her name tag read Marjorie. "How can I help you?" she asked.

"Deputy Miller, Wheaton County. Here to see Sheriff Johnston. I believe he's expecting us."

"Oh, yes. Have a seat and I'll let him know you're here."

Wynn and Miller chose seats against the far wall so as not to be looking directly at Johnston while he finished his call. Instead, they got a good look at the daily workings of the Norfolk County Sheriff's office. The reception counter, specifically.

There wasn't much walk-in traffic, but the phones were surprisingly busy, keeping the receptionist hopping like an old-time phone operator. After a few minutes, Wynn could see the rollover calls went to the female deputy at the desk behind her. He presumed the male deputy acted as a second backup.

Or maybe he was the muscle. The guy was huge. Not so much in height, but in width. And it wasn't fat. Huge biceps strained against his short-sleeve uniform. His neck so thick there was no way his collar was ever going to close tight enough to accommodate a tie. His hair was buzzed into a flat crew cut and the phone looked small in his hands. A nameplate on the front of his desk read *N. Craig*.

Sheriff Johnston hung up the phone and came out of his office. "Deputy Miller," he said as he approached. "It's nice to see you again." He turned to Wynn, "I assume this is our witness?"

"It's nice to see you too, sheriff. Yes sir," said Miller as she stood and shook his hand. "This is Sean Wynn."

The two men exchanged greetings and Johnston led them back to his office. He settled in behind the desk. "Close the door, would you?"

Miller, who'd come in last, closed the door. Wynn's spider-sense tingled.

"Before I show you the video," Johnston said to Wynn, "I wonder if you wouldn't mind telling me the story."

"Why?" Wynn asked.

Johnston paused and leaned back. "It feels like an awfully big coincidence, that a good Samaritan, one with highly acute powers of observation, happened to be in the right place at the right time to pick up on an abduction. Not to mention following them almost seventy miles before losing them. It seems just as likely to me that part of the plan might be to have someone pretend to be a good Samaritan, to send us off on a misdirection."

"Believe what you want," Wynn said.

Stalemate.

After an awkward pause, Miller jumped in. "Listen, Wynn, regardless of any alternate theories, if I was in Sheriff Johnston's place, I'd want to hear it first-hand from the witness also. Standard police procedure."

Wynn looked at her a moment. Then, deciding to cooperate, re-told the story for the fourth time. When he got to the part about the Fresh Start, Johnston leaned forward but didn't interrupt.

When he finished, Johnston simply said, "Okay." He seemed satisfied. He tapped the space bar on his computer keyboard and a large, flat-screen monitor came to life. Johnston entered his ID and password, then pulled up a video program.

"The Fresh Start remodeled a few years ago, upgraded their video system to digital storage. Allows them to keep several months' worth of video on file instead of just twenty-four hours. They've got two cameras inside, and two outside. The two outside are on either end of the canopy looking inward at the pumps. This one facing south," he nodded toward the screen, "shows the missing woman pulling in at 1:22 yesterday afternoon."

Wynn and Miller watched a surprisingly high-quality, color video play on the screen. A timer rolled in the lower right corner as the black Subaru pulled up to the pump.

Johnston continued, "We ran the plates to confirm it is Ms. Davies. It takes her three minutes to fill her tank and then she runs inside. That's when you come along, Mr. Wynn."

Johnston's narration had gotten ahead of the video. It still showed the brunette filling her tank. Even though Wynn now knew her name, it felt awkward to think of her as either Jessica or Ms. Davies. The anonymity felt better.

While the video quality was way better than the grainy black and white Wynn had expected, it covered a large area, making her appear small. It was hard to distinguish the features he had seen during their brief conversation yesterday. They saw Davies replace the nozzle in the pump, screw on the gas cap, then walk inside. A few moments later, Wynn saw himself pull in.

When the brunette returned to her car, Wynn hoped to see the smile she'd directed at him, but quickly realized the camera angle was wrong. This camera was facing him, meaning it caught the back of her head as she passed by. They watched him pause as they spoke briefly, then the Subaru pulled out of the frame. Wynn saw his head turn to follow it. Johnston was about to stop the video when Wynn said, "Wait. Let it play."

Within seconds, the video showed the mid-sized RV pull away from the pump at the next island over, going in the opposite direction. Wynn saw his video image appear to focus on something off-screen, then hurry to replace the fuel nozzle, mount up and speed away. He checked the time counter on the screen. It read 1:29 p.m.

"You said there was a second camera on the other end of the canopy?" he asked.

"Yes."

"Do you have it?"

"Right here." Johnston clicked a file.

"Go to 1:27."

Wynn and Miller waited while Johnston found the right spot and hit play. This time it showed Wynn from the back, looking north. Wynn leaned forward in his chair and focused on the upper right corner of the screen where a small portion of the intersection was visible.

"There. Stop it."

Johnston hit pause.

Barely visible at the top of the screen were the tires and bottom quarter of a long white vehicle.

Wynn tapped the screen. "That's it."

"But we can't tell anything about it," Miller said. "Not enough there."

They looked at each other, disappointed, until Johnston said, "We're not done yet. We may have something else."

CHAPTER 16

WYNN AND MILLER waited a half hour while Johnston called the post office. It was located on Third, a half-block west of Main. According to Johnston, they had a video camera pointed toward the street that should, if everything worked right, catch any vehicle approaching the intersection.

He sent Deputy Craig, the bodybuilder from out front, to get the tape. When Craig returned, they moved to a conference room next to Johnston's office that had a TV and VCR. Old school. Apparently, the post office hadn't been remodeled recently.

Johnston put the tape in. It also had a digital clock in the lower right corner that started at 8:01 a.m. He fast-forwarded until he got to 1:22, then hit a button, and the video began to play. Less than two minutes later, a white van with *All Season Plumbing* on the side drove from left to right across the screen.

"That's it," Wynn said.

Johnston paused the playback. This video was black and white and grainy just as Wynn had expected, but there was no doubt that was the van.

"Play it forward," Miller said. "Maybe it'll catch the plate."

"It won't," Johnston said. "We've looked at these before." He ran the tape anyway, but he was right. The angle was all wrong.

But they did catch one break. For most of the time the van was onscreen, the early afternoon sun reflected off the side window, obscuring the passenger's face. But at the last moment, the van drove into the shadow of the four-story building next door, allowing a quick glimpse of the passenger's profile. Wynn immediately recognized the prominent nose.

"Those are your guys," Wynn said. "Find them and you'll find Davies."

"We'll get on it," Johnston said. Then to Miller, "I'll get this converted to digital, send it and the Fresh Start videos up to Smitty so you guys can be on the lookout. We'll also send them to Rapid City so they can add them to the case file. If they want to transfer the case down here, which I suspect they will, we'll send out the APBs and alert the folks on the main thoroughfares asap. They usually want to move them right away, so time is of the essence."

Wynn looked at Johnston. "You're thinking what I'm thinking?"

He nodded. "Sex trafficking. No ransom request, random victim, multiple suspects. What else? Rapists and murderers usually work alone. And if they are trafficking, they can't do much with them around here. They want to isolate these women, make them dependent on their captors. The best way to do that is to move them away from anything familiar. Get far away from here as quickly as possible. Considering this happened almost twenty-one hours ago, they could be anywhere by now. But we'll coordinate with Rapid City and put out a BOLO on the van. I saw you already did one for the Subaru."

"Yeah," said Miller. "But one on the van, with a photo of it, would be good." She paused. "There is one other thing."

"What's that?" Johnston asked.

Miller pulled out her phone and found the pictures. She handed the phone to Johnston. "Up around rattlesnake creek there's an access road that leads off into a field to the west. There were fresh tire tracks from at least two vehicles that went all the way from 85 over to county road 27."

"So?"

"I'm betting that was them."

"Because of tire tracks? Shit, ranchers are out there driving those fields all the time. Looking for lost cattle, broken fences, all kinds of things. That could've been anybody."

"You're right," Miller said. "But if it wasn't them, the question becomes, where'd they go? Why didn't Wynn catch them? Why haven't we gotten a hit on that BOLO? They didn't just disappear, so where'd they go?"

Johnston sat back and paused, then spoke slowly. "So the theory is they nabbed her somewhere between the construction zone and rattlesnake creek, then hightailed it through the field to 27."

"It's one possibility," Miller said.

"Where'd they go from there?"

She shrugged. "No way to know. My gut says south to 18, then over to I-25. From there they could go anywhere."

"I don't know," Wynn said. "The fact they even knew about that path tells me these guys know the area."

Johnston's voice turned hard. "Anyone with a computer and Google Earth could find that road in ten minutes. I'm gonna need a lot more than that before I start accusing people around here."

"Nobody's accusing anyone of anything," Miller said. "Wynn's just making an observation."

The three sat silently for a moment.

"Anything else?" Johnston said.

Wynn and Miller exchanged glances, but when it became clear no one had anything more to say, they got up, said their goodbyes, and left. Wynn's spider sense tingled as they walked back to the cruiser. "That was odd."

"What?"

Wynn opened the passenger door and stopped, looked over the

top of the cruiser at Miller. "You don't think he was a little overly defensive?"

"He's territorial. I told you, a little like Crower. If we actually had something that pointed to someone local, he'd pursue it, but in the absence of any hard evidence, he's going to defend his people."

Wynn raised his eyebrows. "I guess. What now?"

"I don't know if I'm hungry or feeling sick for this girl, but I could eat," Miller said. "You want to grab some lunch before we head back up?"

They stopped for a quick bite at a small diner a block north of the Fresh Start. As they waited for their food, Miller seemed particularly quiet and subdued.

"What are you thinking?" Wynn asked.

Miller let out a long sigh. "Honestly? I've got an internal battle going on. Professionally, I'm supposed to be detached from this kind of thing. Don't make it personal, they always say."

She paused, and Wynn could tell she was struggling with what to say next. After a few moments, he prompted her, "But personally?"

"I'm kind of freaking out," Miller admitted. "I mean, this girl grew up in Rapid City, same as me. We could've gone to the same high school. Our families might know each other. Maybe a friend of a friend. Hell, in a town that size, there can't be too many degrees of separation. If it can happen to her, it could happen to anyone."

"I get it," Wynn said. "In the Marines, they told us to compartmentalize. In the heat of battle, be disciplined, stick to your training, and do what you need to do. But afterward..."

"Yes! This morning we had a path, something to do." Miller paused. "Now, it feels like she's lost in the wind. And the longer she's in, the less her chances of ever getting out. The mind games they play on these girls are terrible. They threaten their families, get 'em addicted, starve them. By the time they're done they don't even need physical restraints. The psychological bonds alone are enough to keep them in line. If she's not found soon, she's a goner."

Wynn agreed, but had nothing to add as silence fell over the table. The waitress brought their food, but they just picked at it, both having lost their appetites.

A half-hour later they were back on the road, and fifteen minutes after that they approached the one-lane construction area.

"Damn," Miller said as she pulled to a stop behind one other car that had been stopped by the flagger.

"What?"

"We just missed it. We're going to be waiting a while."

"Why? You're a cop. Throw your weight around," he teased. "Tell him you're on important police business and need to get through."

"Bad P.R.," she said. "We'll wait."

"Your call." Wynn looked ahead at the long line of cars moving away in the distance. He looked at the flagger. Same guy. Skinny, curly blond hair, unimpressive beard.

"How much do you suppose those guys get paid?" Miller asked, pointing toward the flagger. "I mean that's got to be the most boring job in the world. I keep debating if they get paid nothing because there's no skill involved, or if they get paid decently because they've got to entice people to do it."

"Never really thought about it," Wynn said.

They watched quietly for a few minutes, while in front of them the earthmovers, loaders, and dumpers all went about their business. Men in yellow vests and hard hats directed the heavy equipment with extra sets of eyes and ears. Eventually, a long line of cars and trucks made their way past in the southbound lane.

Wynn counted seventeen vehicles go by before the flagger finally turned his sign from "stop" to "slow," and allowed them to proceed. Miller once again gave the flagger a small two-finger wave as they rolled past. Wynn leaned forward to look in the side mirror as another long row of cars behind them crossed over the double yellow lines, going north in the southbound lane. The flagger leaned on his sign as he watched the cars go by.

Wynn wondered how much he got paid.

———

Wynn and Miller made comfortable small talk as they drove the next hour. He liked her. She was smart and easy to talk to, and not too full of herself or her job. By mid-afternoon they were back in Newbury and Miller took Wynn directly to the impound yard to get his bike. It sat in a gravel lot surrounded by a chain-link fence with a padlocked gate. A small shed that served as an office sat nearby. The same tow truck driver came out of the office holding a clipboard and a large set of keys. He unlocked the gate, allowing Wynn to walk in and around the bike, slowly examining it for any chips or dings he didn't recognize. There weren't any. He turned back to the tow driver.

"Keys?" he said, holding out his hand.

"How would you like to pay for it?" the driver asked.

Miller jumped in, "Sorry, no one must've told you. Bill the department." She grabbed the clipboard and scribbled a note and a signature.

The guy handed Wynn the keys. He took them and opened the saddlebags on each side, checking to make sure nothing was missing. When satisfied, Wynn nodded to the driver. He turned and spoke over his shoulder. "Have a nice day," he said as he walked back to the office.

"So, finally heading to Sturgis?" Miller asked.

"Yeah."

"Let me know if Randy doesn't have that room for you." She handed Wynn her business card. "Or if you think of anything else."

He put the card in his wallet. "Will do."

"And thanks again for your help. I'm sorry for the hassle we put you through, but if we can find that girl..."

"It'll all be worth it," he finished for her.

"Yeah." She paused, not knowing what else to say. "Well, I better get back. Ride safe out there." She walked back to her cruiser, got in, and drove away.

When she was gone, Wynn reached into his inside left pocket and pulled out his Glock. He checked the chamber, took the magazine from his right pocket and eased it home, then slid the weapon back inside his jacket. He pulled out his phone and searched for a local store. Finding what he needed, he swung a leg over the bike and pulled on his gloves. He rode slowly through the gate, onto the side streets, and eventually to a small home supply store. He parked, went in, made a purchase, and was soon back on his way, pulling onto the main drag that led back to the highway. When he reached the four-way intersection he coasted to a stop. To his left, Sturgis. To his right, back to Linert.

He turned right.

CHAPTER 17

Wynn cruised down the highway at seventy miles per hour. The speed limit. Not a mile over. He didn't want to risk another run-in with Crower.

On the ride back with Miller, he'd developed a theory. Testing it meant he had to get past the construction zone sixty miles away before quitting time. He'd left Newbury at 3:45, but wasn't worried. Construction sites are ruled by the sun, not the clock. They'd work as long as they had daylight. He had plenty of time.

Thirty minutes later he buzzed past Mule Creek Junction, now sure that Davies had never made it that far. He eased back on the throttle, dropped his speed to sixty. Once again he scanned for skid marks on the pavement, or tire tracks along the shoulders, or in the grass. He and Miller had found nothing south of the dirt path that led into the field, meaning Davies may have made it past rattlesnake creek, forcing her abductors to double back. Maybe there was a clue to the north that they had missed.

If there was, he didn't find it.

An hour after leaving Newbury, he came to the north end of the construction zone. As expected, there were several cars already lined up. For the fourth time in two days, he took his place in line and waited. A few minutes later, confidence in his theory morphed into something just shy of certainty as a long line of northbound cars accelerated past, finally free of the delay.

Within moments, the glowing brake lights in front of him dimmed, and the caravan moved forward. Three minutes later he passed the skinny blond flagger. He no longer cared how much the kid was paid.

As he cleared the construction zone and approached the staging area, Wynn kept his speed low. The drivers behind were getting impatient, so he waved them around. He looked for a place to pull over, ideally a dirt road that would allow him to get away from the highway, but he'd take a wide shoulder if that was all he could find.

Two hundred yards past the staging area, he found a barbed-wire-gated driveway heading off into a field on the west side. It wasn't ideal but it would have to do. He parked and dismounted, then dug into his saddlebag and pulled out the purchase he'd made in Newbury. Binoculars.

He carried the binocs back toward the fence line and sat down with his back against a gate post. He turned his body to face northeast, back toward the staging area and the south end of the construction zone. Lifting the glasses to his eyes, he focused on the skinny blond flagger. He was still there. Wynn lowered the binoculars and settled in to wait.

———

One hundred thirty miles north, Brandon sat sulking in the front passenger seat of the Plymouth while Andy drove them to their destination outside of Sturgis. Carlos kept an eye on the three Latina girls in back. They'd gotten a late start as Brandon cleaned up after his run-in with Tomas.

They had also taken the long way. Instead of the paved highway that could have gotten them there in a couple of hours, Andy insisted on a circuitous route of backcountry roads. Probably fewer vehicles to run into, and definitely fewer cops, he had said.

When they were still several miles out, Andy took out his cell phone and made a call. Yes, he had the cargo, he said, followed by a pause and then, no, no problems. He listened for a moment, then said okay, and disconnected.

Andy pulled the van off the highway, onto a paved two-lane road, then made a series of turns as the road wound up into a hilly forest. Eventually, he pulled into a dirt driveway that for eleven months out of the year was very similar to the one leading to Tomas's ranch back in Wyoming.

In early August, however, it couldn't have been more different. Hundreds of tents and maybe a thousand bikers created a tent city in an open meadow on either side of the driveway. After a quarter-mile, the tents ended as the driveway rose up a small hill through a thicket of pine trees.

Another quarter-mile in, the trees gave way to a clearing containing two houses. The first, a large main house out front, and a smaller, two-story guest house fifty yards beyond. A dozen Harleys sat parked in a natural grass front yard, while the dirt driveway stretched all the way back to the second house.

Andy pulled the van into the clearing and was immediately met by a half-dozen bikers, dressed in jeans and black leather, all sporting various tattoos and carrying guns. Brandon quickly counted two shotguns, one rifle, and three pistols. Too far away to see exactly what kinds, but it didn't matter. The message was clear.

The man closest to them, a buff thirty-something sporting a thick goatee, skull cap, and sunglasses, stepped forward as Andy slowed the van and rolled down his window.

"All the way back," the biker said, pointing to the guest house.

Andy eased the van past the main house as the bikers fell in step behind. He stopped the van, positioning the side panel door directly in front of the guest house a few feet away. When the side door opened, the man with the goatee stuck his head inside. He glanced over the "cargo," the three Latina girls, still blindfolded with their hands tied, and nodded.

"Bring them in," he said. "Take them to the first bedroom upstairs on the left."

While the bikers formed a human wall on each side between the van and the house, Brandon jumped out of the passenger seat as Carlos guided the blindfolded girls out of the van, and into the house. They led the girls up an L-shaped staircase immediately left of the entryway to a small bedroom at the top of the stairs. The girls sat on the bed while Brandon removed their blindfolds and Carlos cut the zip ties from their wrists.

"*Baño?*" Carlos asked.

They all nodded eagerly.

"Hey, man," Carlos said to Brandon. "Find a bathroom."

Brandon stepped into the hallway and found a bathroom across the hall, then checked out the rest of the upstairs. There were two more bedrooms further down the hall, all sparsely furnished, containing a bed, a single chair, and nothing else.

When the girls had each taken their turn in the bathroom, Brandon and Carlos closed the bedroom door and left them while they went back downstairs. They didn't bother to lock the door. Where would they go?

Andy and the goateed biker sat at a small kitchen table while two other bikers leaned against the counters. It sounded like they were finishing up.

"We have people constantly patrolling the grounds out to the tents. We'll know before anyone gets here," the biker said. "Any questions?"

"Where's the RV?" Andy asked.

"Already in position. Space D-thirteen. You just take them out there."

"Wristbands?"

"Right here." The biker handed Andy six white wristbands. "Anything else?"

"We're good," Andy said.

"Then I'll leave you to it." The three bikers got up and left.

Andy looked at Brandon and Carlos. "Let's get these girls something to eat, then hopefully they can get some sleep. It's going to be a long week."

CHAPTER 18

Around 6:30, Wynn finally began to see signs of the road construction site closing down for the evening. Machinery was being parked, roads were being swept clear of debris, and most importantly, portable traffic lights were being rolled into place.

As the sun sank slowly behind him, it continued to light up the site, but also created long shadows that made reconnaissance difficult. With the wide-open spaces, he was easily the tallest thing around, and therefore cast the longest shadow. He couldn't exactly stand there and stare with his binoculars without being noticed or raising suspicion. Instead, he took off his jacket and draped it over the fence post behind him, then sat down in its shadow. Anyone looking in his direction would be blinded by the sun's glare, yet he now had a clear view of both the staging area and the construction zone.

As he'd done for the past hour, Wynn focused the binoculars on the blond flagger. Once the portable lights were in place, the flagger stowed his sign, then hurried to the side of the road. He picked up a lunch pail and thermos, then hustled over to a pickup that was beginning to pull out. The pickup stopped just long enough for the flagger to climb into the open rear bed.

After being driven back to the staging area, the flagger jumped out and walked over to a beat-up, old red Honda Civic. Wynn stood up, removed his jacket from the post, and put it on. He ambled the thirty feet or so back to his bike, keeping an eye toward the flagger in the Civic the whole way. He had pulled out of the staging area, down through the ditch, and up onto the highway. The Civic was now picking up speed as it approached, no doubt heading back to Linert for the night.

Wynn stuffed the binoculars back into the saddlebag and swung a leg over the seat as the Civic sped past. He fired up the Street Glide and waited for two other cars to pass before easing onto the highway.

Maintaining his position three cars behind, Wynn followed the flagger as he drove back to town. He watched expectantly for the Civic to turn onto one of the side streets, but it continued through, almost to the south edge of town. Finally, at the last possible street, the Civic turned left at a small truck stop café, went a block east, and pulled into a dirt driveway in front of a lone mobile home.

Wynn pulled up to a gas pump at the truck stop and watched as the flagger got out of the Civic, trotted up the stairs of the trailer, and went inside. Dusk was now settling as the lights came on inside the trailer, which was a good sign. It meant there was likely no one else home.

Wynn considered topping off the Street Glide's gas tank but didn't want to leave a record that he'd been here. If he was wrong, he was about to cross a line.

He eased the bike to the edge of the parking lot across the street from the Civic, then walked up the front steps of the trailer. He kept his sunglasses on as he knocked on the door.

It took a moment, but the flagger eventually opened up. "What?" he asked impatiently.

Up close, the guy was just a kid. Wynn leaned forward, slowly. Got as good a look as he could inside the trailer. Seeing no one, he launched his left hand forward, grabbed the kid by the neck, and pushed him back into the room. Instantly the flagger raised both hands to Wynn's wrist, trying to break the grip. Another good sign. It meant the kid wasn't going for a weapon. Wynn flung the door closed and spun the kid around, slamming him against the wall inside the trailer.

"Where is she?"

"What?" The kid was scared, his fingers clawing at Wynn's grip.

"Where is she?" Wynn's voice rose.

"Who? What are you talking about?"

"Yesterday, the girl. The black Subaru. Where is she?"

The flagger's eyes darted up and right, confirming Wynn's theory.

"What girl? What Subaru?"

"Don't fuck with me." Wynn said. "I know you did it. You isolated a girl in a black Subaru with a couple of guys in a white van when they came through your checkpoint yesterday. I want to know where she is."

"I swear, I don't know what you're talking about!"

Wynn reached up with his right hand and peeled the flagger's left hand from its grip on his wrist. He twisted it back forcing the kid to release his hold and down onto his knees.

"Last chance," Wynn warned.

"Fuck you!"

Wynn twisted the hand further until he heard the wrist bone snap and the kid scream. He quickly covered the kid's mouth with his left hand. "I can do this all night, asshole," he whispered.

Desperation flashed in the kid's eyes as he looked toward the kitchen. He flicked his head and bit down hard on Wynn's gloved hand. He spun under Wynn's arm and twisted out of his grip, making a quick dash toward the kitchen. Wynn wasn't sure what he was going for but knew he had to stop him before he got it.

Wynn lunged as the kid opened a drawer, driving his body into the flagger's back. The kid crashed forward, slamming the drawer on his remaining good hand. The kid screamed in pain. Wynn spun him around, ensured his hands were empty, then unloaded a massive punch to the stomach. Followed that with a brutal uppercut to the jaw. The kid went down, out cold.

Wynn knelt and checked to make sure he was still breathing, then checked the kid's pockets. Pulled out his wallet. The ID said the kid's name was Matt Lester. Wynn returned the ID and wallet back into his pocket, then tapped the other pockets and pulled out not one cell phone, but two. The first was a several generations old iPhone with a badly cracked screen. Wynn pushed the button on the right to bring it to life.

Nothing happened.

Collateral damage from the fight.

Lester wasn't going to be happy about that, but that was the least of his problems. Wynn slid the phone back into the kid's pocket. The second phone was an old-fashioned flip phone, the small screen immediately lit up when Wynn flipped it open.

Wynn checked the menu and opened the contacts list. None. He checked for text messages. Not easy on a phone like this, but doable. Still none. Finally, he checked the call history. There were no outgoing calls at all. The last three incoming calls had all happened yesterday. From the same number. All received in the early afternoon, between 12:30 and 1:40 p.m. The same time Wynn had been following the white van. He slipped the flip phone into his pocket.

Lester was beginning to come around.

Time to go.

Wynn got up and stepped out the front door, closing it behind him, and quickly walked across the street to his bike. Dusk was deeper, but not yet fully dark. As quietly as possible, at least for a Harley, he fired up the Street Glide and was soon heading north out of town. Fifteen minutes later he passed through the construction zone and twenty-five minutes after that he pulled into the rest area at Mule Creek Junction. He pulled out his phone and Miller's business card. There was no cell number listed; he called the main office.

As expected, Miller was off duty, but the male deputy who answered was mostly helpful once Wynn explained who he was.

"Listen," the deputy said. "It's against department policy to give out personal cell phone numbers, but I'll call her and have her call you right back. Will that work?"

"That'll work." Wynn confirmed his phone number for the deputy and disconnected.

Two minutes later his phone rang. "Yeah?"

"Wynn? It's me, Sam. Don't tell me Randy didn't have your room?"

"No. I haven't made it to Sturgis yet. I had a hunch and it paid off. I think I have a lead on Davies."

"What? What'd you do? What've you got?" She was all ears now.

"Well, as far as what I did, I don't think you want to know. But what I have is a cell phone with a number. I think whoever that number belongs to was involved."

"Shit, Wynn. That was a lot in a short sentence. Not sure if I should be busting you or hugging you, but let's start with the number."

Wynn gave it to her.

"Okay. Where are you?" she asked.

"Mule Creek Junction."

"Can you meet me at the office, say thirty minutes?"

"That depends. Are you going to bust me or hug me?"

"That also depends on what I find on this number. I'm going to go down to the office and run it, see if we can find out who it belongs to. Most likely it's a burner, but I've met some dumb crooks over the years. Maybe we'll get lucky."

"Maybe."

"So I'll see you in a half-hour?"

"Sure."

"I also want to hear the story of how you got this."

"Maybe." Wynn disconnected. He put the phone in his pocket, fired up the bike, and pulled onto the highway.

———

Back in Linert, Matt Lester lay on his kitchen floor as he struggled to clear the cobwebs from his head.

This guy knows, he thought. *How the hell did he find out? Who the fuck is he?*

He moved his right hand to his front jeans pocket, but when he tried to reach inside his fingers burst with pain. Barely moving his left arm was a battle. Slowly, he rolled over onto his elbows and knees, and stood up, cradling both arms against his body. Fighting through the pain, he reached into his pocket and pulled out his iPhone, then set it on the counter. Reaching in again he searched his pocket for the burner, but it was gone.

"Shit," he said out loud.

He picked up his iPhone and fumbled with it, tried to turn it on. Nothing happened.

"Shit!" he yelled again.

Lester found some loose change on the counter and staggered out of the kitchen. Even opening the front door was a challenge; the gripping and twisting of the knob caused streaks of pain to shoot up his arms. Eventually, using both hands, he was able to get the door open and stumble down the steps.

Hunching over, he crossed the street to a payphone outside the truck stop cafe. He lifted the receiver, cradled it between his ear and shoulder, and struggled to insert a coin. When the dial tone sounded, he gently punched in a number with his thumb. He let the call ring nine times before disconnecting. He fished the coin out of the return slot and reinserted it back at the top. He dialed again. This call was answered on the second ring.

"Hey, it's me," Lester said, fighting back tears. "He knows. He knows everything."

Lester listened. "Some guy, he knows! Some guy came to my house and broke my arm. He knew I helped get that girl yesterday."

Another pause, then, "How the fuck should I know? I didn't tell him shit, but he knows."

He listened again. "My arm, man, and my hand. I gotta get to a fuckin' hospital."

He paused to listen. "I don't know, he was dressed like a biker. He was wearing leathers and sunglasses. I didn't see his face. It hurts, man. I gotta get to a doctor."

He listened longer this time as he received instructions.

"Okay man, I'll wait. But tell them to hurry. I'm hurting bad here."

Lester hung up the phone and staggered back across the street to his trailer.

Within moments two additional phone calls were made. One call launched a car south. The second stirred a flurry of research including phone numbers, cell towers, and GPS satellites. When the research was complete a third phone call was made, and a second car was launched.

To the north.

CHAPTER 19

IT TOOK A little more than a half-hour for Wynn to make it to Newbury. He rode slower in the dark, especially on wide-open country roads. With wildlife becoming more active at night, he didn't need an encounter with a deer or antelope.

Forty minutes after hanging up with Miller he walked into the Wheaton County Sheriff's office. Same as yesterday, but without the handcuffs. He had to be buzzed in through a side door to the garage, then again into the lobby. It felt unusually bright with its fluorescent lights and off-white floors and walls. Probably because he'd spent the last hour riding in the dark. Miller was sitting at her station at the second window of the curved, raised platform.

"Hey," she said by way of greeting. "For a minute I thought you might've ditched me."

"Didn't want to give Crower a second chance," Wynn replied. "What've you got?"

She sighed. "They're not as dumb as I'd hoped. It's a burner, confirmed. Not registered to anyone. But they're not as smart as they could be. It was used an hour ago, so we have an idea where they're at."

"Where's that?"

"Before I give you that, why don't you tell me how you got this number?"

"From this," Wynn said. He pulled out Lester's flip phone and set it on the counter.

"Okay," she said without touching the phone. "And where'd you get that?"

Wynn looked around the room. The waiting area was empty but the same two deputies were at their desks against the wall behind Miller. He looked over at Smith's office. It was dark. "Can we talk in there?"

Miller tilted her head to the side as if trying to see where this was going. "Okay."

Wynn followed her back to Smith's office. It was unlocked. She flipped on the light and went around behind the desk but didn't sit. Wynn closed the door and leaned back against it.

"Spill it," Miller said.

"It was the flagger," Wynn said. "I didn't catch it until we came back this afternoon, thanks to you."

"Me? What did I do?"

"You asked how much those guys got paid, which got me thinking, probably not much. I was four cars behind the van yesterday and there had to be five or six cars still behind me. Why only let the first three through? Because he could use some extra cash. Someone paid him to only let those three cars go through. Hold everyone else back."

"You said a dump truck blocked the road."

"It did, but now I'm thinking that happened after the flagger stopped us. It was quick, for sure, but now I'm thinking after."

"So, what, the flagger lets three cars through. They can't do it along the construction zone, too many workers. They can't all be involved. So it happens after they clear the zone? How?"

"The first car was in on it, too. There's still an element of chance, but if they can clear the construction zone, they know there won't be anyone coming up from behind for at least seven or eight minutes because the flagger is holding them. If they can find an open area where they can see that no cars are coming toward them, the first car somehow blocks the road and gets her to stop while the van jams her in from behind. I didn't pay attention to the first car, so I don't know how many guys were in it, but if we assume two, then that's four guys against one girl. They could've grabbed her in less than a minute."

Miller paused. "And from there they got away on that dirt road near rattlesnake creek."

Wynn nodded. "It fits."

"Okay," Miller said, buying in. "Tell me about the phone."

"It was the flagger's. His name is Matt Lester. When I left here this afternoon, I rode back and watched him until he got off work. I followed him back to his place in Linert and got the phone from him there."

"He just gave it to you?"

"He didn't object when I took it."

Miller looked skeptical, as if she knew he was evading the implied question, but she didn't push it. "So why are we looking at this specific number?"

"Lester received three calls from that number yesterday, all between 12:30 and 1:40. That would've been right around the time the guys in the van started following her, until right before they hit the construction zone. The first was a heads up that something might be coming, the second a confirmation, and the third was specific instructions on who to stop."

"Where's Lester now?"

"When I last saw him, he was in the kitchen of his trailer."

"And he let you walk out with his phone?"

"He wasn't resisting."

"Stop dickin' around, Wynn." She was getting angry with his evasiveness. "Tell me what happened."

"Okay, okay. At first, he denied everything, but when I told him what I suspected he went for a weapon. I don't know what he was going for because he never got there. He's probably got a black eye and I suspect he'll be sporting a cast on his arm tomorrow, but that's it. When he was down and no longer a threat, I searched his pockets, found the phone, saw the timing of those calls, and took it."

"Why didn't you call Sheriff Johnston?"

"I've already experienced the hospitality of a Wyoming county jail, thank you very much. As much fun as that was, I don't need to do it again."

"Is Lester hurt?"

"Nah, not seriously. He was already coming around when I left."

"If he is involved, he sure isn't going to call the sheriff. But if he goes to the hospital, they might. Depends on the injuries and how good a story he comes up with to explain them." She was on his side again.

"You said you know where these guys are," Wynn said.

Miller nodded. "Sturgis. Or that general area. Cell towers are scarce around the hills, plus if they're in a valley or wooded area it can sometimes cause interference, so it's tough to pinpoint them exactly, but they're in that area. Or at least they were an hour ago."

"I'm out of here," Wynn said, opening the office door.

"Wynn, wait. This is good. But you've got to let us take it from here. I'll give Smitty a call right now and he'll have Johnston send someone over to Lester's. I'm guessing he'll also want to bring in the Meade County Sheriff. I know all of them will want to talk to you. Hell, if she's up there, then this thing crosses state lines and becomes an FBI case, and *they* may want to talk to you. But this is serious shit. We need you to stick around and tell your story. We, hell, I appreciate all you've done, but you've got to stand down, let us handle it. Please."

He paused but didn't respond.

"Tell you what," Miller said. "Stick around here tonight. Let me get you a room at the finest place in town. On us. We'll talk to Smitty tonight and whoever else we need to in the morning, and you can be on your way after that. How's that sound?"

Wynn acquiesced. He knew she was right.

Fifteen minutes after finishing his conversation with Miller, Wynn was back in Smith's office, this time with the sheriff himself, retelling the story of the past few hours.

As Miller suspected, Smith wanted all hands on deck. Now. A half-hour after finishing the second telling to Smith, Wynn began the third recounting of the story on a conference call with both the Meade and Norfolk County Sheriffs, as well as the Rapid City police department on the other end.

When he finished, there were several questions to clarify this or that minor detail, but for the most part, they were all satisfied with Wynn's story. Johnston said he'd send someone over to Lester's trailer to bring him in, but that was it for tonight.

It was after one in the morning by the time they were done. Miller had already called and gotten Wynn a room, even had the key brought over. It turned out the finest place in town was a two-story motel on the main drag, five blocks from the sheriff's office.

Miller escorted him to the motel and made sure he didn't have any trouble getting settled in. His room was on the first floor at the far end of an L-shaped building opposite the motel lobby. Inside was a typical motel room with all the standard furnishings; a bed, a chair, a dresser with a flat-screen TV on top, a desk with another chair, and toward the back, a closet alcove next to the bathroom. It was all clean and newly furnished. Not the nicest place he'd ever stayed, but far from the worst.

"The finest place in town, huh?"

"What, are you getting picky on me now?" Miller said. "Besides, the owner gives us a deal."

Wynn gave a tired smile. "It's great. Thanks."

"I'll meet you at the office at nine a.m. tomorrow and we'll see if the Meade folks have any more questions," she said. "I think there's a good chance they'll have the FBI in on it by then, but hopefully we can finish up by noon and you can get on your way."

Wynn nodded.

"Okay. If that's it, I'll get out of here and let you get some sleep." She paused with her hand on the doorknob and turned around. "You did good today, Wynn. Yesterday too. If we catch these guys and can get her back, she'll have you to thank."

He nodded again.

Miller opened the door and left.

Wynn pulled a small bathroom bag from his duffle and brushed his teeth, stripped to his boxers, and crawled into bed. He wondered if Randy at the Boulder Canyon Motel Inn would hold his room another night, then cursed himself. At least he could leave if he wanted to. He doubted Jessica Davies had the same choice.

CHAPTER 20

Tuesday

FOUR HOURS AFTER going to bed, Wynn was awakened by a polite but insistent knocking on his door.

"Mr. Wynn. Deputy sheriff. Please open the door." It was an order, not a request.

Wynn rolled over and looked at the bedside clock. 5:32 a.m. Through the edge of the curtains, he could see it was still dark outside.

The pounding came a little louder. "Mr. Wynn. Deputy Miller sent us. Please open the door."

"Alright, alright," Wynn said loudly. He got up and pulled on his jeans, then walked shirtless to the door.

"Shit, guys," he said as he opened the door, "Can't this wait til..."

His words were cut off as the door burst open, pushing Wynn back into the dresser. Two sets of hands grabbed for him as he slid to his right, then backpedaled furiously. The narrow space between the dresser and the bed caused one of the men to fall back, forcing them to approach in single file, evening the odds.

The first guy was big. Not NFL linebacker big, but close. He held something in his right hand. Not a gun. Not a knife. Wynn wasn't sure what the hell it was until a bright blue arc of electricity crackled across its end.

Wynn's right hand shot out and grabbed the wrist holding the stun gun. He pivoted away, turning his back and using the big guy's momentum to pull him behind, deftly switching positions so that he was now between his two attackers. At the same time, Wynn swung his left elbow high into the air, viciously landing it squarely on the temple of the second man who was rushing in to help. Between their opposing momentums, it was like getting hit with a baseball bat. The second guy went down in a heap.

He then brought his left hand up next to his right and gripped both hands on the wrist that held the stun gun. He pushed it up and away while ducking underneath the first man's arm, changing positions again like a pair of bizarre dancers. He twisted the arm violently behind the man's back. The stun gun dropped to the floor, as for the second time in twelve hours he broke a man's arm. Wynn stood behind the man, twisting his now useless right arm behind his back, but the attacker's left hand skimmed across the floor, found the stun gun, and pressed it hard against Wynn's calf.

Wynn's muscles immediately convulsed. He let go of the man's arm and fell back against the wall, then slid to the floor. The intruder dropped to his knees and crawled away. He paused for a moment next to his unconscious partner, then scrambled to his feet, stumbled out the door, and was gone. Moments later, an engine revved, and tires squealed as the man abandoned his partner and drove away.

Wynn stared dazedly at the man lying motionless on the floor. Another man, older, with gray hair and a mustache, cautiously pushed the door open and peeked into the room.

"What's going on in there?" the old man called out tentatively. "The police are coming so you settle down and stay put."

Wynn closed his eyes.

A few minutes later the screech of tires on pavement came from just outside his room. A car door opened, and quick footsteps stopped outside his door.

"Police!" a voice yelled. "Come out with your hands up."

Wynn cleared his throat. His strength was coming back, but he was still weak. "I can't. It's clear."

The door eased open, and the wide brim of a Dudley-Do-Right hat appeared. It was Crower. He entered the room slowly with his gun drawn. He first looked at the prone figure on the floor, then saw Wynn against the wall.

"What's going on, Wynn?" he asked cautiously. "Is there anyone else here?"

"No. It's clear."

Crower carefully swept the room, stepping over the figure on the floor and past Wynn into the bathroom, making sure no one else was there. When he was satisfied, he went back to Wynn.

"Where are you hurt?" he asked.

"I'll be okay. They got me with some kind of stun gun. Just need a few minutes."

"Okay," Crower said, "I'm sorry to do this, but I need to secure the scene until I get some backup, then we'll get these off." He rolled Wynn onto his stomach and cuffed his hands behind his back. Wynn didn't resist.

Crower moved over to the guy on the floor and thumbed his shoulder microphone. "Dispatch, we need paramedics at the Inn."

Then to Wynn, he said, "You want to tell me what happened?"

"Two guys knocked on the door, said they were police. When I opened up, they barged in and tried to grab me. Not sure what their plans were after that, but I didn't want to find out. I defended myself."

Crower looked at the side of the unconscious man's face. A deep purple bruise was emerging on his temple. "Looks like you did more than that."

"Carl!" Crower shouted. The old man with the gray hair and

mustache appeared at the door. "When the deputies and paramedics get here, tell them the scene is secure and to get their asses in here."

The old man disappeared outside.

Within minutes, both paramedics and deputies arrived. While two paramedics worked on the unconscious man, a third eventually came over to Wynn, who had by now worked himself into a sitting position against the wall. His hands were still cuffed behind his back. The paramedic shone a small penlight into Wynn's eyes and checked his pulse, then used a pair of scissors to cut Wynn's jeans from the cuff to the knee, revealing a pair of nasty circular burn marks on his right calf.

The paramedic applied a salve and bandages as the other two paramedics, along with two deputies, placed the unconscious man on a stretcher and wheeled him out of the room. When they cleared the doorway, Miller stepped in and hurried over to Wynn.

"Sean, are you alright?" Seeing he was cuffed, she said, "Shit, let's get those off you."

Wynn leaned forward and twisted to the right, giving her access to the cuffs and revealing an ugly bruise above his left elbow.

"That looks like it hurts," she said, releasing the cuffs. "You okay?"

He leaned back, rubbing his wrists and twisting his arm to get a look at his elbow. "Better than he's doing," he said, nodding toward the doorway. He flexed and stretched his arm.

"Want me to look at that?" the paramedic asked.

"Nah, it's good," Wynn said.

"Then we're done here." The paramedic packed his bag and left, passing Sheriff Smith as he entered the room. He sighed heavily as he approached.

"Looks like trouble has a way of following you, Mr. Wynn."

Wynn said nothing. He was thinking.

"You want to tell us what happened?" Smith asked.

Wynn looked up. "Like I told Crower, two guys knocked on the door. When I opened it, they rushed me. I defended myself."

"Uh-huh," Smith said slowly. "Well, let's go down to the station and get a statement."

"Uh-uh," Wynn said.

"Excuse me?"

"I'm done here," Wynn said. "I'm going to take a shower then get the fuck out of this town."

"The FBI may still have questions for you."

"Give them my number. I'll be in Sturgis anyway. I can talk to them up there, but I'm done here."

"We need a statement about all this," Smith said slowly, indicating the trashed room.

"You just got it."

Smith paused, studying Wynn intently. "Can you at least give us a description of the other guy?"

"He was big."

Smith raised his eyebrows. "Anything else?"

"That and the stun gun were all I saw."

Pausing, Smith turned to Miller. "Sam, go see if Carl has another room Mr. Wynn can use to shower and clean up. We need to search this one for evidence. Stay with him until he's ready to leave town, and make sure he goes north this time."

While Miller went to get a second room, Wynn climbed unsteadily to his feet and packed up his stuff. It didn't take long. With Smith watching from the doorway, he threw his toothbrush and t-shirt into the duffle, slipped on his boots and jacket, then made sure his phone, keys, wallet, and Glock were all still in their pockets, exactly where they should be. He reached down and picked up the desk chair that had been tipped over during the scuffle, righted it, and sat down.

He sat in silence for a minute or two until Smith finally asked, "What are you thinking, Wynn?"

"Maybe I'll tell you when I know."

They returned to silence.

A few moments later Miller returned and escorted Wynn to a

different room a few doors down. The sun had now risen but was still casting long shadows in the early morning. It was going to be another hot day.

Miller let Wynn into the new room and waited outside while he showered and changed. Wynn took his time but finally emerged a half-hour later with his jacket on and duffle in hand. Smith, the paramedics, and most of the deputies were gone. It was quiet as Miller walked with him to his bike.

"So why the change of heart?" Miller asked. "Yesterday you were all about finding Davies, but today you're running. Did these guys really get to you?"

"Please," Wynn said dismissively. "They'd have booted me out of MARSOC in a heartbeat if I couldn't handle a couple of amateurs like that. This isn't about being afraid."

"Then what? I didn't peg you for the kind of guy who'd give up so easily."

Wynn turned on her angrily. "Don't give me that bullshit. I've done more to find her than all of you. But you tell me: How'd they find me? Who knew I was staying here last night? It's a pretty short list, right? And just about everyone on it carries a badge, including you. Do you think I'm going to stick around here and give you guys a second chance? Fuck that."

"Whoa, hold on," Miller said. "You think someone on the force is involved? Maybe even me? That's crazy."

"Is it? If it makes you feel any better, gender alone puts you further down the list, but there are plenty of other possibilities."

"Like who?"

"Crower for one." Wynn opened a saddlebag and stowed his duffle. "He was patrolling the stretch of highway where she was taken, and he was the first one to show up here this morning. Awfully convenient."

"Crower may be an idiot but he's not a sex trafficker. I've known him for six years. No way."

"When you come up with something better, give me a call. You've got the number."

Wynn closed up his saddlebags, threw a leg over the bike, and started it up. The engine growled to life with a steady, galloping rhythm.

Miller raised her voice to be heard over the rumble. "I'm supposed to follow you. Make sure you go north."

"Suit yourself." Wynn dropped the bike into gear and roared away.

CHAPTER 21

INSIDE THE FARMHOUSE, Tomas, John, and Tony sat around the kitchen table, the cell phone on speaker mode between them. It was early, but what they were hearing had their attention.

"I'm telling you, we got nothing to worry about," the voice on the phone said. "He's one of Nathan's co-workers at the site. Big and dumb and doesn't know a thing about us. Even if he did, Nathan doesn't think he'll be talking for some time. He was hit pretty good."

"And if he does?" Tomas asked.

"He won't get the chance," the voice said.

"Make sure of it," Tomas said, then disconnected.

The three men looked at each other. John finally broke the silence. Looking at Tomas, he asked, "When's the drop?"

"It's been moved to Saturday. In Albuquerque."

"So we've got to hold on to 'em for four more days?"

Tomas nodded.

"What do you want to do?" John asked.

Nodding at Tony, Tomas said, "Get the van ready, but we're staying put as long as we can. We should know more in a couple of hours. Go."

After Tony left through the kitchen door, Tomas said to John, "Nathan's the link. Be prepared to take him out."

———

Jessica woke up hungry on her second morning of captivity. They hadn't eaten since yesterday morning, right before the three Latina girls were taken away. In fact, they hadn't heard a thing. No one had come to the room, nor had there been any sounds outside the door, as if they'd been forgotten. She only knew, or guessed, it was morning by the fact that the lights had come on.

For her part, Jessica was content to lay in the bunk and let her wounds heal. She would need all her strength if she was going to find a way out. The fire from the lashes on her back had now dulled to a low burn every time she moved, and her muscles, especially those across her back, ached worse than ever.

Lying there also gave her time to think, but her thoughts wound in circles. She wasn't sure if the stages of grief were applicable in this situation or not. There was no use in denying what was happening and she was well past being angry. There would be no bargaining with these guys and surrendering to depression was not an option. Only by accepting her situation could she plan her escape. But was clinging to the idea of escape just another form of denial? She tried not to dwell on it.

Ann, she noticed, had been quiet, too. Almost resigned, as if she also knew the playbook. They had both seen how obedient the Latina girls had been. They'd been broken. Whatever was done to them had been so bad that they chose to obey rather than risk punishment.

Jessica knew you didn't get to that point unless all hope was lost. Unless the pain of obeying was more appealing than the pain of resisting. She knew she had to marshal and preserve every ounce of physical strength and mental toughness. She'd need it, not only to resist, but to fight back when the time was right. But for now, it was about healing. That, and mentally preparing for the pain she knew was coming. Hunger was the first play.

Hailey, unfortunately, didn't seem to see it. She had spent an hour yesterday afternoon pounding on the door, screaming that she was hungry, demanding they bring her food. When she finally realized her demands would not be answered, she crumpled onto her bunk, crying softly for hours. She was now sitting up in bed with a blanket pulled up to her shoulders.

"You think they'll bring us breakfast?" Hailey asked. "They have every other morning."

"We'll see," Ann said as she and Jessica shared a look.

They sat in their bunks and waited. Breakfast never came.

———

Miller returned to the office after watching Wynn leave. The assault this morning was Crower's case, so the paperwork was his responsibility. She did, however, add some notes to the Davies' file regarding the assault and potential abduction of the lead witness. Next, she pulled up the phone tracing software and attempted to ping the number Wynn had given her last night. No response. Whoever owned it had likely ditched that phone.

A conference call had been scheduled for 10:00 a.m. this morning between the various agencies and departments involved in the Davies case. In all likelihood, the FBI would take it over. They wouldn't be happy their lead witness was gone, but that was Smith's problem to explain. And besides, Wynn was right, she knew where he was going.

The best lead still out there was Lester. She silently cursed Wynn for not calling Johnston or herself before confronting him. As law enforcement, they had the authority and manpower to take him into custody and try to make him talk, whereas Wynn's approach likely left him unconscious or on the run. She hadn't heard if Johnston's deputies had been able to pick him up last night. She reached for her phone and dialed Johnston.

A female voice answered the call. Miller recognized it as belonging to Marjorie, the receptionist they had met yesterday. After exchanging pleasantries, Miller asked, "Is the sheriff in?"

"Not yet, but I expect him shortly."

Miller looked at the clock. 7:36 a.m. It wasn't that early. "Last night, the sheriff said he was going to have someone go out and pick up a person of interest named Matt Lester. I'd like to talk to whoever interviewed him."

"I don't think anyone's interviewed him," Marjorie said. "I don't think they found him. At least I know they didn't bring anyone in last night. Deputy Craig is here and might know more. Would you like to speak to him?"

"Sure." Miller was put on hold. A few moments later the line was picked up by a male voice.

"Craig." The greeting was short, but it was enough for Miller to recognize the voice of the bodybuilder who had gotten the videotape from the post office yesterday.

"Hi, Deputy Craig. This is Deputy Miller with Wheaton County. I'm following up on last night's conference call. Sheriff Johnston was going to pick up a person of interest named Matt Lester?"

"Yeah. No good. Didn't happen. I went out there myself about midnight. Pounded on the door for a good twenty minutes. No response. Went over to the medical clinic here in town and also called the hospitals in Douglas and Torrington. Nobody's seen him, so we put out a BOLO. My guess is he's probably nursing his arm at some girl's place. I'll go back out when Johnston gets in. Maybe go to his worksite if he's not home. We'll find him."

"Can you have Marjorie drop me a line when you have him?" Miller asked.

"Sure."

She gave him her direct number and clicked off. Craig sounded confident but he didn't know about the attempt on Wynn this morning. She was getting a bad feeling. Across the lobby, Smith was in his office, leaning over his desk with his readers on. Likely reviewing incident reports. She went back and knocked on his door.

Smith looked up. "Did he get out of town?" he asked.

"Yep. Northbound," Miller fibbed, realizing she hadn't actually seen which way Wynn went. To change the subject, she asked, "Did you know they haven't found Lester yet?"

Smith leaned back and took off his glasses. "Come again?"

"They haven't found him. Johnston sent a deputy named Craig to go get him last night. He says Lester wasn't home when he got there. They put out a BOLO and they're going to try again shortly."

Smith nodded. "Did Wynn say anything before he left?"

Miller was surprised Smitty didn't want to hear more about Lester, even though there was nothing else to tell. It seemed her attempt to change the subject away from Wynn had failed. "No," she said. "He was pretty quiet. Wanted to get going."

"Okay," Smith said. "We've got the call at ten o'clock. Maybe they'll have him by then." He put his glasses back on and resumed reading his reports.

"Okay," Miller said. She walked back to her station more confused than ever. Smith's reaction had not been what she expected. Could Wynn be right? Could someone on the force be involved? Could Smith? No, that was crazy. There had to be another explanation.

———

Wynn did go north. He took the scenic route on Highway 85, which also happened to be the fastest, most direct road, all the way to Deadwood, South Dakota.

Leaving Newbury, the road climbed steadily as grassy plains gave way to the Black Hills. The long stretches of straight highway he'd ridden south of Newbury now morphed into winding ribbons of curving asphalt north of town. The wide expanses of scrub brush bled into hills and valleys filled with ponderosa pine. The air was cooler here, both from the higher elevation and the early morning sun's inability to reach below the canyon walls.

Not surprisingly, the hills were already full of bikers. By the time he crossed into South Dakota, he was just one of a hundred riders in a long line making the pilgrimage north.

Wynn decided to stop in Deadwood for breakfast. Originally an old mining town with a storied past that included Wild Bill Hickok and Calamity Jane, Deadwood had tied its economic engine to a new master some thirty years ago when the residents legalized gambling. It also meant there would be plenty of restaurants catering to the all-night binge gamers and partiers, exactly who he wanted to see.

He was looking for a specific type of place. Not too family oriented. He wanted a place where bikers hung out and where a single rider might be welcomed. He rode through town, spotting several possibilities, then turned around and went back to the most promising, a place called the Miner's Gorge.

Inside, the restaurant was connected through a hallway to a large casino on the left. The restaurant itself, however, was exactly what he was looking for. No high-backed booths allowing for private conversations, but rather a large open room with several rows of small tables set for two or four. Small and close enough to be easily moved together to create one long table for big groups. All open to one another, conducive to conversation across tables.

It was a little past nine when he walked in, the place a little better than half full, maybe thirty people inside. Mostly couples or foursomes, but plenty of solo diners also. Almost all were bikers, dressed in jeans and black leather. He fit right in.

A waitress hurried by, told him to sit wherever he wanted, so he chose a table for four in the middle of the room, within earshot of as many people as possible.

He took off his sunglasses and ordered coffee from another passing waitress. He perused the menu, focusing more on nearby conversations than actually making a selection. When she came back with his coffee, he ordered the standard pancakes, eggs, and bacon, and keep the coffee coming. When she left, he turned his chair slightly and leaned back, placing his right arm over the back of the empty chair next to him. All open and inviting. Mr. Approachable.

It worked. Within ten minutes he had a half-dozen people from three different tables engaged in conversation like they were old friends. Swapping stories about their hometowns, how many years they'd been coming to the rally, or where they liked to stay. They talked about the best places to party, where the roughest places were, and where to stay away from.

And where to go if you wanted to get a little action.

He made particular note of those.

The challenge, he knew, was that the type of place he was looking for, the type of place sex traffickers might set up shop, wasn't going to advertise broadly. You had to seek it out, quietly and discreetly. Too loud an inquiry would raise suspicion and could be dangerous. Too soft an inquiry and you would never find it. The best bet was to be in those places where discreet conversations were held, and maybe you could slip into one. The consensus among his new friends was that the most likely place was a campground and concert venue called the Grizzly Butte.

An hour and fifteen minutes later he left a tip large enough for eight tables. He felt bad that he had taken so much time and hadn't allowed the tables to turn over. Not the waitress's fault. She'd kept the coffee coming long after the plates had been cleared and never said a word.

Back on his bike, it was finally time to get to Sturgis. Two days late, but hey, Randy said he'd have a room ready.

Deadwood connected to Sturgis via thirteen miles of winding, mostly four-lane highway. Hundreds of bikers streamed in each direction beneath a deep blue sky, while towering pines, interrupted by patches of rolling, grassy hills, lined the roadside.

He arrived at the motel a little before eleven in the morning.

Considering what had happened earlier he thought about trying to get a room elsewhere, to someplace no one, not even Miller, knew about. But even if he could find a room, unless he registered under a false name, they'd be able to find him. Besides, Miller was the only one he had told where he was staying. If anyone tried to jump him here, the list of suspects would be exceptionally small.

Fortunately, Randy had kept his promise and did indeed have a room ready. Wynn checked in and grabbed a rally guide and area map from a rack of brochures in the lobby.

The Boulder Canyon Motel Inn was a two-story, U-shaped building with five rooms across the middle and ten down each arm. Fifty rooms in total. His was on the second floor midway down the arm opposite the lobby.

He parked his bike close to the staircase, grabbed his duffle, and climbed to his room. It reminded him of the place in Newbury. All the same furnishings, but all a hard-used twenty years older. It showed.

He closed the curtains, shoved the chair against the door, took off his boots, and lay down on the bed. The last thing he did was turn off his phone. Last night had been short, and with any luck, tonight would be long. The kind of people he needed to find were night owls. For Jessica's sake, he hoped his luck would change.

CHAPTER 22

MILLER BUSIED HERSELF with paperwork until shortly before 10:00 a.m., when she hurried into Smith's office for the conference call. Crower was already there. Smith dialed in and put the call on speaker. Since the initial missing person's inquiry had originated in Rapid City, an investigator from their police department led off the call. He confirmed everyone on the line and then, as expected, handed the case to an FBI agent who took the lead. He introduced himself as Agent Will Parker, summarized what they knew so far, then spoke directly to Smith.

"Sheriff Smith, we'd like to talk to Mr. Wynn as soon as we're done here. Can you arrange that?"

Smitty cleared his throat, "Unfortunately no. We had an incident here this morning and Wynn is gone. I'll let one of my deputies, Ed Crower, explain."

Crower relayed what had happened at Wynn's motel earlier that morning. When he was finished, Smith picked up the story.

"Mr. Wynn was pretty upset and uncooperative at that point. We know he was heading to Sturgis and suspect that's where he is now. I think he just needs a little time to cool off. He was very helpful to us yesterday. If we give him a little space, he'll come around."

Before he could continue, another voice jumped in. "There might be another reason he ran. This is Sheriff Johnston from Norfolk County in Linert. My deputy just called in. They found Matt Lester inside his mobile home with a bullet hole in his head. It also looks like he'd been beaten up pretty good. Whatever else is going on, Wynn is now the prime suspect for a murder here in Norfolk."

Johnston spent the next ten minutes answering questions. It was likely the murder occurred before Craig and his partner went to the home last night, but at the time they hadn't noticed anything. When they arrived a little after nine this morning, the hot morning sun had already baked the interior of the mobile home, creating a smell that was readily apparent. When they opened the door, they were greeted by a swarm of hundreds of flies. It was not a pleasant discovery.

"Deputy Craig is still at the scene and the M.E. is on his way to take a look, but that's what we have for now," Johnston wrapped up.

Smitty jumped back in. "Mike," he said, referring to Sheriff Johnston. "I'm sorry you've got to deal with that mess right now, but I think there's another theory here to consider. It's certainly possible that Wynn didn't tell us the full truth about his encounter with Lester last night. He could've killed him, but Wynn's a reasonably smart man. After visiting you and picking up his bike yesterday, we thought he was out of the picture. If he'd gone back and killed Lester, he'd have stayed away. It doesn't make sense that he would come straight back here to tell us about beating Lester up if in fact he'd killed him.

"The other theory," Smith continued, "is that it's the same people who killed Lester, took Davies, and attacked Wynn this morning. If that's the case, we've got some pretty bad guys running around our counties. I don't know, but this thing feels bigger to me."

There were murmurs of agreement on the phone, but nobody said anything else.

Eventually, Agent Parker jumped in. "I assume we have Wynn's phone number?" Miller confirmed they did. It was part of the initial witness report.

He continued, "Let's track him with his phone and keep loose eyes on him. We don't need to bring him in yet, but I want to know where he is. We'll let the M.E. do their exam on Lester and hopefully get that soon so we can focus on one of these two theories. Unless anyone else has another?"

Parker paused, but nobody said anything.

"Okay," Parker continued. "Do we have an ID on that assailant Wynn put in the hospital?"

"Not yet," Crower said. "He didn't have any ID on him, and we haven't been able to run his prints yet. He's still unconscious and the doctors are keeping a close eye on him. We'll try to do so later this morning."

"Okay, let us know when you have something," Parker said. "Let's reconvene on this line at four o'clock this afternoon and see what we have."

They all said quick goodbyes and hung up.

"I agree with you," Miller said to Smith. "I don't see it. I spent all day with Wynn yesterday and he thinks very logically. There's no way he'd come back here if he'd killed Lester."

"How well did you and he get along?" Smith asked.

"Well enough," Miller replied. "He was pretty upset when he left this morning."

"They said to keep loose eyes on him. What about staying close? What if you were to go up there and hang out with him for a couple of days? I'm sure the folks at Meade could find you a place to stay and it'd be nice to have a direct line into him until we know a little more. What do you think?"

"Sure, that's doable," Miller agreed.

"Let me run this past the FBI and then I'll alert the folks at Meade. If it's all good you can head up this afternoon."

———

It turned out it was all good with the FBI, and especially with the Meade County Sheriff, who now didn't have to spend man-hours babysitting a witness. With a half-million bikers in town, he needed all his guys and then some just to maintain order.

Miller debated calling Wynn to let him know she was coming, but based on his mood when he left, thought the odds were just as good he would disappear. Before leaving Newbury, she tried pinging the location of his phone to confirm, but he had turned it off. She hoped he actually went where he said he was going this time.

It was mid-afternoon by the time she pulled into the Boulder Canyon Motel Inn. She had driven her own Ford SUV so as not to scream "Cop!" everywhere she went. Wynn's Street Glide was parked in the lot, near the staircase. Before making contact, she called back to the office and had one of the deputies attempt to ping the number they had gotten from Lester's phone last night. She had hoped to have some good news for Wynn, but there was still no response.

Wynn's Street Glide wasn't parked directly in front of any obvious door, so she couldn't tell which room he might be in. She tried his number again, but he still didn't answer. As a last resort, she went to the lobby to meet Randy, to see if she could get Wynn's room number from him.

Randy wasn't particularly happy to meet her. She didn't necessarily blame him, considering she had cost him the ability to double-book the room and she was showing up in full uniform when she'd implied she wouldn't. Instead of giving her the room number, he called up to the room to see if he should send her up. As Randy was making the call, Miller slipped out toward the entrance to get a view of the rooms. She didn't think Wynn would make a run for it, but you never knew.

Instead, she saw a door open across the way about midway down the second floor, and Wynn stepped out onto the walkway and leaned on the railing. She yelled a quick thanks back to Randy and walked across the lot. She saw Wynn scan the lot as she climbed the stairs.

"Hey," she said as she approached.

"Hey yourself," he replied. "You alone?"

"Just me."

"You have a way of showing up when you're not expected," Wynn said.

"There have been some developments. Can I tell you about it inside?"

Wynn opened the door and they went in. He walked back to the desk and wheeled the chair around the bed so it was opposite the stuffed chair. He offered her either seat and when she took the desk chair, he sank into the stuffed one.

"What's happened?" he asked.

"Lester's dead," she said. "Shot in the head in his mobile home. They found him this morning."

"Am I a suspect?"

"It's a theory," she admitted, "But no one's buying into it except Johnston. The prevailing thought is that the same guys who came after you this morning got to Lester last night. That's part of why I'm here. To keep an eye on you."

"Protection?" Wynn said doubtfully.

"More like assistance." She smiled. "I've seen what you can do."

"What's the other part?"

"As expected, the FBI has taken over the case. They'd like to talk to you. I'm here to ask if you'd talk to them."

Wynn considered her request. "Two things," he said. "First, are there any new theories on how those guys found me this morning? In the absence of a credible alternative, I'm sticking with what I said. At best you've got a leak and at worst you've got someone directly involved."

"No," she admitted. "No new theories."

He sighed. "Second, when are they going to be able to clear me on Lester? I have no interest in talking with anyone if I'm a suspect."

"We might hear something yet this afternoon. The medical examiner was called out as soon as they found him so they may have a preliminary report." She checked her watch. "We've got a conference call in about an hour, so I'll find out then."

Wynn thought for a moment. "Alright, here's what we'll do. You'll make your conference call from here this afternoon, on speaker so I can hear. If they've cleared me, then you can arrange a meeting with the FBI. If not, I'm gone."

Miller agreed, secretly hoping they'd clear Wynn so she wouldn't be forced to detain him.

They spent the next hour discussing various aspects of the case, re-analyzing things they knew, and coming up with new theories for the things they didn't know. Unfortunately, none of the new theories were as strong as the original. Miller kept her concerns over Smitty's reactions to herself. No use throwing gas on that fire.

When 4:00 rolled around, Miller dialed into the conference call and waited while everyone else connected. Parker took the lead again and began by asking Miller if she'd made contact with Wynn.

"Not yet," she said. "I know where he's at but haven't made contact. I'll do so pending instructions and outcome from this call."

"Good," Parker said. "Sheriff Johnston, do you have any preliminary report from the M.E. on Lester?"

"Yes sir," Johnston said. "In addition to the obvious gunshot wound, the M.E. said Lester had a broken left arm, likely due to extreme twisting, and two of the fingers on his right hand were broken as if they had been smashed in a door."

Miller looked disbelievingly at Wynn, who shrugged slightly.

Johnston continued, "He also had a nasty bruise on the left side of his face and another in his abdominal region, consistent with being beaten."

"Could they tell anything about the timing of those injuries as they related to the time of death?" Parker asked.

"Based on the swelling around the broken bones and the development of the bruising, he said the fatal gunshot wound occurred at least an hour after the beating. But that doesn't clear Wynn. The M.E. said Lester was likely unconscious for a time after the blow to the head. Wynn could've stuck around and waited for Lester to regain consciousness, maybe tried to get more info out of him, and then popped him."

"What kind of round was Lester shot with?" Parker asked.

"Nine-millimeter," Johnston said. "Arrest report from Deputy Crower says Wynn carries a Glock 19. Same round."

"Did you recover the bullet?"

"Yeah," said Johnston, "But it was pancaked. Fifty-fifty if they'll be able to pull anything useful off it."

"And we'd still need to match it to Wynn's gun," Parker said. "Nine mil is a pretty common round."

Miller cut in. "Mike, this is Sam, uh, Deputy Miller. Did you happen to check with Lester's foreman at work to see what time he left the job site last night?"

"We did. About seven o'clock. Why?"

Miller paused as she composed her thoughts. "The timing doesn't work," she explained. "If Lester left work at seven, we can assume it took about twenty minutes to get home, meaning the soonest Wynn could have assaulted him was around seven-twenty. If he hung around for an hour or more before finishing him off, that would have been eight-twenty, and yet Wynn was back in our offices in Newbury a little after nine. No way he could've gotten there in forty minutes."

"You guys know the geography," Parker said. "Anyone want to dispute that timeline?"

No one said anything.

"Alright," Parker continued. "Pending forensics on the bullet we're going to back burner Wynn as a suspect on Lester and go with Sheriff Smith's theory that the same group that took Davies also popped Lester. That means we're looking at something large and organized, and potentially active right now in Meade County. Deputy Miller, if you can arrange to have Wynn come in asap, that'd be helpful."

She looked at Wynn, who nodded. "Will do," she said.

The Meade County Sheriff then gave an update on resources and potential hotspots they were going to monitor in the coming days, including the Grizzly Butte.

When he was finished, Parker spoke again. "Deputy Crower, any ID on Wynn's assailant?"

Crower's voice came over the line, "No sir. We got his prints and ran them, but nothing. Still a John Doe."

"He's not cooperating?"

"He's not conscious. Massive swelling on the brain. The doctors have induced him into a coma."

"All right. Can you get a photo of this guy and start showing it around? Maybe someone knows him. Sheriff Johnston, maybe you could do the same. He might be from your area."

Johnston chimed in, "Will do."

"Anything else?" Parker asked.

When no one said anything, he scheduled their next call for 10:00 p.m., and they all disconnected. Wynn walked over to the closet and pulled his Glock out of his jacket and handed it, grip first, to Miller.

"Check it," he said. "Hasn't been fired in a month."

"I believe you, " she said. But she took it anyway, ejected the magazine and cleared the chamber, then held it to her nose. "All good," she said as she re-inserted the magazine and handed it back. "I just hung my ass out there lying for you, *and* I put a big hole in Johnston's theory that you might've killed Lester. Trust me now?"

Wynn nodded.

"Good," Miller said. "Now let's go talk to the FBI."

CHAPTER 23

A HALF HOUR after the conference call ended, Sheriff Johnston's inbox dinged to indicate an incoming email. It was from Crower. The picture of the John Doe who'd tried to assault Wynn and ended up in a coma.

It wasn't a pretty picture.

The guy had oxygen tubes in his nose, his eyes were closed, and an ugly purple bruise covered the side of his face, but his features were still distinguishable. If someone knew him, they should be able to recognize him.

He forwarded the email to Deputy Craig with a quick note to "spread this around." Craig opened the email, read it, and went on to other work.

———

By late afternoon, as best she could tell being locked inside a windowless room, Jessica was sitting back in her bunk. Ann had helped her to get up and move around more today, trying to prevent the injured muscles from tightening up too much as they healed. It was both painful and exhausting.

While they hadn't been given any food since yesterday morning, they were able to drink as much as they wanted from the bathroom sink. The water served double duty, not only filling her empty stomach, but also keeping her hydrated, to help her injured muscles heal.

Ann continued to maintain a steady composure, but Hailey was a wreck. If Jessica had doubted the applicability of the stages of grief to this situation, Hailey was demonstrating them in real-time. She was angry yesterday, had bargained last night, and was in full tilt depression today, having barely moved off her bed. Even when Ann helped Jessica move about the room, they both encouraged Hailey to join in, but she remained inert on her bunk.

For the first time since yesterday morning, they heard movement outside the door. Mixed emotions, equal parts hope and fear, coursed through Jessica. Hunger fed the hope that their captors would bring them something to eat, but fear of all the other things they might do still dominated her thoughts. After a few moments, however, the noise ended, leaving nothing to indicate anyone was out there. She settled back against the wall.

Twenty minutes later there were more sounds outside the door, then the familiar pounding and the shout of "Back off!" as keys rustled and the deadbolt turned. Hailey jumped up from her bunk and ran over to Ann. She huddled close. Jessica squeezed herself back against the wall.

The door opened and two men entered; the older white guy and someone Jessica had not seen before. A younger, Latino guy. Different from the first one. The older guy once again held a gun in his hand and immediately positioned himself against the wall between the exit and bathroom doors. The younger man stood in the open doorway.

"Hungry?" the older man asked.

The three women nodded and mumbled tentatively.

"Here's how it's going to work. When I pound on the door, I want the three of you sitting in a row on that bunk." He pointed to the bunk furthest from the door where the three Latina girls had sat.

"We'll bring something in, set it on the floor, and only when we leave will you get up. Understand?"

They nodded again.

"Let's practice. Pretend I just pounded on that door. Now."

Quickly, but cautiously, the three women got up and went to the indicated bunk. Jessica was last to arrive, both because she was furthest away, and moved slowest due to her wounds.

When they were settled, the older man said, "You all met Tomas when you were brought in. He runs this place. We do what he says, you do what we say. If we all do what we're told, we'll all get along. If not..." He nodded to the younger man who held up a four-inch wide, eight-foot-long leather strap.

"Understand?" the older man asked.

They nodded.

"Good." He signaled to the younger man who disappeared out of the doorway. He returned a few moments later with a tray of microwaved sandwiches. He set the tray on the floor and then looked up at the women, challenging them with his eyes, as if he were feeding hungry tigers. When they didn't move, he stood up quickly and walked out.

"Only when we leave," the older man said. He closed the door and the deadbolt slid back into place.

"How many are there?" Jessica asked Ann when they'd finished eating. Hailey sat quietly on the next bunk.

"At least seven," Ann replied. "But the bigger obstacle is the two locked doors."

"Two?"

"There's always noise from further away before they pound on our door. I'm guessing that means at least one more locked door between us and freedom. Maybe more."

Jessica nodded. "And even if we did get through both those doors, we have no idea who or what might be on the other side."

"Agreed," Ann said. "I don't think we're getting out of here until they decide to move us."

"When do you think that'll be?"

"Graciela said they were held a little over a week before they were moved, which seems long. I've been here four days, so probably any time now. A few more days at most."

"So, we've got somewhere between no time and a few days to figure out how to escape when they move us, right?" Jessica asked.

"Yeah. But we've got one other thing on our side," Ann said.

"What's that?"

"They don't want to hurt us."

Jessica felt the burn on her back. "How do you figure that?"

"Remember the guy with the broken nose? The first night I was here he came for me. The second night he came for Hailey. The third night he was coming for you."

Jessica's eyes opened wide.

"Graciela and I stopped him, put some pretty good scratches on his face. Another guy came in and told him the old guy would kill him if he hurt us. The next morning his nose was broken. My guess is the old guy did it. He doesn't want us hurt."

"What's that mean?" Jessica said.

Ann shrugged. "Maybe we have a little more power than we think. If we fight back, maybe they won't kill us."

"But how? I mean, I've taken a couple of self-defense classes, but nothing that would help us here. How about you?"

Ann laughed bitterly. "I'm an auditor. Unless they give me access to their books, I'm not sure what I can do."

"Too bad. I was hoping you were a cop, or former army, or something like that. What about Hailey?"

"I don't know. Never asked." Turning to Hailey, Ann said, "Hey. Hailey. What do you do for a living?"

Hailey stared back and then closed her eyes and rolled over.

"I'm guessing not a cop," Ann said.

"No," Jessica agreed. "I guess not."

———

A few miles east of Sturgis, Brandon and Carlos loaded two of the Latina girls into the burgundy, wood-panel van to take them out for the night's work. The third, Andy had decided, would stay behind. There were age requirements and she simply looked too young. Not worth the risk. She would stay here and work the house.

Andy gave them instructions and wristbands, and told them two of the bikers would already be in position. The bikers would watch inside while Brandon and Carlos kept things going outside. It was new for Brandon, but Carlos had done it before. He knew the routine.

CHAPTER 24

THEY WAITED TWENTY minutes after the conference call ended before Miller called Parker to arrange for Wynn to come in for the interview. It was only two miles to the sheriff's office, but in Miller's SUV, it took fifteen minutes to get there.

Main Street through Sturgis was closed to non-biker traffic, and the side streets were packed with both bikers and four-wheeled vehicles. Thousands of leather-clad bikers strolled the streets, the men in jeans, t-shirts, and black vests, many of the women in shorts and halter tops.

Tents lined the side streets selling everything from bike accessories to clothing, to tattoos. One street was roped off for a beer garden and several restaurants had commandeered the sidewalks in front of their establishments to create more seating for the masses who were tiring in the late afternoon sun. The steady roar of idling tailpipes was intermittently punctuated by the revving of a single, or sometimes multiple Harley engines.

Miller's badge got them a parking spot in the lot of the Meade County Sheriff's department. With Miller leading, Wynn entered his third sheriff's office building in as many days. Like its counterparts, it reminded Wynn more of a bank lobby than a law enforcement office. Maybe a lot of them were this way. Regardless, they had lost their novelty.

After introducing themselves to the deputy at the reception counter, they were escorted back to a small conference room where two men sat at an oval conference table. The one on the right, a tall, thin, good-looking man with short, dark hair in his mid-forties introduced himself as Agent Parker. He reminded Wynn of Tom Brady. He immediately disliked him.

Within minutes, the small conference room filled with two more FBI agents, the Meade County Sheriff and the Sturgis Chief of Police. The two junior FBI agents stood against the wall when they ran out of chairs. Wynn was getting faster at telling the story, and without any truly new questions from Parker, his statement rehashed many of the things already said multiple times. Wynn had the feeling the real purpose of the meeting was to allow Parker an opportunity to size him up. Judge for himself if Wynn was a credible witness. Forty-five minutes later, Wynn and Miller were on their way out.

"So, what's the plan for tonight?" Miller asked as they walked back to her SUV.

Wynn looked at her cautiously. "Is that as in my plan, or our plan?"

"I've been told to keep an eye on you. Easier to do if we're together, don't you think?"

"Maybe for you, but I don't need a uniform tagging along beside me all night. Not likely to be welcome where I'm going."

Miller looked down at herself and recognition spread across her face as she realized he was right; she was still wearing her full uniform, including her duty belt. No matter where they went, she would stand out. Up the street, there were several booths selling t-shirts and other clothes.

"Wait right here." She took off up the sidewalk.

Miller was back in less than ten minutes with a pair of plastic bags in hand. "Mind if we go back to your motel? I don't want to change in there," she said, nodding toward the sheriff's office.

"Sure." Wynn wanted to get his bike anyway.

When they got back to the motel, Miller took the two plastic bags and a small overnight bag up to the room, then went into the bathroom to change. When she came out, Wynn did a double-take to make sure he was looking at the same person. Gone were the green cargo pants and the baggy tan shirt with its pockets and badges. As was the bulky duty belt with its radio, Taser, flashlight, and gun. Gone too, and most stunningly, was the loose bun that held her hair, which now fell in soft, auburn curls around her shoulders.

Miller, now in jeans, wore a black t-shirt unlike any Wynn had ever seen before. The t-shirt was snug but not tight, the short sleeves made of a black lace that showed off her muscular arms. More black lace filled the deep V-neck, covering the swell of Miller's cleavage, while the requisite "Sturgis Motorcycle Rally" logo stretched across her left breast. The t-shirt was tucked into a pair of tight jeans that were tucked into a pair of ankle-high, brown leather boots.

She looked fabulous.

"Will this get me into wherever you want to go?" she asked.

"Almost," Wynn said. "You got a jacket?"

"No," she said. "But it's warm out. I won't need one."

"Not on a bike at night. It cools off fast."

"We can take my car," she offered.

"Not to where I want to go. We need to blend in. Don't worry, we'll stop and get you one. Besides," he paused, "you'll need a place to hide your gun."

"Why?" she asked cautiously. "Where are we going?"

"Shopping first. Dinner second. The Grizzly Butte third, and hopefully someplace with a white van after that."

Wynn checked his Glock, knowing he had an extra full magazine in his saddlebag. He told Miller to grab her gun, cuffs, and flashlight.

He didn't need to tell her to bring her phone or her badge. When they got down to his bike, he placed her hardware and his jacket in one of the saddlebags, then handed her an extra pair of sunglasses.

"Put these on," he said. "And hold on tight."

The passenger portion of the Street Glide's seat was small, and with no sissy bar or backrest, Miller was forced to clasp her arms around Wynn's midsection as they rode back to town. It'd been a long time since he'd had anyone on the back of his bike. He liked it. It took a little getting used to the extra weight, but she was light; he adjusted quickly.

Traffic was still heavy, but now on two wheels, with all the roads open to them, it didn't take long to get back downtown. Rows of Harley-Davidsons, Indians, and a smattering of other bikes were parked on both sides of the street at the curb, as well as two rows down the middle, leaving a pathway on each side barely wide enough for two bikes to ride abreast. They cruised down the main drag at a leisurely pace, tightly packed with other riders ahead and behind, until they found a parking spot.

"Wow," said Miller as she stepped off. "I mean, I've been here before, but never on a bike. This is crazy."

"It's different," Wynn agreed.

They found what they were looking for on a side street about a block and a half away. Inside a steel-framed booth enclosed by dirty, white polyester walls, they found t-shirts and jackets, vests and chaps, gloves and hats and helmets and all sorts of riding paraphernalia.

Wynn went straight to the jackets, but Miller looked skeptical. "It's still over ninety degrees out here. We're going to be the ones standing out if we wear these things."

Point conceded. Even though it wouldn't be quite as easy to hide a weapon, they turned their attention to the leather vests and eventually they found one for each of them with a concealed carry pocket. Wynn also made her buy a pair of riding boots. They weren't as fashionable as her ankle-high brown leather ones, but they were much more functional.

"You'll fit in better," Wynn told her. "First thing someone checks are the shoes. It's the hardest part to change, and the biggest giveaway if someone isn't who they say they are."

"Should I be worried you know all this?"

He shrugged. "Make sure you scuff them up a little when we get outside."

When they had made their purchases, they went off in search of someplace to eat. The Gilded Queen, a large, three-story, log-cabin style bar with outdoor seating overlooking Main Street fit the bill perfectly. More than a few guys turned their heads when Miller walked past as they weaved through the crowd to find a table.

Once they were seated and settled with drinks in hand, Wynn asked, "Have you been able to get anything more from that number I gave you?"

"No. I checked it twice today and got nothing. At best they just turned it off, but likely they've ditched it."

Wynn nodded, "But their last known location was somewhere around here, right?"

"Yeah," Miller said. "But look at all these people. It's like looking for a needle in a haystack."

"Not exactly. I think it's a fair assumption that if the guys who grabbed Davies are here, they're hoping to make some money off her. Second, ninety, maybe ninety-five percent of the people here are good, honest, hard-working folks. They're not into buying sex. That means we need to find where the five to ten percent of people who are into it hang out.

"And think about it from the bad guys' perspective. If you had a product that you couldn't advertise, how would you get customers? Word of mouth, one-by-one, right? And yet you need to make sure those same customers don't rat you out, so you want them to be loyal, have some kind of code. An honor-among-thieves, thing. Who has that?"

"The motorcycle gangs," Miller said.

"They prefer to be called clubs, but yes."

"And we'll find them at the Grizzly Butte?"

"As good a place to start as any."

CHAPTER 25

AFTER DINNER, WYNN and Miller walked back to his bike. Shielding themselves from prying eyes, they each tucked their guns inside their vests and placed her brown leather boots in one of the saddlebags. Guns weren't allowed in the Grizzly Butte, but Wynn hoped Miller's badge would ease the way if challenged. Then they joined the long, loose procession of bikes heading the five miles east out of town.

When they arrived, Wynn was reminded once again that the word "campground" didn't do the place justice. The South Dakota courts had been wrangling for years as to whether the "Griz," as it was known by its residents, could be incorporated into its own small city. He understood why. Set on a single square mile of mostly unde-veloped plain, for two weeks at the beginning of every August, the Grizzly Butte boasted South Dakota's third-highest residential popu-lation. It was without a doubt, a tent and RV city.

They parked in a lot that, for fifty weeks out of the year, was just a grassy field east of the campground, then walked to the main entrance. They stood in line to purchase their wristbands, then entered through a large set of chain link gates. When a big, bald guy in a black "Security" T-shirt attempted to wand her down, Miller flashed her badge and motioned to Wynn. "He's with me."

The guy nodded and let them in.

When they were thirty feet away, Miller said, "I hope that's not representative of the security in this place. He didn't even bother to check if my badge was real."

"Unfortunately, I'm afraid it probably is," Wynn said. "I'll bet at least a third of these RVs have some kind of weapon inside."

"Lovely thought. Let's be careful."

On either side of the path were huge camping areas with row upon row of RVs and fifth wheelers. The air smelled of barbeque as hundreds of people sat in lawn chairs arranged in small groups around smoking grills. Most, it seemed, with a beer or beverage in hand.

Straight ahead on the main stage amphitheater, a heavy metal rock band was inciting the early crowd. Like downtown, booths ringed the concert area selling all kinds of food, drink, and clothing. Skirting left, away from the amphitheater, they followed a paved roadway as it bent to the south, wove through a group of small cabins, then U-turned back north to rejoin the main road. To their left, they passed a swimming pond, aptly named Bikini Beach, complete with a sundeck and rope swing. Dusk was slowly fading to dark, but that didn't appear to bother the hundred or so people still partying in the sand.

Another half-mile west, they passed more areas designated for tents, RVs, and small cabins. Further on were areas for races and riding exhibitions, a general store, the campground office, and of course, the obligatory bikini bike-wash area. There was even a veteran's memorial field with hundreds of U.S. flags arranged in precise rows to honor those who had died in service.

When they finally reached the west end, they turned north for a quarter-mile. The paved road turned to dirt, and then meandered south and east. They made their way back toward the main stage, passing through a maze of tents and RV's. All told it took more than an hour to walk through everything, and Wynn still wasn't sure they'd seen it all.

As they approached an intersecting road, Wynn stopped and turned around. He was now facing north with the amphitheater to his right, the Bikini Beach pond slightly behind, and multiple rows of RVs to his front left.

"What do you think?" he asked.

"This looks good," Miller said. "It's a crossroads. Eighty percent of the campers are either behind us or to our left, so they'll have to come by here to get into the concert, which we have to assume is the big draw. On the other hand, a good percentage of the visitors who are only here for the concert will want to check the rest of the place out, so they'll come by in the other direction."

"Agreed," Wynn said. "But we'll stick out like sore thumbs if we just stand here all night." He looked around. Spotted a couple of lawn chairs leaning against an RV. "You grab those chairs. I'll get us a couple of beers. We'll blend right in. Sit here as long as we want."

"What if the owners want their chairs back?"

"Flash your badge and flex that muscle," he teased.

While Miller grabbed the chairs, Wynn walked the outskirts of the amphitheater. He wanted a better feel for the layout and where small groups were set up. In particular, he looked for the motorcycle clubs. They weren't hard to find. There were small gatherings of Hells Angels, Outlaws, and Sons of Silence, among others. The largest group, he noted, were the "Aces" who had passed him on the interstate outside of Cheyenne two days ago.

When he had completed the circuit, he stopped at a booth and bought two beers. Returning to Miller, he saw that she had moved the chairs underneath a tree just off the main intersection. It was a great spot to observe while still maintaining some obscurity themselves.

"You see all kinds of things here, don't you?" Miller said. An abundance of scantily clad women walked around the Griz. Many wore Daisy Dukes and cowboy boots, halter tops, or back-baring leather vests. Some wore variations of leather and lace lingerie, while a few brave ones decided that body paint alone was enough.

"That you do," Wynn replied.

"We're looking for something unusual, right?" Miller asked. "I've seen a lot of unusual stuff in just the last ten minutes. What's going to stand out?"

"Unusual in the context of where we are. Clothing or lack thereof probably won't do it. I'm thinking we should be looking for behaviors that don't seem right. Most people aren't that hard to read. Take those two for example," Wynn nodded to a pair of young women. They wore cowboy boots and hats, shorts, and spaghetti strap tops. "Out for a good time tonight, right?"

"Yeah," Miller agreed.

"So, if we saw them do anything too serious, almost like a negotiation, that would be out of context. That's what we're looking for."

"Got it."

They continued to make small talk throughout the next two hours, simply watching the people go by. For Wynn, it was no hardship at all. Miller was bright, funny, and easy on the eyes. The hardest part was keeping his eyes focused outward.

They'd each gotten up to use the restroom and walk around the amphitheater, looking for anything unusual. Wynn saw a couple of small-time drug deals go down but nothing worth mentioning. Not what he was here for. Several of the motorcycle clubs swelled in numbers, but they seemed to be chilling for the most part. After two hours, it looked like a bust. Nothing stood out.

The third band of the night had finished up their set and stagehands were preparing for the headline act when Miller reached over and tapped Wynn on the arm.

"What's up?"

She nodded toward a young Latino couple. A dark-haired guy held fast to the girl's elbow and seemed to be talking sternly as they walked toward the amphitheater. The girl looked afraid. She wore fishnet stockings underneath a tight leather skirt and vest. With the only light coming from the stage area, it was hard to tell their ages, but they looked to be in their early to mid-twenties.

"That's the third time I've seen her come by. I didn't notice who she was with the first time, but the second time she was going the other way with one of those guys you call the Aces. And I think the guy's been with another girl too."

"You sure?"

"Not a hundred percent, but yeah, I think so."

"How many Aces have you seen come by here tonight?"

"Five or six."

"Alone or together?"

Miller thought for a moment. "Shit. They've either been alone or with one of those girls. They're customers."

"Stay here. Look for the other girl." Wynn got up and jogged a couple of quick steps to the road, then fell in pace thirty yards behind the couple. They entered the amphitheater and veered away from the stage in the direction of an area where Wynn had seen a group of Aces gathered earlier. As they approached, the guy suddenly stopped and turned the girl to face him. Wynn stepped in line at a beer stand to avoid being seen. He tried to listen in but was too far away to hear anything. One thing was clear, however. It was a short, one-way conversation.

Almost like instructions. Or a threat.

Unusual.

When he finished, the girl turned and walked on toward the Aces. The guy watched her go, then turned back, passing only a few paces behind Wynn who had moved up in line. Wynn waited a beat before ducking away and trailing the guy toward the exit.

Three minutes later Wynn passed by Miller, giving her a quick hand signal to join him.

"Have you seen the other girl?" he asked when she caught up.

"Not yet. But I did see another Ace."

"Which direction?"

"Going toward the concert." Miller hustled to keep up with Wynn's pace.

"Alone?"

"Yeah."

"Okay. Go back to where we were and keep an eye out for that first girl we just saw. I'm guessing she'll be coming this way in the next twenty minutes, probably with another Ace."

"Should I call Parker?"

"Not yet. Let's let this play out a little more. I'll text you if I find something."

"Okay," she said. "Be careful."

Miller peeled off and went back to the lawn chairs while Wynn tailed the dark-haired Latino as he turned down a mostly deserted row of RVs and fifth wheelers. Ambient light from the amphitheater bled between the RVs near the front, but the further down the row the guy went, the harder it was for Wynn to keep him in sight. He had become just a black shape moving in the shadows. Then he was gone.

Wynn stopped, listening for footsteps or voices, but heard nothing. He jogged up to where he had last seen the guy and flattened himself against an RV. A pair of voices came from behind him.

"Is she ready?"

"Almost. Give her a minute."

"The dude's gone?"

"Yeah, ten minutes ago."

Wynn slipped between two RVs and hustled back to the row behind him, then lowered himself to the ground. Peering beneath the RV he saw two sets of feet standing in front of the second RV to his left. Rising to a crouching position, he peeked around the corner.

Two guys stood next to a door outside a large fifth-wheel camper. Further away, seven or eight other campers were sitting out on lawn chairs down the row, back in the direction they had just come from. Seeing them, Wynn understood. The guy he followed had overshot the row he wanted to go down to avoid passing by the other campers.

Once he got safely past them, he cut between the rows and doubled back to where he wanted to be.

Eventually, the fifth wheeler's door opened, and a splash of light illuminated the ground. He peeked around the corner again to see another Latina girl, dressed very similarly to the first, step carefully out the door. A hand from inside the fifth wheel helped her down the steps.

There are more inside.

The two guys outside had their backs to Wynn, but as the dark-haired Latino took the girl by the elbow and directed her across the lane, the second one turned to close the door, illuminating his face for a brief instant.

But the one moment was all Wynn needed. Dark hair. Prominent nose. It was the passenger of the white van he'd seen following Davies.

Wynn's mind raced. He needed a plan. He could go rush the guy but had no idea how many more were inside. As easily as he'd gotten his gun in, it was highly likely these guys were armed too. And besides, he had no idea if Davies was even in the fifth wheeler.

He crept two rows further away, then raced back toward the main road. Slowing to a brisk walk he followed the path toward Miller and the amphitheater, searching for the couple who had just left. Scanning the crowds, he finally saw them taking a shortcut across the grass, bypassing Miller. He pulled out his phone and dialed her number.

"Hey," she answered urgently, "What's up?"

"This could be it. I followed the guy to a fifth-wheeler parked about two hundred yards from you. He picked up another girl and is heading back to the concert. Looks like you were right. They found a pool of customers in the Aces. They're bringing them back here to consummate the transaction. There are at least two guys here at the RV, one of whom was the passenger in the van that followed Davies."

"Did you see her?"

"No, just this other girl, but the RV was big enough. She could be in there."

"Where are you?"

"Following these two back to the concert. They took a shortcut. You won't see them."

"Okay, Should I call Parker?"

"Yeah, do it. Night rules."

Miller sounded puzzled. "What's that?"

"Marine slang. Means you come in silent and heavy. Bring everything you've got. But don't let him take them down until we know for sure we've got Davies. I'm going to try to get inside. I'll keep you posted."

Wynn put his phone in silent mode and slipped it into his pocket. The pair in front was twenty yards ahead and approaching the same cluster of Aces he had seen a short time ago. Once again, the guy stopped and gave the girl some kind of instruction.

Wynn veered left and kept walking to get a better view of the pair, and the Aces. He stayed back a safe distance as the guy finished up, then nudged her toward the bikers. She took a hesitant step forward, paused to take a deep breath, then pulled her shoulders back and walked on. The guy watched her for a few seconds, then turned and walked toward the exit. Wynn let him go. He turned his attention back to the bikers and scanned for the first girl but didn't see her anywhere.

Wynn pulled out his phone and texted Miller: *First girl?*

Miller's reply was immediate: *Came by 5 minutes ago. With an Ace.*

He put his phone away and walked toward the girl, hoping to reach her before she engaged with the Aces, but no luck. She bravely approached a group of four, two of whom stepped aside, opening a space to welcome her into their conversation. The two guys on either side put an arm around her, closing the circle like a Venus flytrap closing on its prey.

Now that she was in, Wynn needed a change of plan, which was pretty much being made up on the fly anyway. Scanning the scene again, he changed course to approach two Aces standing side-by-side on the outskirts of the concert area. Wynn took a deep breath and strolled up beside them.

When he was sure they had noticed him, he said simply, "Hey."

The one next to him nodded, cautiously.

Still looking at the stage, Wynn said, "Nice colors. Where you from?"

The guy looked at Wynn, curiously. "Cheyenne."

"Your president here?" Wynn asked.

The guy turned, squaring himself. Wynn stood calmly, looking at the stage. The second guy also turned and stepped forward. They were now at Wynn's nine o'clock and eleven o'clock positions, facing him, while he looked past them at the stage.

"Who wants to know?" the first challenged.

Wynn turned his head, finally looking the guy in the eye. "Someone who can save you guys a lot of trouble."

"What if we like trouble?"

"With me? Fine. But with undercover cops? You look smarter than that."

The first guy paused a moment, then turned and nodded. "Come on."

Wynn followed, with the second guy falling in pace behind. They walked around the outskirts of the assemblage which now included thirty or so bikers and another seventeen or eighteen women. Close to fifty people in all.

They stopped next to a group of six people. Four Aces and two women, who stood on either side of a mountain of a man. He had to be at least six-four and close to three hundred pounds. Not all of it muscle, but he carried more of it higher, rather than lower. He had a shiny bald head with a trimmed goatee. He wore a sleeveless collared shirt underneath a black leather vest, showing off arms as thick as Wynn's thighs. As they approached, the big guy looked questioningly at the first man who leaned in and spoke quietly.

The two men separated. The big guy looked at Wynn and asked, "Save us some trouble. How so?"

"Can we talk privately?" Wynn said.

The big guy looked around, then back at Wynn. He took a few paces to the side, out of earshot. "What?"

Wynn nodded toward the Latina girl who was still in the group with the four Aces. "Your guys have been enjoying the company of that girl and her friend tonight, right?"

The big guy stared back at him.

"Her handlers are gonna get stung tonight. My guess is you and your guys don't want to be anywhere near that when it happens."

"And how would you know this?"

"Let's just say I've got contacts," Wynn said.

"Why warn us?"

"Because her handlers also have something of mine. I need to get it back before this goes down. I need to take your guy's place."

The big guy paused, his poker face not revealing what he was thinking. He looked over at the girl, then back at Wynn. Finally, he looked past Wynn and called out, "Chase! Dom! Come here."

The two guys who had escorted Wynn stepped over. The big guy pointed to the girl. "Bring her over."

The two guys walked over and interrupted the conversation. Based on their reactions, the other four Aces were none too happy as Chase and Dom took hold of the girl's elbows and escorted her away from the group. Her face was pale as they approached.

The big guy made his way back to the larger circle of bikers, then motioned to Wynn, inviting him to join their group. He put his huge arm around Wynn's shoulders.

"I want you all to take a good look at our new friend here," the big guy said ominously. "He's either our newest friend or newest enemy. We'll know tomorrow. But either way, I want you to take a good look so if you see him around later in the week, you can greet him accordingly."

He then turned to Wynn and squeezed his shoulder "Understood?"

Wynn nodded.

The big guy released Wynn's shoulder and pointed at the girl. "She goes with him."

Wynn stepped across the circle, grabbed the girl by the elbow, and led her away from the Aces.

The girl stopped and turned to Wynn. "You pay?" she asked with a heavy accent.

"*Sí,*"

In broken English, the girl said, "Two hoondred?"

"*Sí,*" Wynn said again. Then gestured forward, "*Vamonos.*"

CHAPTER 26

THE GIRL LED Wynn back toward the fifth-wheeler. She followed the same path that the guy had gone, first overshooting the intended row, then walking past their destination, cutting back between a couple of dark RVs, and finally circling back. The van passenger, who was sitting in a lawn chair, stood up as they approached.

"New blood. That's good," he said to the girl. Then to Wynn, he said, "Two hundred for a half hour. That's the entrance fee. What you do once you're in there is up to you."

Wynn studied the guy's face. His nose was swollen even bigger than Wynn remembered. He had a big cut on his forehead and scratches all over his face that looked to be a couple of days old. Now that he saw him up close, even in the dark, Wynn was sure. This was one of the guys who had picked up Davies. It turned his stomach to give this guy money, but he had to get inside. He handed the guy two hundred dollars.

"Wait two minutes," the guy said.

Wynn stepped back and looked up and down the row. He knew he was in the fourth row of RVs, but hadn't been able to accurately count how many down the row he was.

Three minutes later Wynn heard movement as the door opened and a guy with an Ace's vest stumbled out.

"Come again," the van passenger said sarcastically, laughing at his double entendrè as the Ace walked away. He then held the door open and helped the girl up the steps and into the fifth wheeler as Wynn followed.

Two bikers sat at a table immediately to Wynn's left as he entered. A pair of Rugers sat on the table between them.

Across from the table was a small kitchen, and beyond that, a short hallway led past a couch and TV area to what Wynn assumed was a bathroom. The door was closed but light leaked from underneath.

The girl took Wynn's hand and pulled him to the right, past a blanket that had been hung to create privacy. Wynn crouched to avoid bumping his head as he climbed three steps that led up to the bedroom area.

Rather than a single queen bed, two single mattresses had been pushed to each side creating a small walkway in between. Another old blanket had been hung from the ceiling above the walkway to separate the two beds and further divide the cramped space. The blanket was pushed back, allowing Wynn to see that the other side was empty. He assumed he had just seen its male occupant leave, and its female occupant was in the bathroom. Classic Led Zeppelin blared over a beer-can-sized Bluetooth speaker, probably to mask other sounds the bikers below had tired of hearing.

The girl sat down on the bunk and scooted across the bed to the left, while Wynn did the same toward the far back wall. Once he was settled, she leaned toward him and reached her hand toward Wynn's crotch. He quickly grabbed her wrist and moved her hand away.

"No," he said as he shook his head. "English?"

She shook her head.

Shit.

He picked up the speaker and placed it at the end of the bed, pointing it outward so it wasn't blasting in his ear. He then turned to the girl who was looking at him, confused.

Wynn held his hands up in front of him and waved them back and forth. "No, no."

He didn't know much Spanish, but he was hoping he could communicate well enough to at least get some information from her. He tried to remember how to say "how many" in Spanish.

"*Cuantos?*" he said, pointing at her.

She looked at him, confused, "Two hoondred," she said.

"No, no." He pointed at her. "You, *uno*."

He pointed at the blanket and the bed on the other side, "*Dos?*" He held up two fingers.

"*Si,*" she said cautiously.

"*Bien, bien,*" he said. He then pointed at her and said, "*Uno.*"

"*Si.*"

He pointed at the blanket and the bed on the other side, "*Dos?*"

"*Si,*" she said, her voice rising as she understood.

Wynn put a finger to his lips, "Shh," he said. He then held his hands out, palms up, and shrugged his shoulders, "*Tres?*" he asked.

"*Si,*" she whispered urgently.

"*Cuatro?*" He asked as he held up four fingers.

"*No.*"

"*Bien, bien,* that's good," he said. "*Tres,* here?" he asked as he pointed down with both index fingers.

"*No,*" she shook her head.

Wynn sat back, frustrated and confused. She had just said there were three of them, but then she said no when he tried to confirm.

She reached out and grabbed his hands to get his attention. "*Uno,*" she said as she tapped her chest. "*Dos.*" She pointed to the other bed. She then put her arm in the air and repeatedly pointed away with one finger, "*Tres.*"

He finally got it. There were two of them here tonight, but there was one more out there somewhere. He didn't know if that meant somewhere else here at the Grizzly Butte, or elsewhere in all of Sturgis, or throughout the Black Hills. He knew the second girl wasn't Davies, but it was still possible the third girl might be. He had no idea how to ask.

Instead, he changed tack. "Okay." He pointed toward the two bikers sitting at the table, made a mean face, and pointed his hand like a gun. "*Cuantos?*" he asked.

She pointed two fingers down with both hands and spun them in a circle. "*Cuatro,*" she said. She pointed two fingers on one hand at the two men below in the kitchen, "*Dos*." She then reached her other hand as if indicating outside and "*Dos,*" again.

Wynn repeated the hand motions and said it back to her to confirm. There were four guys here, the two at the table plus the two outside. He pulled out his phone and sent a text to Miller: *Two girls, four bad. One more girl not here. Maybe JD.*

K. Where R U?

In RV.

Where? Parker on way.

Hold. Need to find JD.

"Ten minutes!" a loud voice called from the other side of the blanket.

The girl grabbed onto Wynn's arm. She was frightened. He gently removed her hands and then mimed with his own that she should stay here and that he would be back with help.

She understood. She put her hand on Wynn's arm, indicating he should wait. She started slowly bouncing on the bed and moaning. Wynn was embarrassed as she kept at it for a few minutes, before faking a climax and stopping. She then removed all her clothing, bundled it up in her arms, and went down the steps and through the hanging blankets, walking naked past the two men into the bathroom.

Smart, brave girl.

Wynn followed a minute later and nodded to the two guys sitting at the table. He opened the door, stepped outside, and walked across the lane.

"Come again," the van passenger called out. He laughed as Wynn disappeared between a couple of RVs to the row beyond.

CHAPTER 27

Wynn slipped between a pair of RVs and doubled back. He jogged to the far end of the row, then peeked around a large Winnebago to look back at the fifth wheeler. The guy from the van had resumed his position sitting in the lawn chair. Wynn pulled out his phone and dialed Miller.

"Yeah," she said.

"Where's Parker?"

"On his way."

"Okay. Target is a fifth-wheel RV in the fourth row, thirteenth one on the north side. Two guys inside, armed, and two guys outside. Assume they're armed also. Just the two Latina girls here, and it looks like they alternate their time in the RV. Right now, the surrounding vehicles appear to be deserted, but that'll change when the concert ends."

There was movement down by the fifth wheeler. The dark-haired Latino guy had returned, hustling the other girl along with him. Their voices were excited.

"Sean, you there?" Miller asked.

"Something's up. Hold on."

Wynn rushed up the row, staying quiet and hidden in the shadows. He ducked behind an RV forty feet away and strained to listen.

"What should we do?" the van passenger asked.

"Let me call Andy," the Latino guy said. He dialed the phone, then paced back and forth waiting for it to be answered.

"Hey, it's Carlos. We've got a situation here. We were hooked up with a group of bikers who turned cold. They were lining up all night and now suddenly want nothing to do with us. It's weird."

He paused, listening. Then to the van passenger, Carlos said, "Brandon! That last guy. Was he an Ace?"

"I don't think so. He wasn't wearing colors."

"Shit!" Carlos said into the phone. "The last guy wasn't part of the club." He paused. "On our way."

Carlos turned to Brandon as he stuffed the phone back into his pocket. "We're done. Let's get out of here."

Brandon swung the door open and jumped into the fifth wheel. Carlos grabbed the second girl by the arm and held her tight against the side of the RV. Pounding and yelling came from inside. Suddenly the two bikers burst out of the open door and quickly hustled away in Wynn's direction. He ducked out of sight as they jogged past.

As Wynn turned back toward the fifth wheel, Brandon and the girl stepped out. She was still pulling her top on. Brandon and Carlos shoved the two girls between a couple of RVs and disappeared from view. Wynn sprinted down the side of the RV and peered down the next row to see them hustling in Miller's direction. He realized the phone was still in his hand.

"You there?" he asked.

"Yeah, what's going on?"

"They're spooked and running, but I've got eyes on them."

"Where?"

"Coming your way. Two minutes tops."

Wynn had to hang back a little further than he liked. The van passenger, Brandon, had seen his face, and was constantly looking over his shoulder. It would be harder to stay in the shadows the closer they got to the amphitheater.

Miller caught up as he hurried past their intersection.

"What do you think?" she asked.

"They're leaving. Probably have a car in the lot. When we get there, I'll go for the bike. You follow 'em. Slow 'em down 'til I pick 'em up. Maybe they'll lead us to Davies."

"Got it," she said.

They continued to follow as Brandon and Carlos hustled the two girls straight through the amphitheater toward the east gate. The crowds were thick as heavy metal music pounded from the stage. Wynn closed the gap, knowing that once they broke through the other side it would be a race to get out of the lot.

Miller dialed Parker's number. When he answered, she said quickly, "They're moving. Track my phone. I'll follow as long as I can."

She disconnected, then dialed Wynn's number and held her phone up for him to see. "Keep the line connected. Even if we can't talk, we'll be able to hear each other."

Wynn tapped the answer button and stuffed the phone back into his vest pocket. They came out the other side of the amphitheater. The foursome was exiting through the chain-link gates. They crossed the road toward the grassy lot.

When they came through the gate themselves, Miller followed the foursome deeper into the lot while Wynn sprinted to the left to where his Harley was parked some hundred yards away. As he approached the bike, he put the phone to his ear.

"You got them?" he asked.

Miller's breath came in heavy gasps. She was running. "They're in a dark, wood-paneled van coming your way. I couldn't stop them. Looks like they're heading toward the west exit."

"Where are you?" he asked as he swung a leg over the bike.

"Behind, but I'm losing them. Don't wait for me. If you see them, just go!"

Wynn didn't wait to hear more. He fired up the bike and took off, clearing the last row in time to see a dark Plymouth Grand Voyager turning south out of the lot. He bumped over the grassy field toward the exit as fast as he could.

Approaching the road, Wynn had to wait to let two cars and several bikes go by. When he finally pulled out, it was difficult to keep the van in sight with so many taillights weaving in and out in the dark.

A mile ahead, however, traffic cleared at an intersection where half the vehicles turned left, while the other half, including the van, continued straight ahead.

Wynn followed a safe distance back as the geography changed from open fields to wooded hills. The long, straight road began to twist and turn, as lengthy driveways spurred off from the main path. He was surprised at the amount of traffic in such a rural area.

Rounding a curve, a sea of tents appeared in a sparsely wooded acreage on one side of the road. The van pulled into a long, dirt driveway that led east through the tents. Several of the bikes followed, but veered off toward individual campsites while the van pushed all the way through.

At the far end of the makeshift campground, the trees thickened as the path climbed a small rise. The van went up the slope and disappeared out of sight. Wynn pulled into the grass next to a campsite at the edge of the hill and shut down the bike.

Grabbing his phone out of his pocket, he checked to see if he was still connected with Miller. "You there?"

"I'm here. Where are you?"

"A temporary campground about two miles south of the Griz. The van went through it. I'm guessing there's a ranch or permanent building further in, but I've got to walk from here."

"Okay, good. We've got one of Parker's guys tracing your phone. We're a couple minutes out. Stay put 'til we get there."

"I'm gonna get a better look," Wynn said.

"No, Sean. Stay put. Wait for us."

"There's no time. These guys are spooked. No telling what they'll do."

Miller growled. "Ugh. Just be careful. Keep the line connected."

Wynn turned the volume all the way down before he put the phone back in his pocket. He stepped off the bike, pulled out his Glock, and scrambled up the hill into the woods.

After forty yards he reached the top of the hill and stopped behind a large tree. The road was twenty yards to his left. It'd been ten years since he left MARSOC, but his training would be ingrained forever. He paused to listen but heard nothing unusual. Ahead, the trees momentarily glowed red from the van's brake lights, but otherwise, all was dark.

Wish I had some night goggles.

He stayed still for thirty seconds, listening for any sound, scanning for any movement. Hearing and seeing nothing, he crouched low and moved through the trees, always keeping the road a steady distance to his left. A few hundred yards in, lights glowed from a house that was sitting in a clearing another hundred yards ahead. He crept forward until he was outside the clearing, still hidden in the trees. He crouched behind a fallen tree to assess the situation.

Two houses stood in the clearing: one close, the other set fifty yards back. More than forty bikes sat parked outside the main house and several people were moving in and around the front door. The wood-paneled van was parked in front of the smaller house farther back.

A hard, cold steel barrel pressed against his left temple.

"Don't move, fucker."

Wynn stayed still.

"Drop it."

Wynn released his grip on the Glock and let it fall to the ground.

"What are you doing here?"

"I heard this is where the real party is. Thought I'd check it out."

"So you sneak up?"

"Didn't know if I needed an invitation."

The guy paused, then said, "Get your ass up. Let's go see if you're invited or not."

Wynn stood, careful to keep his head pressed steadily against the rifle. When he was finally standing and gained solid footing, he spun his head to the right. Pivoting on his left foot, he brought his right elbow up and back, smashed it into the guy's right jaw. His left hand shot up and grabbed the barrel of the rifle. Pushed it up and away as he pivoted back to face the guy. His right fist swung up in a brutal uppercut that landed squarely on the guy's lower left jaw.

A vicious one-two combination. Right side. Left side. Game over. The guy went limp, releasing whatever grip remained on the gun and crumpled to the ground. Wynn put the gun to his shoulder, a Heckler and Koch MP5. He peered through the sights and spun in a quick circle, searching for more targets.

Wynn cursed himself. He'd gotten careless. This guy never should have gotten close, let alone got the drop on him. Satisfied there was no other immediate threat, Wynn checked the magazine. It was full, thirty rounds. He slapped it back into position, then knelt and put his fingers on the guy's throat, feeling a faint pulse. He might make it. Might not. One thing was for damn sure, the stakes had been raised.

Wynn was now in full-on, special operations mode. He searched the ground for his Glock, then stuffed it in the back of his jeans. Crouching low, he skirted to the right, staying ten yards back in the trees. He circled the clearing and made his way toward the smaller house where the van was parked out front, its sliding side door still open.

Along the near side of the house, two windows leaked dim light around the edges of their closed shades, preventing him from seeing inside. He crept around to the back of the house where a sliding glass door exposed much of the downstairs interior.

Immediately inside was a small dining room. A kitchen sat to the left, and a living room took most of the space to the front. The front door was almost exactly opposite the sliding glass door, with an L-shaped stairway on the right, leading to what Wynn presumed were bedrooms upstairs.

As he watched, a man in his mid-forties came out of the kitchen with a drink in hand and sat at the dining table. Moments later, the two guys from the Grizzly Butte, Brandon and Carlos, came down the stairs and joined him. Wynn couldn't hear exactly what was being said, but it was clear by the loud voices and angry gesturing that the older man was pissed. After a few minutes, Brandon ran up the stairs and soon came back down with the girl Wynn had been with inside the fifth wheel. He shoved her out the front door while Carlos followed. The older man remained seated at the dining room table with his drink.

Wynn raced to the far side of the house. Stopped at the front corner. He was about to peek around when he heard the van engine start up. The tires moved toward him. As it passed, Wynn could see Carlos driving the van, but no one else inside.

He stole a look around the corner to see Brandon and the girl walking up the flagstone path toward the main house. He turned back as Carlos parked the van thirty feet away. Wynn ran over and hid on the passenger side as the driver's door slammed shut.

When Carlos came around the back of the van, Wynn leapt out and clubbed him in the face with the butt of the rifle. Using both the rifle and his heavy boots, Wynn unleashed a furious attack. He kicked and beat the man as he fell to the ground. Eight years of special ops training came back as Wynn instinctively kept up an enraged assault around the man's head and neck. It was a brutal attack, kill or be killed, and Wynn had no intention of dying.

When there was no longer any resistance, Wynn knelt and checked for a pulse. Finding none, he dug into the dead man's pockets and pulled out a short switchblade that he flicked open. Six inches long with a slim handle. Big enough for the job, but just barely.

After dragging the lifeless body back into the trees, Wynn circled the house and approached the front door. Using his gloved fist, he pounded urgently. He wanted the older guy to come to him.

Moments later, the guy inside opened the door, saying, "Can't you fuckers—"

Wynn's left hand shot out, caught him solidly in the throat and cut off any further sound. He pushed through the door, turned, and slammed the older guy against the wall. Wynn stabbed the knife upward, entering just below the guy's sternum. The man stood for a few seconds, Wynn's forearm tight beneath his chin. Wynn felt a thick, warm wave of blood flow over his hand, heard it splash on the floor, then the body went slack. He let it slide silently down the wall.

Wynn wiped his hand on the guy's shirt, closed the front door, and climbed the stairs, the Glock extended in a two-handed grip. Four doorways lined the hall, two on either side. The first door, on his left, was open. Except for a bed, the room was empty.

The second door, on his right, was a bathroom. Also empty.

The third and fourth doors were closed. He put his ear to the third. It was quiet.

He slipped over to the fourth door and listened. Bedsprings creaked in a steady rhythm. Whoever was in there was preoccupied. *Slow to react.*

Wynn stepped back to the third door. Using the heel of his boot, he smashed just below the latch, sending splinters flying into the room as the door crashed open. The second girl from the Grizzly Butte screamed and jumped back off the bed toward the far wall. She was alone.

Wynn stepped into the room, locked eyes with the girl, and raised a finger to his lips.

Quiet.

She nodded.

He motioned her to get down behind the bed, then pressed himself against the wall next to the doorway and peeked around the corner to the fourth door.

The steady rhythm of the bedsprings had stopped.

Wynn crouched low and waited. Within moments, the fourth door cracked open. The boxy barrel of a Glock eased through. A male voice came from within. "Who's there?"

"Drop it," Wynn said.

The Glock stayed elevated. "What the fuck's going on?"

Wynn still couldn't see the guy. "I said drop it."

"You a cop?"

"Worse."

The gun hovered in the doorway.

Wynn was torn. The last thing he wanted was gunfire that might alert the others there was a problem. "Last warning," he said. Keep it in sight and put it on the floor. Then slide it away."

"Okay, okay."

The gun slowly lowered, a male Caucasian hand becoming visible. "Finger off the trigger," Wynn said.

The hand lowered the gun to the floor and pushed it away.

"Good. Now come on out."

"Can I get some clothes on?"

"No. Just come out."

"C'mon. Let me get some pants on. You can watch." The door swung open. Inward. A middle-aged man, naked and hairy, stood in the opening. His left hand was hidden behind the door, his right behind the wall.

"Let me see your hands," Wynn said.

The guy's eyes locked Wynn. Stayed a beat too long.

The drywall next to the door exploded as a shot thundered from just five feet away. Wynn pointed his Glock at the guy's center mass and pulled the trigger. Three times. Quick. And deadly.

Three holes appeared in the guy's chest as he stumbled backward and fell onto the bed, then slid to the floor. Wynn rushed forward and kicked a small pistol out of the guy's hand and stood over him, pointing his Glock at the man's face.

There was no need. The man's eyes stared, unmoving, at the ceiling.

Wynn ran a mental check of his body: arms, legs, torso. He wasn't hit.

Another girl crouched behind the bed against the far wall. She appeared, well, not fine, but unharmed by any bullets. She had dark hair, dark eyes, and dark skin. Not Jessica Davies.

Wynn stepped back into the second bedroom. The girl there was also unharmed.

He looked at the bullet hole in the drywall opposite of where he'd been standing. The drywall itself had been blown away, revealing a dark two-by-four. The bullet was embedded in the stud.

He let out a relieved breath, then looked up. The girl from the last room was naked, clinging tightly to a sheet she had pulled from the bed to cover herself. He turned to the girl from the second bedroom and pulled at his own shirt, then to the naked girl. The message was clear. Get her dressed. Quickly.

He waited at the top of the stairs while the girl got dressed. Kept his gun trained on the front door. Someone must have heard the gunfire. When no one appeared, he led them down the staircase, past the older man's body on the floor, and into the galley kitchen. Pushing them down onto the floor between the cabinets and appliances, he used more hand signals to indicate they should stay there. It was the safest place he could think of for the moment.

Slipping out the glass doors, Wynn made his way around the far side of the house to the same corner he'd been at moments before. He glanced around the corner, then settled in to wait. Sure enough, within less than two minutes, Brandon came out of the main house with the girl from the fifth wheel and another biker, heading down the flagstone path toward the small house.

As they approached, the low, faint chopping of a helicopter pulsed the air. The trio stopped at the end of the flagstone path, across the driveway from the front door of the small house. They looked up.

The woods around the main house suddenly exploded with light. The air filled with sirens and the whir of helicopter blades.

Searchlights illuminated the grounds. Dark figures with "FBI" printed boldly on their backs emerged from the woods. Their guns up and ready as they converged on the main house. Panicked gunfire came from inside.

Glancing around, Wynn realized the small house was being ignored.

While the biker sprinted away into the woods, Brandon grabbed the girl and turned back to watch what was happening at the main house. Wynn leapt out from behind his corner, Glock drawn in a two-handed grip as he stepped forward.

"Brandon!" he yelled. "It's over. Let her go. Get down on the ground."

Brandon turned toward the voice, one hand gripping the girl by the arm while the other reached behind his back.

"Don't do it!"

Wynn waited a half-beat, until he saw a flash reflect off the gun Brandon was bringing around, then pulled the trigger. The Glock spat once. A small red circle appeared just left of center on Brandon's forehead. His body, still turning from momentum, spiraled down in a heap.

Wynn rushed forward. Kicked the gun out of Brandon's lifeless hand, then grabbed the girl by the arm. They sprinted back inside the house as gunfire blasted all around. He raced to the kitchen and pushed her down beside the two girls already cowering there, then covered their trembling heads with his arms as they waited for the barrage to end.

CHAPTER 28

An hour later, Wynn sat in the back of an ambulance, being checked out by a paramedic for the second time that day. Miller sat beside him, quiet.

"Everything looks good," the medic finally said.

"Told you," Wynn replied.

"Well, we had to get you checked out," Miller said. "It's been a busy day."

As they stepped out of the ambulance the full aftermath was revealed. Portable lights had been set out, lighting up the area like a Friday night football stadium. There were ambulances and coroner trucks, cop cars and FBI vehicles parked all around. Even a helicopter had landed on the other side of the main house. Cops in uniforms from almost every imaginable jurisdiction were either hustling back and forth or huddled in small groups, examining various aspects of the scene. Parker was engaged with two other agents near the front door but looked up when the ambulance pulled away. He and another agent walked toward them.

"Hell of a mess here, Wynn," Parker said.

"What's the tally?"

"Six girls recovered safely. Seven suspects taken into custody. Nine killed, including the five you got."

"I only killed four."

"Five. The guy who got the drop on you in the woods suffocated on his own blood."

Wynn looked at him, confused. *How do they know...*

"Your phone was still connected to Miller, remember?" Parker said. "We heard everything."

Wynn's stomach dropped as he tried to remember if there was anything incriminating in what they heard.

"But no worries," Parker said. "You helped us take out a big link in an even bigger sex-trafficking chain. Everything you did sounded like self-defense to me."

Relieved, Wynn realized what Parker had just said. "Six girls recovered? Was Davies one of them?"

"Unfortunately, no. They're all Latina and speak very little English. Which makes us think they were brought up from Mexico. It also makes me worry that Davies is being taken south, in trade. We'll stay on it."

Wynn nodded.

"Listen Wynn. I know you want to get Davies back, but this is good work. You did good tonight. These girls owe you their lives. And with this link taken out, there are going to be several other girls over the next few months who'll make it safely to wherever they're going. I know it's not exactly the outcome you hoped for, but this is good."

Wynn nodded again.

"We'll need you to come in tomorrow. Give a formal statement. But for now, why don't you go get some sleep. You too, Miller. We'll also need a statement from you."

They both nodded, then Parker pivoted and re-entered the chaos. Wynn and Miller watched him go, pausing to take in the full scene. They looked at each other, then silently turned and started walking down the long driveway back to Wynn's bike.

———

It might have been his imagination, but it felt like Miller was holding on a little tighter than necessary as they rode back to his motel. Wynn was almost disappointed when they pulled into the lot. Imagination or not, he liked the feel of her arms around him.

"You know," he said as they got off the bike. "All your stuff is upstairs. You're welcome to stay here if you want."

Miller smiled. "I'd like that."

She took hold of his arm as they climbed the stairs and went down the walkway to his room. He unlocked the door and held it for her, then followed her inside. After closing the door, he spun the deadbolt and put the chain in place, then turned toward her.

It took a moment for his eyes to adjust. Ambient light from the lamps outside snuck in around the edges of the closed curtains. She hadn't moved. Still right there, standing in front of him. She reached up, put her hands around his neck, and kissed him. He wrapped his arms around her thin waist and leaned back against the door, pulling her toward him, pressing the cold steel of their guns between them.

"Maybe we should lose the hardware," he said when they finally separated.

She put her hands inside his vest, pushed it off his shoulders. "Maybe we should lose everything."

And for a little while they did. They lost their clothes, their inhibitions, and most importantly, the memories of the last few hours.

———

Inside the farmhouse, Tomas sat at the kitchen table surrounded by John, Nathan, and Tony. The burner was once again on speaker in the middle of the table. Tomas grew angrier with each word.

"It sounds like it was this guy, Wynn, and that lady deputy. The one that was here with him yesterday," the voice on the other end of the line said. "Somehow, they found Brandon and Carlos, tracked them back to the main house and called in the Feds. Sounds like they came in with a damn battalion."

"The girls?" Tomas asked.

"The Feds got them."

"The crew?"

"All dead. Our three plus six of theirs. They got seven in custody, but they don't know anything."

Tomas was relieved. His customers in Sturgis didn't know enough to be a threat, and with Brandon, Carlos and Andy already dead, he wouldn't have to send anyone after them.

"Who is this guy?" Tomas asked. He looked across the table at Nathan, whose right arm was in a cast, resting on the table.

"Wynn?" the voice on the other end asked. "Former marine, now an unemployed biker. He's nothing special."

"And yet this morning, he disabled one of our guys," Tomas locked eyes with Nathan as he said it, "and put another in the hospital. And tonight, he busted an operation we've been running up there for years. That is special. What's his interest in all this?"

"Best I can tell it's a hero complex," the voice on the phone said. "Claims he doesn't know the girl, but maybe he feels responsible. Maybe he thinks he should've saved her."

"Let's find out. I want you to come talk to the girl. In uniform. If there's any relationship between the two, she'll tell you."

The voice on the phone hesitated. "I'm not sure that's a good idea. If my cover's blown, I won't be of any use."

"If your cover's blown," said Tomas, "You'll be dead. Get out here. Now."

Tomas stabbed the phone to disconnect the call, lowered his head for a moment, then looked up, scowling at the three others.

"We've suffered losses tonight," he said as he got up from the table. He stepped over to the counter and opened a drawer.

"Andy..."

Tomas pulled a hammer from the drawer.

"Carlos..."

He closed the drawer and turned back to the table, stepping up behind Nathan.

"And Brandon. All dead. The girls gone. You want to know why?"

The three men seated at the table didn't say a word. A bead of sweat slid down the side of Nathan's face. He sat, staring straight ahead with Tomas holding the hammer behind him.

"Because you failed!" Tomas wound his arm above his head and slammed the hammer down on the cast of Nathan's broken arm. Nathan howled in pain as the cast cracked down the middle. John and Tony jumped up, their chairs tumbling over as they sprang away from the table.

Tomas grabbed Nathan by the back of the head and smashed his face down onto the table, breaking his nose, blood spurting in all directions. He raised the hammer again, crashed it down onto the table, an inch from Nathan's head.

"You fail me again," Tomas said menacingly, "I won't miss."

He dropped the hammer on the table and stormed out of the room.

———

A half-hour later, Nathan sat under the light of a single bulb on the front porch of the farmhouse. Darkness enveloped the surrounding forest. He had tissues stuffed up his nostrils and silver duct tape wrapped around the cast on his arm.

A Norfolk County Sheriff's cruiser pulled to a stop in front of the house. It was almost one in the morning. Deputy Craig was in full uniform when he stepped out of the car.

"He blames you?" Craig asked as Nathan approached.

"Isn't it obvious?" Nathan held his arm up near his face. Dark, ugly bruises were forming around both eyes.

"Fuck him," Craig said.

The two men clasped palms in a bro-shake and embraced momentarily, awkwardly.

Separating, Nathan said, "They're waiting for you." He nodded toward the large barn.

"Let me handle it once we get in there," Craig said.

They entered through the small door on the east end, next to the large double doors. Tomas, John, and Tony sat at a table near the bay where Jessica had been lashed when she was first brought in.

"You're late," Tomas said as they approached. "I thought maybe you weren't coming."

"I'm not late," Craig said. "Just needed to get dressed. I don't normally wear this getup at one in the morning."

Tomas smiled slightly.

"You still want me to do this?" Craig asked.

"Of course," said Tomas. "Go into the bunkhouse. Tony will bring her to you."

———

Awakened by the sudden brightness as the lights came on, Jessica tensed immediately when the deadbolt moved inside the door. She had no idea what time it was but knew it couldn't be morning yet.

Something was wrong. This wasn't the pattern.

Across the room, Hailey scrambled out of her bunk and ran to Ann.

Jessica pulled the blanket around her as she sat up and brought her knees to her chest. The door eased open as Tony stepped quietly into the room. He held his index finger to his lips, then crept over to Jessica's bunk, motioning for Ann and Hailey to join them.

"I have someone here who can help you." Tony looked Jessica in the eye. "But I need you to come with me. And you two," he indicated Ann and Hailey, "to stay here."

"Where are you taking her?" Ann demanded.

"Like I said, I have someone who can help. Otherwise, you can spend the rest of your lives fucking strange men in the hope of getting something to eat."

Jessica didn't trust him, but hope is a powerful incentive.

"I'll be alright." She got up from the bunk.

Tony led her out. She waited in the laundry as he re-locked the deadbolt. Then he opened a door opposite their own, and ushered her into a space that was a perfect mirror of the one she'd spent the last two days in. Except this one was furnished like an apartment, complete with a couch, TV, and a small kitchen.

Jessica blinked to make sure she wasn't seeing things. Next to the table stood a cop.

"Oh my God!" Jessica rushed past Tony to reach Craig, "Help us!"

"It's all right," Craig said in a soothing voice. He took hold of her arms and guided her into a chair at the table. "We'll get you out of here real soon. I just need your help with a couple of things."

"Anything!" Jessica leaned forward. "Just get us out of here!"

"Great. Okay, calm down," Craig eased into a chair across the table. "I need answers to a couple of questions first."

Jessica looked at him, her eyes pleading with him to hurry. "What?"

"Sean Wynn. Who is he?"

Jessica's eyes turned from pleading to confused. "Who?"

"Sean Wynn. Your boyfriend."

"I ... I don't have a boyfriend. I have no idea who that is."

"You don't know a biker named Sean Wynn? Maybe he's a friend?"

"No!" Jessica whispered urgently. "I have no idea who that is. Let's get out of here!"

"You're sure you don't know a biker named Sean Wynn?"

"No!"

Craig sat back in his chair.

Jessica's mind swirled. *Who is this guy? Why is he just sitting there? Why aren't we leaving!*

Craig called over his shoulder, "She doesn't know him."

Out of the corner of her eye, Jessica saw movement behind Craig. Tomas and John stepped out of the bathroom. Her heart sank.

"Unless she's lying," Tony said from behind her.

The realization that it had all been an act crashed down on her.

"You fuck!" She lunged across the table at Craig. Tony and John were on her in an instant, pulling her back to her chair.

Tomas approached. He bent down next to her face, his crooked teeth and cigarette breath rekindling the terror of her first night. "Are you lying?" he asked.

She clamped her eyes shut, frozen with fear.

"Do you remember me?"

Jessica cracked open her terrified eyes and nodded.

"Do you remember when I said you're mine?"

She closed her eyes and nodded again.

"Then tell me, who is this boyfriend?"

"I don't have a boyfriend."

"Maybe we can help you remember."

Tomas nodded to John and Tony. They lifted her off the chair and carried her, kicking and screaming, through the laundry and out into the main barn. They took her back to the bay where the rope with the leather wrist straps hung over the rafter. Where she had been beaten when she was first brought in.

Nathan joined in and helped Tony place the leather bindings on Jessica's wrists. John grabbed the opposite end of the rope that hung looped on the wall.

With her wrists secured, John hauled on the rope, raising Jessica's arms above her head. She sank against the rope, her knees bent as her feet dragged across the floor.

Like before, Tomas seized a handful of hair at the back of her head and pulled it down, causing her face to lift, her eyes to stare into his. "I will ask you one more time. Who is this boyfriend?

"I swear I don't know! I don't have a boyfriend."

"You're lying!" Tomas slapped her hard across the face. "He's causing trouble! Who is he?"

"I don't know, I don't know…"

"She doesn't know anything," Craig said again.

Jessica opened her eyes, finding hope in Craig's voice. Maybe it wasn't an act.

"Help me," she begged.

"Help you?" Tomas laughed. "No one is coming to help you. Not your boyfriend, not the police, not anybody. I own you. I own everything."

Tomas stepped back and addressed Craig. "You ask her."

Craig stepped forward. "Sean Wynn. We know all about him, except one thing. Why is he so interested in you?"

Jessica looked at him, confused. "I have no idea what you're talking about. Help me!" Her hope turned to anger.

Craig raised his voice, "Why is he following you?"

Jessica paused as the last drops of hope drained away and a new realization dawned. She saw what was happening now and was beyond angry. "You fuck!" Jessica seethed through clenched teeth. "What kind of man are you? Take an oath to protect but you're just his little bitch, doing whatever the fuck he says."

Now it was Craig's turn. He raised his hand and swung it toward her face.

But this time Jessica was ready. She squeezed her arms together and tilted her head back, causing Craig's attempt to slap her to breeze harmlessly past her face.

"You pig!" she screamed. "You're supposed to help me!"

Craig stepped forward and grabbed her hair, yanking her head back just as Tomas had done. He put his face next to hers. "I'm helping you stay alive, bitch."

Hatred boiled from Jessica's eyes as she stared at him. Gaining her footing, she spat in his face and kicked upward with her knee as hard as she could, catching Craig squarely in the crotch. It was a good effort, but she had no momentum, no force. It might have stung, but it wasn't crippling.

"You bitch!" He backhanded her across the face, this time catching her full on. Stars exploded across Jessica's vision as her knees buckled. Craig reached up and grabbed the rope, pulled it down and wrenched the other end from John's hands. With one giant arm, he picked her up and carried her to the table. Dropping her feet to the floor, he ripped at her jeans and yanked them down to her knees. He spun her around so she was facing the table, then smashed her face down onto it. Pressing his body against hers, he pinned her bare legs against the table, then swung the rope over the far edge. Reaching underneath, he grabbed the rope and pulled hard, stretching her arms taut and lifting her heels from the floor.

He ripped off her panties and unbuckled his pants. Leaning over her back he whispered in her ear, "I'll show you what kind of man I am, you bitch."

Jessica was helpless. There was nothing she could do. No way to stop it.

When it was over, Tony and John half-carried, half-dragged Jessica back into the bunkhouse and dumped her on the floor.

CHAPTER 29

Wednesday

T HEY SLEPT LATE, at least for Wynn. It was past eight-thirty by the time he checked the clock on the nightstand. Last night's ambient light was now full-on sunshine leaking in from around the curtains. Miller was still asleep, her naked body pressed against him. He savored the feel of her smooth skin against his.

As quietly as possible, he got up and went into the bathroom, took a quick shower, and brushed his teeth. He examined his reflection in the mirror. His long hair and beard stuck out in all directions. *Nicole would hate this.*

He rummaged through his bathroom bag for a razor, with no success. Instead, he finger-combed his hair and beard as best he could. When he came out ten minutes later with a towel wrapped around his waist, Miller was sitting up in bed, the sheet pulled loosely around her.

"Good morning." He walked over and sat on the bed.

"Good morning," she said sleepily. She paused a moment, then said, "I want you to know I don't normally do this."

"Of course," he said, "It was an intense night. We both needed to let off a little steam."

"No, not that," she said. "This."

She leaned forward and kissed him, pushing him back on the bed. She let the sheet fall away and loosened the towel at his waist, then climbed on top.

———

Afterward, they both showered and dressed. Wynn, in a clean version of his standard jeans and t-shirt, Miller in her uniform. They stopped at a small diner up the street for breakfast and eventually made it to the Meade County Sheriff's office around 11:00 a.m.

Parker and the FBI had commandeered three offices. They started by having Wynn and Miller give their formal statements in separate rooms. The agents interviewing them hadn't heard the open phone line between Miller and Wynn the night before, so they had a lot of questions. It took more than an hour to get the statements on record. When they were finally finished, they were led into an office where Parker sat behind a desk and two other agents sat in chairs in front. Parker motioned for the two agents to get up so Miller and Wynn could sit.

"How are we feeling this morning?" Parker asked.

"Good," they both replied, giving nothing away.

"Okay, here's where we stand," Parker said. "As suspected, all six of the girls are from Mexico, either Sonora or Chihuahua provinces. They were all abducted between two and four weeks ago. Four of them were promised passage into the U.S., while the other two were flat-out abducted.

"None of them know where they've been, or where they are, for that matter. They've either been blindfolded or moved in windowless trucks. They were brought up in two separate groups of three. The three that you rescued last night, Wynn, were from Sonora, said they arrived here the day before yesterday. They also said that the night before they got here, they were held with three other white women, one of whom was just brought in that day. We showed them a picture of Davies and they think it was her, but she'd been whipped and was barely conscious, so they couldn't tell for sure, but yeah, they think it was her."

"Whipped?" Miller asked.

"Sometimes it's not a pretty world," Parker said.

Miller nodded once and looked down.

"They have no idea where they were being held?" Wynn asked.

"None," Parker said.

"Do they remember how long it took to get here, or any details about the trip?" Miller asked.

"Their recollection of time is sketchy," Parker said. "They think it was more than four but less than five hours. That's based on the fact that they didn't stop to use a restroom and they all had to go pretty bad by the time they got here."

"That's one way to tell time. Pretty clever, actually," Miller said.

"The one I was with in the RV last night was plenty smart," Wynn said. "What else?"

"They said most of the trip they were traveling relatively slow. Only the last hour or so felt like they were going fast and straight. Otherwise, slow with lots of curves."

"Backroads," Miller said.

"That's what we figure," Parker agreed. "We also assume an average speed of no more than fifty, for five hours max, means they were within two hundred fifty miles."

"That's a big circle," Miller said.

"It's a donut," Wynn said. "They wouldn't risk being on the road any longer than necessary, so if they were on the road three hours even at forty miles an hour, that means they were at least a hundred and twenty miles away. We're looking for someplace between one-twenty and two hundred fifty miles out, within roughly two hundred miles of Linert."

Parker picked up the phone and dialed an extension. When it was answered he asked if he could get a regional map brought in, including all of South Dakota, Wyoming, and Nebraska, along with a few feet of string.

"What about the guys?" Wynn asked when Parker hung up.

"Two distinct groups," said Parker. "A dozen bikers, part of a small club, and the three that brought the girls in. Unfortunately, the three can't tell us anything, thanks to you Mr. Wynn. The seven bikers we have in custody aren't talking."

"Do they have any association with the Aces?"

"Nah. We know about the Aces. These guys aren't up to that level."

"Any ID on the three that brought them up?"

"Two of them. The one you shot was from Nebraska and the one in the house was from Ohio. We're running background checks on them now but so far nothing that helps. No ID on the guy outside. Probably an illegal."

"Phones?"

"Got a burner off each of them. The two guys outside only called the guy inside. He must have been in charge. His had several numbers on it, but they're all burners."

They were interrupted by a knock on the door. A deputy came in with a map that he laid out on the desk between them, then handed Parker a spool of string. Parker tied the string around a pencil from his desk and measured out the equivalent of one hundred twenty miles against the distance legend on the map. With his finger, he anchored one end of the string to Sturgis and drew an arc on the map, south of the city, stretching from east to west.

"I doubt they would have gone north and come back," he said.

He doubled the length of the string and drew another half-circle arc further out, representing the outer limit of their search area almost two hundred fifty miles away. Finally, he used the legend again to shorten the string by fifty miles, and then placed the anchor end on Linert. He drew two lines perpendicular to the two he had just drawn, to the east and west of Linert, representing the two-hundred-mile outer limit.

"Your theory, Wynn, is that Davies was held in a location some-where inside that arc."

Miller stood and leaned over the map.

"Rattlesnake creek?" Wynn asked.

She pointed to a spot on the map. Inside the arc. "Right there."

Wynn looked at the map. Other than a few county roads, there wasn't much there. "That's a lot of empty space."

"That's good," Parker said. "Fewer places to search, but I agree, it's a big area."

"So what's next?" Wynn asked.

"What's next is that if you have any other ideas or information, I'd love to hear them."

Wynn sat back, his mind visualizing the wind-swept grasslands where he'd last seen Davies. After a few moments, Parker continued, "In that case, we take it from here. Like I said last night, you've both done great work and you should be very proud. But now it shifts into a new phase. I think your theory makes a lot of sense, but that was two days ago. She could be anywhere by now. And with what happened last night, this is bigger than Jessica Davies. We've got teams all over the country working on this. It's time to let us handle it."

"What about the guy Wynn put in the hospital yesterday morn-ing?" Miller asked. "Can he tell us anything?"

"He's still a John Doe. No ID and no match on the prints," Parker said. Then to Wynn, "Still unconscious. You must have one hell of a hard elbow."

Wynn shrugged.

"Before we go," Wynn said, "I was hoping we could see the girls. The one I talked to last night was really brave. I want to thank her for being so helpful."

Parker smiled. "They're out at the hospital at Fort Meade. I'll call out there and tell them you're coming, but it'll be up to the doctors if they let you see them."

CHAPTER 30

WYNN AND MILLER left the sheriff's office and walked out to Miller's SUV.

Rally activities hadn't ramped up for the day yet, so it took only eight minutes to drive to the Veteran's Administration hospital at Fort Meade. When they arrived, they were met by a guard at a security gate, who directed them to the correct building, where another guard told them someone would be with them shortly.

A few minutes later, a woman in her late forties, wearing a white lab coat and stethoscope, came out to greet them. She introduced herself as Dr. Anderson, and led them through a pair of heavy wood doors, down a hallway with a floor of speckled white tile and tan brick walls. There was a distinct smell of antiseptic that reminded Wynn of every military hospital he'd ever been in.

"We're keeping them three to a room," she explained. "After what they've been through, they've developed quite a bond, so we figured it best to keep them together as much as possible. Agent Parker said you wanted to see the group from Sonora?"

"Yes, please," Miller said.

Anderson stopped at a golden-oak-colored wood door. She turned back to Wynn and paused.

"Listen," she finally said, "I'm just going to say it. These girls have been through a lot. Most of it at the hands of men dressed just like you. I speak Spanish myself, so deputy Miller and I are going to go in first. I'm going to ask if they want to see you, and if it's okay, Deputy Miller will let you in. If there's a bad reaction, I want you out of there. Are we clear?"

Wynn nodded.

Anderson turned and knocked gently on the door, then she and Miller went in. Less than a minute later, Miller opened the door and motioned Wynn inside.

The girls were sitting in three separate beds, wearing hospital-issue pajamas. Two of the beds had their heads pushed against the wall to the right, while the third looked as if it had been wheeled in temporarily, perpendicular to the other two. It was pushed against the far wall, which was mostly windows. The girl he had spoken with last night was on the bed in the middle.

"*Senoras, esto es Senor Wynn,*" Anderson said.

The three girls looked at him for a moment, then the one he had spoken with in the RV jumped out of the bed and ran toward him, embracing Wynn in a huge hug. The other two quickly joined her. The sounds of laughter, crying, and "*Gracias, muchas gracias*" filled the air.

"Or not..." Anderson said, relieved.

"*De nada, de nada,*" Wynn repeated over and over.

They made their way over to the beds, where Wynn sat at the foot of one, while the girl from the night before, whom Anderson introduced as Graciela, sat next to him, clinging tightly to his arm. The other two, Lucy and Cristina, sat on the bed opposite while Miller and Anderson stood in the walkway between. With Anderson translating, each of the girls detailed how they had been abducted, and how the men had threatened their families back home if they didn't do as they were told.

When the girls finished telling their stories, Wynn got to the questions he had come to ask. What were the first few days of your captivity like? Did they move you right away, or did they keep you in one place? Beyond the threat to your families, what else did they do to get you to comply?

The answers were not comforting. They told of being whipped with a thick leather strap. Cristina turned her back and lifted her shirt so he could see the faint outline of the welts that had not yet fully healed. They spoke of hunger and how food had been withheld for days at the slightest sign of resistance. How the strap was always used as a threat.

"What about their captors?" Wynn asked. "What can they tell us about them?"

Anderson translated the question, then listened while Graciela spoke. When she finished, Anderson said, "The guys who first abducted them held them for a couple of weeks before handing them off to the guys who brought them here. In this new group, one of the guys was really big, and another had rotting teeth, but they were only there overnight, so don't know much more."

Wynn probed a bit more about Davies but there was little more to add. When they stood to leave, each of the girls gave Wynn a long hug, which he politely returned.

"You've got fans," Anderson said as she led them back down the hallway toward the exit.

"Right place at the right time is all," Wynn said.

"A bit more than that," Miller said under her breath.

———

Jessica spent most of the day in her bunk. After being dumped on the floor, Ann and Hailey had helped her onto the bed where she slept until the lights came on. Shortly thereafter came the ritual pounding on the door and the call of "Back off!"

Jessica remained still, not caring what else they did to her, but Ann and Hailey helped her over to the bunk where they'd been instructed to sit, and positioned her between them. When the door opened, the older guy came in and pointed the gun, while the big guy set a plate of microwaved breakfast sandwiches on the floor.

She couldn't help but notice the big guy had evidently crossed somebody. Large purple bruises surrounded both eyes, and his nose was swollen to almost twice its normal size. A cast held together by silver duct tape covered his right arm. He glanced at Jessica as he set the plate on the floor, before quickly turning and leaving.

Without a word, the older guy followed him out the door, then closed and locked it.

Jessica felt Ann's eyes on her.

"Was he...?" Ann asked as Hailey brought the sandwiches back to the bunk.

"No," Jessica said quietly, "but he was there. They all were."

"Was the guy with the bad teeth there?"

Jessica nodded.

Ann's face paled, "Did all of them...?"

"No. It was just one, but they all watched," Jessica said. "I hadn't seen this guy before." Her voice cracked as she tried to get the words out. "He... He was a cop."

An hour later, the sandwiches were still untouched.

———

Wynn and Miller drove back into town and had a late lunch, lingering at the table, knowing that at least as far as the case was concerned, there wasn't much else they could do. Miller had no real reason to hang around another night and Wynn was at a dead end.

"One thing we forgot to get from Parker," Wynn said as their plates were being cleared, "are the numbers from the lead guy's cell phone."

"He said they were all burners."

"Yeah, but that guy was stupid enough to keep his. Maybe they're in such a remote area that new burners are hard to come by. Maybe some of the others will keep theirs."

"Maybe," Miller agreed. "There'll be another briefing call tonight. I'll get the numbers from him then."

She paused, then said, "You still think she's in the area, don't you?"

"You heard Graciela. They were all kept in one location a week before being moved. Why change your M.O.?"

She didn't have an answer for him. "Well, Parker's got it now."

Wynn paid the bill and they went back to the motel so Miller could grab her things before heading back to Newbury. They made love once again, knowing this might be the last time their paths crossed. Afterward, Miller took a quick shower, then left, leaving Wynn alone and lonely in a rundown motel room.

———

Jessica sat on her bunk, her back against the concrete wall, forcing herself to eat. She knew she needed the calories, regardless of what had happened. She'd seen several rape victims come into the ER over the years, some beaten and bruised, others with barely a mark on them.

On the outside, anyway.

But inside, mentally and emotionally, they were all devastated; afraid of becoming pregnant or catching a disease, afraid of ever being able to trust a man again. Knowing their lives would forever be delineated as the time before it happened, and the time after.

She'd also seen, however, various paths on the other side. While no one was ever the same, she'd seen some women harness their strength, resolve to never be a victim again, and move forward. It was a choice. Remain a victim or become a survivor.

"How are you doing?" Ann asked.

Jessica returned a weak smile.

"You said you hadn't seen this guy before. That he was a cop?"

"He was wearing a uniform, whatever that means."

Ann sat back. "It means there are at least eight of them."

Jessica nodded.

"I know this is hard," Ann said, "but what did you see when you were out there?"

Jessica paused. "On the other side of that door is a laundry room with two doors. One goes into an apartment-type room directly opposite this one, the other leads out to a garage."

"A garage?"

"Not like on a house, but like an auto shop. Where they fix cars."

"Were there any windows? Could you see outside?"

"Yeah, but it was dark. I couldn't see anything."

Ann paused. "How awake were you when they first brought you in three days ago? Right before they took you out of the van, I mean."

"I was fairly awake by then."

"Was the road bumpy?"

Jessica paused as she thought back. "Yeah. It was."

"I thought so, too," Ann said. "Which means we're probably out in the country somewhere."

"So?"

"It means even if we get out of here, we're probably a long way from anyone who can help."

———

An hour after Miller left, Wynn hopped on his bike and rode into town. If he was going to be lonely, he might as well do it with a beer in hand. He went back to The Gilded Queen, not out of any sense of melancholy or sentiment, but because they had one of the best open-air bars in town. The perfect place to sit and watch the people.

The late afternoon sun was stretching into evening as Wynn found a stool at the bar looking out onto the street. He ordered a Corona from the twenty-something bartender wearing a black leather corset, cat ears on her head, and very little else. He kept the tab open.

People of all shapes, sizes, and ages passed by on the street. A five-piece southern rock band played on a stage inside, the volume increasing every time the door opened, which was almost constant. Eventually, he ordered another beer and some dinner, striking up an occasional conversation with the cat-eared bartender, but mostly keeping to himself.

Coming down off the adrenaline rush of a dangerous mission had always had this effect on Wynn. It made him contemplative, wondering about the fragility of life, of right and wrong. How tiny choices, or fractions of a second, could mean the difference between life and death. How people can come into your life, turn it upside down, and then be gone.

He wondered why he hadn't told Miller about Nicole. It was the one big part of his life story he'd left out. Maybe he hadn't felt comfortable enough when the subject came up during their first visit to Sheriff Johnston. Was that really just two days ago? It felt longer.

After leaving the Marines, Wynn had enrolled at the University of Southern California to study computer systems. He'd met Nicole during his junior year while she was working on her master's in biochemical engineering. They hit it off right away. He was a couple of years older, even though she was ahead of him in her schooling. They started dating early in the semester and were virtually inseparable during his senior year.

After promising her father he'd take care of his little girl, they got married the summer after graduation. They found jobs in Ventura County, north of L.A., and settled into a domestic bliss.

Until a stray bullet, while they were celebrating their fourth anniversary at a posh new restaurant, ended all that.

Nicole died at the scene.

Wynn had failed to keep his promise.

He had tried throwing himself into his work. A little cybersecurity company he owned that had grown nicely. Employed twenty people, including a couple of his former platoonmates.

He'd almost let them down, too.

Thankfully, they'd convinced him to sell it before he ran it into the ground. While it still had value. Significant value, it turned out. Enough to get out of the place he'd shared with Nicole and buy a new home next to the water, and still make work optional.

But the change of scenery hadn't helped. So he bought the Harley. Spent the past twenty months on the road. A psychologist friend said he was running. He said he was searching.

They both knew that was bullshit.

The presence of a large man sitting on the stool next to him pulled Wynn out of his reverie. It was the president of the Aces, the big, bald guy he talked to in the amphitheater of the Grizzly Butte last night.

The big guy looked straight ahead. The bartender with the cat ears and corset was leaning over the other end of the bar. Without taking his eyes off the bartender, the big guy said, "Heard there was some trouble over at the Little Griz campground last night."

"So I heard," Wynn said, also looking straight ahead.

"Heard they busted a sex-trafficking ring. Nine guys capped. A bunch more arrested."

Wynn didn't respond. Took a draw from his beer.

"How'd you know?" the big guy asked.

"Like I said, contacts."

"You a cop?"

Wynn laughed softly. Shook his head. "No."

The big guy paused. "Did you get back what they had of yours?"

"Nope."

The cat-eared bartender came up and asked the big guy if he needed anything. He said no. Wynn shook his head before she could ask, so she moved on down the bar.

"What's your name?"

"Wynn."

"What do you do, Wynn?"

"Unemployed."

"You ride with anyone?"

"Nope."

"Well, Wynn, I'm Damon. If you ever want to ride with someone or even need a favor, give me a call. We owe you."

He slid a business card across the bar. It had a picture of the club logo, the grey ace of spades with a knife blade trailing red blood, along with the words "Damon Styre, President, Dead Aces" and a phone number. It was a Colorado area code.

Dead Aces. At least I was close with the name. "I'll keep that in mind."

The cat-eared bartender placed a ticket down in front of Wynn. Damon picked it up, pulled out his wallet, and put two twenties on the bar.

"Hope you get back what you're looking for," Damon said. He nodded, got up, and left.

Wynn took another draw from his beer.

He always found it interesting how, when he struggled with a problem, it sometimes helped to get his mind off it. To think of something else, just as he'd been doing for the last couple of hours. Sometimes he'd get flashes of clarity when he came back to the problem. In this case, clarity came in the form of more questions.

About phone numbers. And information. And motivations and actions. And how information was passed, and actions resulted. And what the motivations were for those actions.

He still wanted to know about the phone numbers picked off the burner phone last night, and he still wondered if they had moved Davies yet. But who killed Matt Lester? Why? And why did they send two guys after him yesterday morning? How did they know where to find him? He knew he was asking the right questions, which more often than not, was the most important part.

And now, he also had a plan.

CHAPTER 31

Thursday

WYNN GOT ON the road early the next morning. He cruised west out of Sturgis, through Deadwood, and followed the highway as it turned south, backtracking the exact course that had brought him to the rally two days earlier. The air was crisp, and the shadows shortened as he wound through the canyons, a dazzling mixture of blue skies, green pines, and red sandstone. Gaining elevation until he crossed the state line, he gradually descended over the next thirty miles as he made the transition out of the Black Hills onto the open plains of Wyoming.

A little after nine a.m., Wynn cruised through Newbury. He thought about Miller but didn't consider stopping. She wasn't likely to approve of what he was about to do.

South of Newbury, he opened it up, setting the Street Glide at an easy seventy-three-mile-per-hour cruise. Fast enough to get where he was going, but not too fast to risk another run-in with Crower. Wynn could tell the weather had been dry, the fields on either side going another shade closer to brown since he had last come through only three days ago.

He passed by Mule Creek Junction and once again slowed his pace, scanning the road, ditches, and fields to either side. Not that he expected to find anything new, but he wanted to be watchful just in case. As he approached the construction zone, a line of cars had already stacked up to wait. He slowed to a stop and turned his attention to the workers milling about. He'd broken two men's arms in the last three days, one of whom had been working on this project and was now dead. Who's to say the other might not work here also?

When the line of southbound cars was released, Wynn cruised through the mile-and-a-quarter work zone slowly, keeping his eyes open. He didn't know if he'd recognize the guy who'd hit him with the stun gun, but there was a good chance he'd be wearing a cast on his right arm. He saw nothing of note, except perhaps a new flagger at the south end. Both his arms seemed to be working fine.

Wynn continued to go slowly as he passed by the staging area on his left, and the short driveway where he had watched Lester on the right. Two miles further on, a dirt road led off to the east.

It isn't much, but it may have to do.

At twenty minutes after ten, Wynn rolled into Linert. He rode all the way through town until he came to the last possible street, then turned left at the small truck stop café and parked in the lot across the street from Lester's mobile home. The beat-up, old red Honda Civic sat in the driveway. Yellow police tape crisscrossed the front door.

Wynn got off the bike and walked up the street and around the block so he could see the back of the mobile home. He knew that all mobile homes were required to have at least two entrances, which was confirmed when he saw a flimsy set of metal stairs leading up to a back door. There was no police tape on this one.

Glancing around the sparse neighborhood, Wynn noted a few other homes across the street to the north and east but didn't see any people. He quietly strode up the metal stairs and tried the doorknob.

As expected, it was locked.

But also as expected, the door hung slightly askew, revealing a single spring-latch, and no deadbolt. Wynn pulled a credit card out of his wallet and slipped it between the door and the frame, then leaned into the door with his shoulder while twisting the knob and jamming the credit card against the lock. Within seconds the latch released. He pulled the door open, quickly slipped inside, and closed the door behind him.

Inside, it was already hot and stuffy. A putrid smell like rotting meat hung heavy in the air. Hundreds of flies buzzed within the space, swarming largely around a dark brown stain on the arm of a ratty old couch. Johnston had said they found Lester with a bullet hole in his head. Wynn could imagine Lester collapsing on the couch, cradling his broken left arm and smashed fingers until someone came in and shot him.

But how did they know Lester needed to be silenced? How did they know Wynn had been here? He had taken Lester's burner and his other phone was smashed in the fight. Maybe he got it working? Johnston hadn't said anything about recovering a working cell phone. Was there another burner somewhere?

Wynn spent the next ten minutes searching for a phone or anything that Johnston and his deputies may have overlooked, but there was nothing. Disappointed, he slipped out the back door and nonchalantly strolled back to the front of the house.

Walking back to his bike, his gaze drifted to the café beyond. He paused at the intersection, taking a moment to look back at Lester's front door, then across the street to the café. He followed the side-walk until he was in a straight line between the two, then, scanning the ground, went across the street and through the parking lot toward the restaurant. Rounding the corner, he spotted a payphone attached to the side of the building.

He picked up the receiver but there was no sound when he put it to his ear. He hadn't used one of these in years, but seemed to remember you had to put coins in before you heard the dial tone. Fresh out of coins, he pulled out his cell, and dialed the number on the phone.

It rang. He disconnected.

Wynn looked back across the street at Lester's front door. He could imagine Lester coming to his senses and wanting to call for help. He'd check for his burner first, but it was gone. He'd check his iPhone next, but it was smashed. Maybe then, Lester would stumble out of his trailer and come over here to make a phone call. He could imagine Lester telling someone what had happened, asking for help. Someone telling him to sit tight, that help was on its way. Lester would go back to his trailer, leaving the door unlocked for whoever might be coming.

Wynn searched his contacts, found Miller's number, and dialed. She answered on the second ring.

"Hey, it's me," he said.

"Hey," she said. "Didn't expect to hear from you. What's up?"

"I was hoping you could research a phone number for me. I need to know what numbers were called from a particular phone this past Monday between seven-thirty and ten o'clock in the evening."

"Monday evening, huh? Does this have anything to do with Lester?"

"It's a payphone across the street from his trailer. He called somebody, but I had his burner and his personal cell was smashed. He had to find a phone somewhere."

"And whoever he called becomes a prime suspect in his murder, your assault, and Davies' kidnapping," Miller mused.

"It's a theory," Wynn agreed.

Wynn gave her the number and Miller said she would get back to him within a couple of hours. He disconnected the call and went inside the café. It was a little early for lunch, but he'd skipped breakfast. And besides, it was never too early, or too late for that matter, for coffee.

A sign inside the front door read 'Seat Yourself', so he went to a table near the back along the far wall. Only three other tables were occupied, but it was a habit. He liked to see who else came in.

A waitress in her late fifties came around with a pot of coffee and a menu. She was wearing a surprisingly vintage uniform, complete with a lace skirt, apron, and striped hat. Probably the same uniform they wore when the place opened thirty years ago. Hell, probably the same waitress.

She flipped over a cup already on the table, filled it, and said she'd be back in a few minutes. Wynn perused the menu, eventually settling on his standard fare of pancakes, bacon, and eggs. He pulled out his phone and opened the map app. Using his fingers to pinch and zoom and swipe, he eventually found the dirt road two miles south of the construction zone. He zoomed in to study the area more closely.

As promised, the waitress returned in a few minutes and took his order. As she turned to leave, Wynn asked, "What do people do for jobs around here?"

"Besides working for the county or the schools, it's mostly farming or construction. Why? You thinking about joining us?"

"Maybe."

"Where do you live now, hon?" She was one of those. Called everybody hon.

"Southern California."

"Stay put, sweetheart. You'd be crazy to move here."

Wynn smiled and said thanks, then turned his attention back to his phone. The map app didn't have the detail he needed so he switched to Google Earth. Hearing the door open, he looked up to see Sheriff Johnston and Deputy Craig walk in. Johnston spotted him and ambled over.

"Mr. Wynn, I'm surprised to see you here," Sheriff Johnston said. "I heard you were busy up in Sturgis."

Ignoring the implied question, Wynn said simply, "Good to see you, sheriff."

"You might remember Deputy Craig," Johnston said. "He's the one who found Lester."

"Nice to see you again, Deputy."

Craig nodded but said nothing.

"Speaking of Lester," Wynn said, looking back at Johnston, "Any progress on finding his killer?"

"It's funny you should ask," Johnston said. "I was wondering if you wouldn't mind stopping by the office and maybe fill us in a little more on what happened between the two of you. Maybe there's something we missed."

"Am I a suspect?"

"Oh no, no," Johnston said, feigning an apology. "Miller's time-line cleared you. We'd just like to have a firsthand conversation with the last person known to have seen him alive. Shows we've conducted a thorough investigation. And like I said, maybe there's something we missed."

"Uh-huh," Wynn said cautiously.

"We could go now if you want," Johnston offered.

"Tell you what," Wynn countered. "I just ordered. Let me finish here and I'll swing by in an hour. How's that?"

"Sure, that'll be fine," Johnston said. He and Craig stood there for an awkward moment.

"Is there anything else?" Wynn asked.

"No, no. We'll see you in an hour."

Johnston and Craig turned and walked back to the front counter where they spoke quietly to the waitress. She jotted something down on her order pad, and then they left. Wynn went back to his phone.

Thirty minutes later he was finishing breakfast when his phone buzzed. Miller's name popped up on the screen.

"What did you find?" he asked by way of greeting.

"Looks like you were partially right, but I'm not sure it's the result you expected," Miller said. "There were two calls made from that phone Monday evening. The first went unanswered to one of the numbers we got off the guy's burner Tuesday night. The second was connected to the Norfolk County Sheriff's department."

"Why wouldn't I expect that?" Wynn said. "I told you someone with a badge is involved."

"Because a guy who was assaulted called the cops? That's not proof of anything. That's what we'd expect him to do."

"How long was the call?"

"A little under two minutes. Why?"

"When was the last time you took an assault call in less than two minutes? Whoever he talked to wanted to get him off the phone. Do you guys record incoming calls?"

"On our budget? Not hardly. I'm sure they don't either."

"What about a report? If some guy called in and reported an assault, you'd have paperwork on it, right?"

"Yeah," Miller admitted.

"And yet," Wynn continued, "When we talked to Johnston on the conference call Monday night, he didn't know anything about it. If they'd had an assault reported, Johnston would've known."

"Shit," Miller said.

Wynn knew he was convincing her.

"What do we do now?" she asked.

"First, whatever we do from here on out has got to stay off the books. There's a dirty cop in this but until we figure out who it is, we can't tell anybody what we're doing. Not even Smith."

"That's a big ask. He's my boss."

"Are you willing to bet your life he's not involved?"

She paused, recalling Smitty's reaction to the news Lester was missing. "No. What else?"

"Text me the number of the first call, the one for the burner."

"What are you gonna do?"

"I'm not sure yet. Johnston found me sitting down here at a diner and asked me to come in for an interview. Says it's for his file, but I think I'm still a suspect. Or a fall guy."

"He hasn't said anything like that for a couple of days, but I don't know. He was quiet on the briefing call last night, and we were dismissed this morning."

"Dismissed? Why?"

"None of the crimes related to Davies occurred in Wheaton County. Except your assault, but we don't know that's related."

"What about the guy in the hospital?"

"Still in a coma. Swelling hasn't gone down. They're going to keep him induced until it does."

"What about his photo? Has Crower passed that around?"

"Yeah, he and a couple of others. They put it up in the post office, at the grocery store, diners, and gas stations, but so far nothing."

"Shit," Wynn said. "Okay. Text me that number then quietly check if there's a report on Lester's assault. If there is, it blows this theory, but if not, we've got to proceed as if a cop somewhere is involved."

"Okay," Miller said. "Call me when you're done with Johnston. And be careful."

"You too."

Wynn finished his coffee and walked to the front counter to pay his bill. On his way out, he stopped in front of a bulletin board hanging on the wall in the foyer. There were flyers for babysitting services and horse training, cars for sale and handyman services. There were business cards for insurance agents and multi-level marketing schemes, but no police posters asking, "Have you seen this man?"

CHAPTER 32

WHEN WYNN FIRST floated the theory that a cop was involved, he understood Miller's skepticism. Hell, considering he'd been more angry than rational at the time, even he might have been talked out of it. But the fact that the Norfolk sheriff's office was called from the café's payphone on Monday night added new credence.

It also made his upcoming meeting with Johnston that much riskier.

He sat outside the café for an extra twenty minutes, waiting for Miller's text and developing a strategy for handling the interview. When the text finally came in with the number, he rode over to the sheriff's office.

After the receptionist told him to take a chair in the waiting area, he chose a seat against the front wall, giving him a mostly unobstructed view of the bullpen. Sheriff Johnston was in his office, visible through the glass wall, in a closed-door meeting with Deputy Craig. Wynn settled in to wait.

It was another busy afternoon at the sheriff's office. Three of the four desks in the bullpen, except for Craig's, were occupied by deputies either on the phone or with people in front of them. It wasn't the sheriff's full staff, but it was a good portion.

Which gave Wynn an idea.

Making note of what the three deputies were doing, he pulled up the burner number that came off the payphone, then hit the 'Call' button. To avoid putting the phone to his ear, he instead put it on speaker and lowered the volume so only he could hear it above the general office din.

As the muted buzz of a phone ringing on the other end came across the speaker, Wynn watched the three deputies for any reaction. Seeing none, he hung up and dialed again, this time focusing his attention on Johnston and Craig in the glass office. No response. Finally, he tried a third time, keeping an eye on the receptionist. Still no reaction.

Would've been too easy.

Not that his little experiment truly eliminated anyone, but it might've narrowed the focus had anyone reacted or picked up.

Johnston finally stood up from his desk and came out of his office.

"Sorry to keep you waiting, Mr. Wynn," Johnston said as he approached. "As you can see, we're a little busy around here this afternoon."

The sheriff led the way back to his office and held the door open for Wynn, who sat in the same chair he had used Monday. Johnston closed the door, went around the desk, and sat down while Craig remained standing in the corner. Johnston pulled out a small, digital recorder.

"You don't mind if we record this, do you?" Johnston asked.

"Not at all. Do you?" Wynn pulled out his phone and opened the voice recorder app. He set the phone on the desk.

Johnston smiled slightly and nodded his agreement. He turned on the recorder, stated his name, the date and time, the occupants in the room, and the purpose of the conversation.

When he finished, Wynn jumped in. "Before we begin," he said, "I'd like it on the record that Sheriff Johnston has indicated I am not a suspect in Mr. Lester's murder, and that I have immunity from any charges that may result from the information I am about to give."

Craig groaned audibly.

Johnston paused a moment, then said, "I'm sure you understand, that only the county prosecutor can grant immunity. That's beyond my pay grade. But as the head of law enforcement in Norfolk County, I can confirm that you are not currently a suspect in Mr. Lester's murder."

It wasn't as much as Wynn wanted, and he knew the chances of that statement preventing any charges were next to nothing, but getting it on tape could create one hell of a problem for any future prosecutor. Besides, with his role in what happened in Sturgis two nights ago, he knew the FBI needed his cooperation more than any real or imagined charges Johnston might come up with. Not perfect, but he was satisfied.

They spent the next hour asking and answering questions, going over the same story Wynn had already told at least four times before. Johnston tried to trip him up a couple of times, but the truth was easy to remember, so he told it, patiently correcting Johnston when he assumed too much. Craig stood in the corner, glaring angrily.

When finished, Johnston thanked him for coming in while Craig remained silent. Wynn didn't bother saying goodbye; just picked his phone up off the desk and left.

————

"What do you think?" Johnston asked Craig as they watched Wynn walk out the front doors.

"I think the bastard did it," Craig replied.

"What about Miller's timeline? No way he could've made it to Newbury based on the M.E.'s assessment."

"Fucking doctors don't know everything. If both the doc and Miller were off by fifteen minutes, it'd work. He could've done it."

"Well, keep working it," Johnston said, ending the meeting.

Craig went back to his desk and sat down, pulling a small flip phone from the drawer. Opening the phone, he saw he had missed three calls.

———

Ann sat on her bunk, outwardly quiet and stoic. Inside, her mind raced, trying to reconcile the new information from the past day and a half.

Something's changed. The old guy either allowed Jessica to be raped or had no power to stop it. By a cop, no less. And it's my fault. I told her they wouldn't hurt us. But they did. And they'll continue. Over and over again.

Then her own words came back to her. '*We're a long way from help.*'

Which means we have to help ourselves. Go on the offensive. Fight our way out of here. Either succeed, or what did the guy say? Spend the rest of your lives fucking strange men.

I'd rather die.

"Ladies," she said, looking first at Jessica, then at Hailey, "I've got an idea."

———

Wynn rode back to the Fresh Start to refuel. He stepped around the side of the building to call Miller.

"It's me," he said when she picked up.

"How'd it go?"

"Fine. Not sure what Johnston was looking for, but I didn't give him anything. That guy Craig sat in but didn't say a word. He seems worse than Crower. You guys got an asshole quota or what?"

"There's a lot of testosterone in a Wyoming sheriff's department, for sure. And by the way, there's no report of an assault on Lester. I hate to say it, but your theory is getting stronger."

"What do you know about Craig?" Wynn asked.

"Never met him before Monday. Why?"

"I don't know, he gives off a vibe. Very angry."

"Be a lot easier if that guy in the hospital woke up," Miller said. "But even if he does, it'll be a couple of days before we can talk to him."

"Yeah," Wynn said, just to fill the space while he was thinking. "So what's next?"

"Got to try to find his partner. Any way we can contact the hospitals around here and see if someone came in with a broken arm on Tuesday morning?"

"Broken arm? I thought you said it was self-defense?"

"It was. That doesn't mean he may not have gotten hurt in the process."

Miller sighed. "I'm glad I'm on your side. Would he have any other injuries that might help identify him?"

"No, just the arm."

"Hmm. We'll need to check all the doctor's offices and medical clinics in addition to the hospitals. Too many other places where he might've gotten it x-rayed and set. Do you think Rapid City to Cheyenne is a big enough area?

"I would think so."

"Okay, I'll get on it, but it'll take a while. What are you going to do?"

"Hang around down here. Keep digging. See if I can uncover something."

Her voice turned flirty. "Come up here and I'm sure you will."

He smiled. "Tempting, but I'll let you know."

Wynn disconnected and walked back to his bike, still parked at the pump. He hopped on, and took off north in search of an old dirt road.

CHAPTER 33

Wynn cruised north on Highway 85 until he found the dirt road heading off to the east, two miles before the construction zone. He turned and slowed his pace considerably as the tires crunched over a combination of sand and loose dirt. Washboard bumps appeared intermittently on either side of the road. Not good on a street bike. No traction at all.

He followed the road through a sea of tall brown grass, looking for a turnout or other side road that might lead further north. About a mile in, the road dipped into an arroyo. Approximately fifteen feet wide with softball-sized stones littering the sandy bottom, it was dry now, but Wynn could imagine a powerful flow after a spring thunderstorm.

Easing the bike down into the dry bed and going at no more than a walking pace, Wynn slowly made his way north up the wash. Thirty yards in, the arroyo turned to the right and the road behind was lost to sight. He found a relatively flat, level spot and shut down the bike.

Stepping off, Wynn dug into his saddlebags for the binoculars and a bottle of water. The afternoon sun was beginning its downward arc toward evening, still a few hours away. He climbed out of the arroyo to get his bearings, the huge piles of sand and gravel near the staging area visible like small mounds off in the distance.

It was a two-mile hike to reach the southern edge of the construction zone, and another mile and a quarter to reach the north end. Simple math and geometry told him there and back would be a minimum of seven miles in the hot sun.

No other way to do it. He started walking.

Wynn soon realized the grass wasn't as tall or thick as it appeared from the road. It made the hiking easy, but only came up a little past his waist, meaning he would have to crouch as he got closer. Not a problem. He had done plenty of recon in the Marines. He knew what to do.

What he didn't know was if he'd find what he hoped. He was going on the hunch that the guy who zapped him two mornings ago would be working on this site. Lester had worked here, and the waitress in the diner said most guys either did construction or farming. The guy hadn't struck Wynn as the farming type, and there wasn't a lot of other construction around. If he was here, he'd be easy to pick out. He'd be the one with a broken arm.

Ahead, clouds of black exhaust rose from the heavy machinery. The size of the massive piles of sand and gravel becoming more apparent when he was finally able to compare them to the now visible row of semi-trailer box cars. Beyond that he knew, were rows of personal vehicles, not yet visible from this angle.

He crouched low and moved swiftly as he made his way to within a quarter-mile of the staging area. Using the binoculars, he scanned for activity. For now, the area was quiet. A half-mile to his left cars were slowing on the highway as they approached the construction zone.

Staying low he made his way around the staging area and worked his way north past the massive piles of sand and gravel, then eased his way back to the west, closer to the road.

He spent the next ten minutes watching the workers in the area, examining each for a telltale cast. Seeing nothing, he slowly backed away to the east, getting well out of sight before continuing north.

Wynn repeated the process every couple hundred yards. Slowly creeping in from east to west, watching for ten minutes, then creeping back out before moving north and doing it all again.

He quickly eliminated the guys operating the heavy equipment, the loaders and dozers and scrapers. It was obvious they needed two good arms to keep those things under control. He also eliminated the guys carrying shovels or brooms. Again, two good arms were needed.

That left the runners, the guys shuttling light equipment and supplies back and forth in the beds of their pickup trucks. Which raised another problem. Wynn had broken the guy's right arm, which would be inside the pickup, not easily visible through the driver's window. They were also the most mobile, moving from one end of the site to the other, causing Wynn to evaluate the same vehicle multiple times.

Eventually, Wynn settled in a little more than midway through the zone and started counting the pickups, mentally distinguishing one from another. If he saw the driver's left arm hanging out the window, the guy was obviously driving with his right and therefore wasn't likely his man. Hard to drive with a recently broken arm. With this strategy, he was able to eliminate several of the pickups fairly quickly.

As the afternoon wore on, Wynn was beginning to think he'd guessed wrong when he saw an old white and brown Ford F150 roll slowly in from the north. It stopped near a group of guys with shovels who climbed in the back, then slowly K-turned to head back the way it came. The stops and starts were abrupt and Wynn could see the guys in the back hunkering down and holding on tight.

The pickup proceeded north a half-mile where it eventually stopped and the guys in the back jumped out with their shovels. A couple of the guys seemed to say something to the driver who responded with a well-known hand gesture. The man drew his hand back inside the cab and onto the steering wheel before the pickup drove away.

With signs the worksite was beginning to shut down for the night, Wynn backed away from his recon position and worked his way back to the staging area. The first of the pickup trucks soon arrived, disgorging loads of workers who walked to their vehicles and took off for the evening.

A little while later the white and brown Ford pulled into the staging area. Five guys hopped out of the back while the doors on both sides swung open. The driver rotated his legs out and stepped down from the cab, then turned back and leaned in. A moment later he straightened up and took a step backward. He held a thermos and lunchbox in his left hand.

His right arm was in a cast.

Wynn zeroed the binoculars in on him. The guy was big. Not linebacker big, but close. The guy made his way to a much newer, bright blue Ford F150. The cast was an odd, shiny color, and the guy had dark circles around his eyes.

Wynn searched his memory. *I didn't hit the guy in the face. Where'd the bruises come from?*

The guy climbed into his shiny pickup and pulled onto the highway, then headed south towards Linert. Wynn tried to get the license number off the truck, but even with the binoculars, the jostling of the bumper as the truck bounced through the dirt made it impossible.

Having seen what he had come to find, Wynn backed away and began the two-mile trek back to his bike.

———

After leaving work at the construction site, Nathan drove three miles south on Highway 85. He took a gravel road west that eventually met up with the secondary county road that ran past Tomas's ranch. It'd been a rough day, his first one back since that biker had broken his arm Tuesday morning. Not only did he have to explain the broken arm, but the black eyes and broken nose, too.

Thankfully, John had been there to back up his story of a car accident, but he could tell several of the guys didn't buy it. They'd made comments throughout the day, making it clear they thought it more likely he'd gotten his ass kicked. Even now, his face flushed with humiliation when he thought about it. He was supposed to be the one doing the ass-kicking, not the other way around.

Which put him in a foul mood by the time he got back to the ranch. At least Craig had gotten his rocks off with the brunette bitch last night. Maybe he'd do the same tonight, regardless of what Tomas had to say.

Before they were gone.

———

When Wynn was halfway back to the arroyo, and far enough away not to worry about being seen, he stood up straight and pulled out his phone to call Miller. Only one bar of service. Hopefully enough.

"Where are you?" she asked.

"As best I can tell, the middle of nowhere. Any luck with the hospitals?"

"Not yet. We've called the bigger ones and enlisted help from the locals in each county to reach out to the clinics and individual offices, but so far nothing. Still waiting to hear back from many of them though. How about you? Any luck?"

"Maybe," he said. "I saw a guy working the construction zone with a broken right arm. I was too far away to follow him, but I'm going to cruise through Linert; see if I can spot his truck. If not, I'll stay here and catch him when he goes to the site tomorrow."

"You think it's him?"

"It'd be one hell of a coincidence if not."

"Hmm, alright. But promise me something," Miller said. "If you do find him, call me. Don't go confronting him alone like you did

Lester. Time is running out and this may be our last decent lead. We need him alive."

"Will do. But we're still off the books, right?"

"Yeah," she said. "Way off. And I don't like it."

"You got a better plan?"

Miller paused, her silence answering the question. "Let me know if you find him."

"I will," Wynn said. "Talk to you tomorrow."

Back at his bike a few minutes later, Wynn put the binoculars and empty water bottle in the saddlebag, then slowly turned the bike around and made his way back to the dirt road. The tire tracks he'd left earlier were plainly visible. He wondered if anybody had seen them. Not that it mattered now, but he hoped not. He might have to come back.

He eventually made his way out of the arroyo, onto the dirt road, and back to the highway. The last rays of daylight were filtering between the buildings as he ambled through Linert, in search of the blue Ford. The street in front of the diner where he and Miller had lunch on Monday was packed with cars, but Wynn guessed most of their drivers were at the bar across the street. Regardless, there was no blue pickup in sight. He continued past the Fresh Start, past the grocery store and the Subway, and down to the truck stop café. Still no luck.

He pulled into the café and looked across the parking lot to Lester's trailer. It was quiet, the yellow police tape still crisscrossing the door. He went inside the diner and sat at the same table he had used earlier. It was clear the dinner rush was winding down. There were several dirty tables and quite a few more with patrons sitting in front of empty dinner plates.

A different waitress, younger than the one this morning, in jeans and a t-shirt, came by and offered him coffee, which he gladly accepted. He ordered a burger and fries and by the time she brought it out, the place had nearly emptied.

"Hey," he said to the waitress as she set the burger in front of him. "I wonder if you could help me."

"I'll try. What do you need?"

"I was having a little trouble with my bike earlier and some dude told me about a guy here in town who works on Harleys. He didn't know the guy's name but said he drives a bright blue Ford pickup. Any idea who he might be referring to?"

"Works on Harleys?"

"I don't think that's his full-time job. It was the bright blue Ford that sounded like the real thing he was known by."

"Hmm," she said, thinking. "Sorry, I don't know anybody who drives a blue Ford. Let me ask Roy. He knows everybody."

She went back to the kitchen and came out a moment later. "No. Roy don't know anybody who drives a blue Ford pickup. You sure he's from around here?"

"Maybe not. Thanks anyway."

Wynn finished his burger, paid the tab, and rode up Main Street to a motel he'd seen earlier. He tried the same story with the front desk clerk but got the same result. No luck.

At half-past nine on Thursday evening, he unlocked the door to his third motel room of the past four nights. It was the same as the other two. In fact, his duffel was still in his room in Sturgis. He didn't even have a toothbrush.

Taking a seat on the bed, he knew he had a good lead, but it was dry until tomorrow morning. He considered calling Miller but didn't have any update for her. He figured she would call him if she came up with something. With nothing left to do he stripped down, showered, and went to bed. Maybe he could catch up on some sleep.

CHAPTER 34

JESSICA, ANN, AND Hailey spent most of the day discussing Ann's plan; debating its strengths, which were few, and its weaknesses, which were many. But in the absence of better alternatives, even a bad plan was more appealing than what they imagined their captors had in store for them.

By mid-afternoon, they'd talked themselves out, and hunger was once again becoming an issue. They spent the rest of the day sitting quietly on their bunks.

Assuming, of course, it was daytime. With the only thing distinguishing day from night being the lights that seemed to automatically turn on and off, Jessica worried that the cycle had been either accelerated or delayed, warping their sense of time to further disorient them. Last night, she'd gotten her first look outside and as expected, it was dark. She was confident that meant today was Thursday, her fifth day of captivity. It also meant it was getting late in the evening. The lights should be going out soon.

She was startled by an unexpected bang on the door.

"Back off!"

The three women looked at one another.

"Are we doing this?" Ann asked.

Jessica nodded, followed by Hailey. Jessica rushed over and sat on the bunk where they'd been told while Hailey poured a paper cup of water onto her face and curled up in her bunk. Ann rushed into the bathroom and lie on the floor.

The deadbolt slid back, and the older skinny guy entered the room. He looked at Hailey in her bunk and Ann on the floor. "What the fuck is this?"

"We're sick," Jessica said, her voice a hoarse whisper.

"With what?"

"F... Food poisoning. We need ice and antibiotics."

The old guy looked at each of the women. "Tony! Get in here!"

The young Latino appeared in the doorway and looked at the three women. "Jesus. What happened?"

"Says they've got food poisoning."

"No way. They've been eating the same shit we have."

Jessica nodded toward Hailey. "Check her out," she whispered.

Tony stepped over to Hailey and poked her arm. She rolled toward him. "Shit, John. She doesn't look good. She's all sweaty."

Jessica moved her mouth but no words came out. She swallowed and tried again. "We... we need ice and antibiotics."

"Ice?" John asked. "What for?"

"To bring the fevers down." She nodded at Ann on the floor. "If you don't, she could die."

John paused as he continued to look back and forth. Finally, to Tony, he said, "Go get Nathan and a bag of ice."

Tony darted out the door. He left it open.

"She might be dead already," Jessica said.

John crept over to Ann and pushed her leg with his foot. She didn't move. He crouched beside her.

Ann spun onto her back and drove her fist, with the bolt protruding like a knife, toward the soft spot at the base of John's neck. Jessica launched herself across the room, pushing John into the bathroom, causing him to drop to his hands and knees while Ann battered away beneath him with the bolt.

The first swing missed its intended target, his carotid artery. Ann kept at it, kept stabbing with the dull bolt, anywhere she could connect. Bright red marks appeared on John's face and neck, while Jessica climbed over his back and wrestled for the gun.

Hailey ran to the door and slammed it shut just as Tony was about to come through. She put her back to it, leaned against it, and pushed her legs with all her might to keep the door closed. She had to keep Tony out. Their whole plan was to somehow get the gun away from the old guy, then they could blast through the door lock and somehow shoot their way out. With Jessica and Ann battling John two-on-one, they stood a chance. If Tony got through, the match would even. Their odds would plummet.

John had kept the gun in his hand when he'd dropped to the floor. Now, his heavy hand pressed it flat to the concrete as it pointed away from Ann. Jessica used one hand to try to pry his fingers from the weapon while she raked her fingernails across his eyes with the other. All to no avail. John used his left hand to slap Ann across the face, then pinned her right hand to the floor and twisted the bolt from her grasp.

Hailey slid her back down the door, extending her legs, gaining better leverage when something heavy slammed against the door, sending her flying across the room. The big guy with the cast, followed by Tony, rushed into the room.

Tony leapt on top of Hailey and jammed the stun gun into her side, the current crackled as it flowed. Nathan rushed to the bathroom and pulled Jessica off of John and threw her across the room. Tony turned the stunner on Jessica, its thousands of volts erupting like fire through her limbs.

Nathan pulled John away from Ann and swung his heavy boot twice, violently, into her ribs. He turned and held John back as he attempted to rush toward her.

"You bitch!" John screamed. "I'm gonna fucking kill you!"

"No, you're not." Nathan held him back until John calmed down. "But you can make her wish you would."

John pushed away from Nathan and stalked over to Tony. "Go get some zips."

Tony disappeared out the door, then reappeared moments later with several zip ties in hand. John pointed his gun at Jessica and Hailey while Tony and Nathan approached Ann cautiously.

Ann squirmed into the corner of the bathroom, trying to hide behind the toilet. Tony and Nathan squeezed into the tiny room. Ann kicked and swung her arms, but Tony avoided them and jammed the stunner into her shoulder. Jessica and Hailey screamed as the stunner crackled. Ann's muscles convulsed as Tony kept the pressure applied.

"Get her tied and bring her out." John looked at Jessica and Hailey. "Don't you bitches move unless you want to join her."

Using a zip tie, Nathan secured Ann's hands together. He removed a three-inch bed bolt from her right hand and tossed it to John. "Souvenir for you."

John caught it with his free hand and examined it briefly before throwing it out the door. "Bitch is gonna pay. Bring her."

Tony grabbed Ann by the hair and dragged her out the door.

"You stay here," John said to Nathan, handing him the gun. "Keep the doors open. Let these two hear what's about to happen."

Jessica huddled with Hailey on the bunk, hearing nothing for about a minute, until a sharp slap echoed from outside the door, followed by a painful scream. The cry trailed off to gasping sobs before the lash landed again, prompting another gut-wrenching shriek. Again. And again. Jessica and Hailey recoiled from the sounds, screaming and crying in fear and sympathy.

With tears streaming down her face, Jessica locked eyes with Nathan, silently pleading to make it stop. He smiled and looked away. The lash echoed again, followed by silence. A minute later, Tony dragged an unconscious Ann back into the room and dumped her on the floor. Her shirt was in tatters. Purple welts rose across her back.

John came through the doorway, looked down at Ann, then up at Jessica and Hailey. "Any questions?"

The women shrunk away in fear.

"I didn't think so."

CHAPTER 35

Friday

WYNN WOKE EARLY on Friday morning and spent the first forty-five minutes going through his kata. He held the stretch poses until his muscles screamed, then moved rapidly from one form to the next. The combination had the sweat streaming by the time he was done. He showered, dressed, and was checked out by seven-fifteen.

Back at the truck stop café, he lingered over coffee to allow the construction crew time to clear the staging area. Most of the crew would likely start at seven and be out on the site by eight, leaving the area mostly empty by eight-thirty.

By eight-twenty, with the air already warm, Wynn hopped on his bike and rode north toward the construction zone. Fifteen minutes later he rolled the Harley down off the highway and onto the trampled grass path that led through the ditch and into the staging area.

As expected, the place was deserted. He rode slowly between the first two rows of parked vehicles until he came to the end, then turned up to go between the third and fourth rows.

About a third of the way down on his right was the bright blue Ford. Unmistakable. He stopped and pulled out his phone, then took a picture of the license plate. It was from Oklahoma. He forwarded the picture in a text message to Miller: *Can you run this plate? Need name, address, and picture if able. ASAP.*

He looked around and saw a couple of guys getting equipment out of one of the semi-truck trailers to the east, but they paid him no attention. He zoomed out with his phone and took a picture of the full pickup, before putting his phone away and casually riding to the exit. Checking both ways for traffic, he pulled onto the highway and rode back to Linert.

The café was getting tiresome, so he pulled to a stop across the street from the diner where he and Miller had lunch on Monday. He shut down the bike, but before getting off, checked his phone. There was a message from Miller, along with a picture. A driver's license photo. Wynn couldn't be one hundred percent sure, but ninety percent was good enough. It was the guy who'd attacked him Tuesday morning in Newbury. The message was short: *Call me.*

Miller picked up on the first ring.

"What do you have?" Wynn asked.

"Let me ask first," she said. "Is that the guy who jumped you at the motel?"

"I think so, yeah."

"You sure?"

"Didn't get a great look at him but yeah, I think so. Why?"

Miller ignored his question. "Where'd you come up with this plate?"

"He works down here at the construction site, just like Lester. He's got a cast on his right arm."

"Shit," Miller cursed under her breath.

"Who is he?"

"His name's Nathan Craig, brother of Nick Craig, as in Deputy Nick Craig of the Norfolk County Sheriff's Department."

Wynn paused as the pieces fell into place. "It fits," he said. "Lester isolates Davies on the south side, Craig runs interference on the north, brother Nathan and friends make the pickup. When I hit up

Lester, he calls Craig not to report an assault, but to warn an accomplice. Craig kills Lester but then says he can't find him to buy time, then sends his brother and a friend up to Newbury to silence me. It all fits."

"That's what I was afraid of," Miller said, "but we don't have any proof. He could say he broke his arm a hundred ways. And no offense, but a witness who'd been zapped with a stun gun during an assault isn't very reliable. Without him, we got nothing that ties it all together. I can't go making an accusation like that without some proof. Smitty will never back it."

"You got an address on the brother?"

"In Oklahoma. Nothing local."

Wynn thought for a moment, "How busy are you today?"

"As compared to this? Not busy at all."

Wynn smiled. "Tell you what, I need some supplies. Can you come down here and keep an eye on the truck, make sure this guy Nathan doesn't go anywhere?"

"What do you need? Maybe I can bring it."

"Cops don't typically have what I need, and even if you did, you may not want it traced back to you."

Miller paused for a moment while she processed what he said. "Understood."

Wynn texted her a photo of the truck and described the driveway from where he had watched Lester four days ago, a good spot for Miller to keep an eye on the vehicle. It would take her close to ninety minutes to get there, but Wynn wasn't concerned. Nathan was most likely working a full day, but certainly a half-day at a minimum. You don't show up at a construction site for anything less.

They disconnected and Wynn pulled up the browser app on his phone. He had three distinct items he needed to acquire, likely necessitating three different stops. Finding where he could get the first item was easy. The second required a couple of phone calls, but he found it. The third item took multiple searches and phone calls, but he ultimately found it from a private seller. Wynn said he'd be there in less than three hours.

———

The info from Miller had finally given Wynn some direction. He fired up the Street Glide and rode south on Main Street until he hit the intersection he had come in on five days ago. He turned right onto Highway 18, and forty-five minutes later was passing the Prairie Junction rest area, the spot where he first encountered Jessica Davies and the white van. He slowed as he went past, then hit the entrance ramp to the northbound interstate. Fifteen minutes after that he took the exit ramp into the small town of Douglas, Wyoming.

Like so many things in Wyoming, 'small' was a relative term. With barely more than sixty-four hundred residents, Douglas was actually the fifteenth-largest town in the state. But people are people the world over. Fleet managers need to know where their vehicles are, parents want to know where their children are, and husbands and wives want to keep track of wandering spouses. And so even a relatively small town like Douglas had a cell phone store that carried GPS tracking devices, Wynn's first stop.

The cell phone dealer was located inside a strip mall off the main drag. Signs for the various carriers competed for window space in the glass storefront. Inside, a lone employee, a guy with disheveled black hair and a full beard, was helping a woman transfer data from her old cell phone to a new one.

"Be right with you," the guy called out as Wynn entered.

Wynn spent a few minutes browsing at nothing in particular before the guy freed up. "How can I help you?"

"I called earlier about your GPS trackers,' Wynn said.

"Oh yeah. Over here."

He led Wynn to the end of a long display case with the latest phones and tablets and other electronic gadgetry under a glass countertop. The guy explained that there were three options. The first was plugged into a power source inside the car and never needed new batteries. The second was battery-operated, could be magnetically attached to almost any spot outside or under the car, and provided constant, real-time streaming of the vehicle's location, but required a monthly data plan. The third option was also battery-operated and magnetically attached, didn't require a monthly data plan, but would only provide intermittent location data. The shorter the interval between location "pings," the sooner the batteries would need to be replaced. Wynn chose option three. He didn't expect this to be a long-term surveillance.

Thirty-five minutes after entering the cell store, he was on his way out and off to his second destination, a simple hardware store. There he picked up some long, plastic zip ties, batteries, a roll of black duct tape, a couple of bungee cords, and a cinch sack to carry it all in. When he'd secured those purchases into his saddlebags, he pulled out his phone and called the private seller. They arranged to meet in thirty minutes in a truck stop parking lot on the south side of town.

With nothing else to do, Wynn arrived within five minutes. The Broken Bow Truck Stop sat on four acres of perfectly flat land, between two budget motels, and across the street from a Baptist church. The lot stretched more than a football field on each side, with a restaurant and convenience store smack in the middle. Eight gas pumps were spaced generously on four islands out front.

For those who wanted to rest, there were almost three acres of well-used dirt parking on either side and behind the store. Wynn counted more than a dozen rigs currently parked behind it. He pulled to a stop in the deserted northwest corner of the lot, making sure to stay out in the open to be easily seen.

While he waited, Wynn pulled out the GPS tracker, put in fresh batteries, and downloaded the app that would allow him to receive its signal on his phone. He paired the tracker to his phone and a map appeared with a red dot indicating the tracker's position. He zoomed in on the map as tight as it would go, and saw a tree take shape on his phone thirty feet to the right of the red dot. He glanced up and saw the tree in real life, exactly where the map said it would be. Pretty accurate. Looking closer, he saw the faint outline of a blue dot beneath the red one indicating his own position relative to the tracker.

Excellent.

He set the frequency so that the tracker would ping his phone every sixty seconds, which according to the guy at the store meant the batteries would last about ten hours. They might last forty-eight if he set it to ping every five minutes, but too much can happen in five minutes.

Scrolling through the settings he found an option to have the tracker shut down if it hadn't moved in five minutes, and then send an alert when it started moving again, potentially extending the battery life.

The sound of tires leaving the pavement and crunching onto gravel prompted him to look up. An old Chevy pickup pulled around the far corner of the store. He shut the tracker off and placed it back in the saddlebag as the Chevy pulled to a stop ten feet away. The driver, a heavy-set guy with a black mustache and severely receding hairline, had his arm hanging out the window. He didn't bother getting out.

"You the guy?" he asked.

Wynn looked around the dirt lot. "I guess so."

"Let me see the cash."

Wynn pulled five, hundred-dollar bills out of his pocket and held them up.

"Let me back around." The guy turned the wheel hard and pulled a tight U-turn, backing deep into the corner behind Wynn's bike so that the nose of the truck was pointing toward the store, the tail facing an empty field. A dozen eighteen-wheelers sat parked two hundred feet to their left, and to their right across the field was one of the budget motels. Thousands of acres of prairie grassland stretched out behind them.

The guy got out, then reached behind the bench seat. He pulled out a dark gray, four-foot-long, hard-sided case and brought it around the back of the truck. He lowered the tailgate and set the case on it. He unlatched the four clasps and raised the top of the case, revealing a Kel Tec KSG, high-capacity shotgun.

It was a nasty-looking thing. Monochrome gray from barrel to stock, a forward pump handle descended from the barrel to help support its weight and provide added control. Two long, twelve-shell tubes ran the length of the barrel. With one in the chamber, it gave the shotgun a twenty-five-round capacity. Wynn hoped he wouldn't need nearly that much.

"Serial number?" he asked.

"Still there, but it's been passed around. Probably registered somewhere but it's passed through at least three sets of hands since."

Wynn picked it up and opened the chamber, confirming it was empty. He checked the firing mechanism, then turned toward the open grasslands and put it to his shoulder, lined up the sights. He squeezed the trigger once and heard a satisfying click. Pumped the barrel with his left hand and squeezed the trigger again. Another click.

"Ammo?" he asked.

The guy walked around to the passenger side of the pickup and came back a moment later with two small cardboard boxes.

"Fifty rounds, as promised," he said.

Wynn opened both boxes and took a shell out of each. He examined them and put them back in the box.

"I've been thinking," the guy said, "five hundred isn't enough. Let's make it six."

"No," Wynn said. "As hot as this thing probably is, you should be paying me to take it off your hands. Besides, if you could get more, you'd have already sold it. Take the five and be happy. Otherwise, we're done here."

He pulled the five hundred out of his pocket and handed it to the guy, closed the case, and carried it all to his bike. He placed the shells inside the saddlebags and secured the case across the bags with the bungee cords he'd just purchased. Not exactly inconspicuous in L.A., but in Wyoming, nobody would look twice.

The guy spun his tires in a last show of machismo as he left, kicking up dirt and gravel. Wynn ignored him. Two minutes later he was back on the road toward Linert.

CHAPTER 36

WYNN GOT BACK to Linert by early afternoon. He pulled into the Fresh Start to fill his tank and took out his phone to call Miller.

"How's our boy?" he asked when she picked up.

"I haven't seen him, but his truck hasn't moved," she replied.

"That's okay, he'll be back. Is there anyone else in the staging area?"

"No. A few guys came back to grab lunch out of their cars but it's pretty quiet now. You get all your shopping done?"

"Yeah. I'll be coming through in about twenty minutes. Give me a signal if anyone goes in the lot. Otherwise, I'll go straight there and come right back out. When you see me leave, meet me back in Linert behind the diner where we had lunch on Monday."

"You got it," Miller said.

Wynn unfastened the bungee cords holding the shotgun case and pulled the GPS tracker out of the saddlebag. He made sure it was securely attached to its magnetic case, then turned it on and pulled up the app on his phone to make sure it was working. When satisfied, he shut it off and put it in his vest pocket. He refastened the shotgun case across the back of the bike and was soon back on the road.

Fifteen minutes later he saw Miller's SUV parked nose-out along the side of the highway. She gave him a thumbs-up as he went by. Slowing, he turned down into the grassy path that led into the staging area, and rode straight back to Nathan Craig's bright blue Ford.

He kept the bike running as he hopped off. He pulled the GPS tracker out of his pocket and switched it on, then crouched down near the rear of the pickup and spun onto his back. Wriggling under the pickup, he attached the tracker to the heavy iron crossbar of the receiver hitch. Satisfied it was solid, he scooted out from underneath the pickup, stood up, and walked calmly back to his bike.

Barely two minutes after pulling into the staging area, he rumbled past Miller on his way back to Linert.

———

Miller took a left on Second Street, then a quick right into the alley behind the stores that fronted Main. The back half of the block was an empty parking lot, and just two blocks north of the Norfolk Sheriff's Office. Wynn was parked in one of three empty spaces between two deserted pickup trucks, loading shells into a shotgun. She pulled in beside him.

"Successful shopping trip, I see."

"Can't complain," Wynn said.

"I don't want to ask if that thing is properly registered, do I?"

Wynn gave a slight smile and shook his head once. He continued loading shells into the gun.

"I assume you put some kind of GPS tracker on the truck?"

"Like I said, you don't want it traced back to you."

"And we're going to hang out here and follow him when he leaves work tonight."

"That's the plan."

"What if he goes straight to Craig's place? I mean, they are brothers. Would be perfectly natural."

"I don't think he will," Wynn said. "As a deputy, Craig's got to be pretty well-known around here, and yet when I asked around, no one knew anyone who drove a bright blue Ford pickup. That tells me brother Nathan keeps a low profile. I think he's staying elsewhere."

"So, we wait?"

"Yep. For now, we wait."

Miller parked her SUV, then got out and walked around to Wynn's bike. She was wearing her full uniform and duty belt. She opened the rear passenger door and took her radio off. If Craig was involved, she didn't want to use her radio to communicate. She reached under the seat and pulled out an extra ammo clip which she slid in place of the radio. Wynn closed the shotgun with a sharp snap, then checked to make sure the safety was on. He handed the weapon to Miller. "Let's take your car."

While Miller stowed the shotgun in the back seat, Wynn put his other purchases from the hardware store, including the extra box of shells, into the cinch sack. He pulled out his own Glock and ejected the magazine, making sure it was full. He slid it back into place and put it in his inside vest pocket, along with an extra magazine. He grabbed the bulging cinch sack and carried it over to Miller's SUV.

"I hope you're overpreparing," Miller said.

"After what happened Tuesday night up in Sturgis, you've got to figure these guys are on edge. Sure as hell don't want to be under-prepared."

Miller said nothing.

"Listen." Wynn stopped and looked at her. "Not only could this get messy, but I'm not going to promise everything I do tonight is going to be legal. If you want out, it's cool, but now's the time."

Miller gave a weak smile. "You're not getting rid of me that easily. Besides, Davies needs us. I'm in."

They locked up the SUV and walked between two buildings to Main Street, then went south half a block to the diner. Three older gentlemen sat around a table near the front, but other than that, the place was empty. Wynn led Miller to a table against the window as the waitress who had served them Monday approached with a pot of coffee.

They ordered a late lunch and lingered over coffee, Wynn's phone on the table between them, open to the tracking app. They checked the position of the tracker when they first sat down and every thirty minutes or so thereafter, but it hadn't moved. While they waited, they debated whether Davies might still be in the area, or when and how much was needed to bring in Parker and the FBI.

"I've been doing some more reading about what Johnston said the other day," Miller said. "About how these traffickers isolate the women, get them away from anything familiar so they become dependent on their captors."

"And?" Wynn asked.

"I think Parker's right. If those three Latina girls in Sturgis were brought up from Mexico, it's got to be a two-way pipeline. If she's not already there, I'll bet that's where Davies is headed."

"Could be," Wynn agreed.

"But you think she's still in the area?"

"It's a classic double-bluff scenario," Wynn said. "First thought is to get as far away from the abduction site as quickly as possible. They assume BOLOs will be issued and maybe even checkpoints set up, but they also know that eventually, those will come down. So instead of running right away, they hunker down, wait for the heat to cool off, then move. It's a risk either way, but if you've got a place isolated enough, you could sit for a while. Hell, those three girls in Cleveland were held for ten years, and that was in a suburb. As rural as it is out here, they could be held for years."

"But there's no money to be made if they sit on them, and we assume that's the motive, right?"

"Right, so they wait long enough for the heat to cool down, then move 'em. How long does a missing person checkpoint stay up?"

"Only a day or two. The BOLO stays around for a month, but it gets buried within a week."

"And if you've got a guy on the inside who can tell you how long the checkpoints are up, or when the case has lost steam, you'll know when it's safe to move them."

Miller nodded.

Wynn's phone vibrated on the table. An alert flashed on the screen.

"He's moving."

"It's only four-thirty," Miller said. "Seems early."

"It's Friday night. They probably shut down a couple of hours early knowing many of them will be working all weekend. Give them a chance to blow off some steam."

They watched as the red dot pinged on the highway just south of the staging area. Wynn zoomed out on the map until he could also see the blue dot that indicated their position. A minute later the red dot pinged again, another mile and a quarter further south, coming their way. It continued that way for another fifteen minutes, coming steadily toward them. When it was a mile out of town, they looked out the large plate-glass windows of the diner and waited. Within a minute, Nathan Craig drove past in his bright blue Ford.

"Let's give him a minute," Miller said. "We aren't going to lose him, and we don't want to risk being spotted."

They huddled over the phone and waited for the next red dot to appear. When it did, it wasn't on Main Street, but on Elm Street, in front of the sheriff's office.

"Shit, he is going to his brother's," Miller said.

Wynn nodded but said nothing.

They waited another minute.

The red dot pinged, back on Main Street, further south.

"That was quick," Miller said.

"Picking up or dropping off," Wynn said.

They waited another minute. The red dot pinged on Highway 18, heading west out of town past the golf course.

"Let's go," Wynn said.

He dropped some cash on the table to cover the tab plus a generous tip. They bolted out the door and back to Miller's SUV.

Wynn plugged his phone into the charging cable while Miller pulled out onto the street.

"Stop at the sheriff's office," he said.

Miller looked at him questioningly, but pulled to the curb two blocks later. Wynn jumped out and ran inside, then came right back out less than a minute later. "Craig just left," Wynn told her. "Marjorie said I just missed him."

"Could be going home," Miller said.

"I don't think so. Got anyone in Newbury who can get his address for you?"

"Crower's on the desk today."

"Anyone else?"

"Yeah, maybe."

Miller pulled out her phone and punched a number, the ringing sounded over the speakers inside the SUV. When it connected a voice said, "Wheaton County Sheriff's Office."

"Balls, it's me, Sam."

"Hey, how's it going Sammy?" The voice sounded friendly and familiar.

"I need a favor. Can you pull me an address for a Nick Craig, down here in Linert?" Miller turned off Main Street onto Highway 18 and headed west out of town.

"Deputy Craig?" Balls asked.

"Yeah."

"Sure," Balls said cautiously. "What's up?"

"Nothing serious," Miller lied. "I've got a few questions for him regarding the Lester murder, but he got off duty early today. They wouldn't give me his cell number."

"All right. Hold on." Wynn could hear keys tapping in the background.

"Here it is, you ready?"

"Yeah. Go."

"He's at 412 South Oak Street."

Wynn typed it into his phone.

"Need anything else?" Balls asked.

"No, that'll do it for now. Thanks, Balls."

"You owe me, you know."

"Yeah, I know," Miller said, exasperated.

"I can think of one way you can repay me."

"Think again, Balls. I appreciate the favor, but think again."

She disconnected.

"412 South Oak is only a block from the sheriff's office," Wynn said. "He wouldn't need a ride home, and he's already well past it. They're not going there."

"So where?"

"Keep following and we'll find out." Wynn paused a moment. "So, Balls?"

"Ugh, don't start."

"Interesting nickname. Just curious is all," he chided.

"The dude ran into a burning meth house to save a kid who was sleeping. The place could've blown at any minute. In fact, it did, right after he got the kid out. That took balls."

"Impressive," Wynn said.

"It's either that or the fact that he's bald as a cue ball."

Wynn smiled and nodded. She'd gotten him. It was a good tactic to ease the tension. He checked his phone. "They're about ten miles ahead. Looks like they took a right, going north on county road 27."

"Shit," Miller said.

"What?"

"That's the road we came out on when we drove across that field the other day. I'll bet we were close."

"Can't worry about that. Let's focus on now."

"Agreed."

They drove in silence for a few minutes until Wynn saw the red dot appear well left of the county road. "Looks like they turned off," he said. He zoomed in on the map. "Looks like a long driveway. Three buildings at the end."

Wynn waited for the dot to ping again while Miller turned right onto 27.

"How far?" she asked.

"Seven or eight miles."

The dot pinged again right next to one of the buildings on the screen.

"I think they've stopped," Wynn said.

They continued on for another few minutes while the red dot remained stationary on the screen.

Wynn glanced up from his phone. "Look for a driveway on the left."

The road, which had been arrow-straight and flat for the first five miles, slowly curved to the right and climbed a small bluff. It reversed back to the left and then right again in a lazy s-turn switchback as the bluff grew steeper. A thin forest of pine trees appeared on either side of the road and grew thicker as they climbed. As they crested the hill, a dirt driveway snaked away to the west.

"Is that it?" Miller asked.

"Probably." Wynn looked at his phone and saw that the red dot was now almost directly west of them. "Let's go a little further to make sure there's not another one."

They drove another two miles as the road straightened. The pine forest thinned then disappeared, and they found themselves on another flat, grassy plain, a hundred and twenty feet higher than the first one.

"That had to be it," Wynn said. "Turn around. Let's go back and find a place to park. We'll go in on foot."

Miller found a wide spot, and with no other cars coming from either direction, k-turned in the middle of the road and sped back toward the driveway. About a mile out, the trees thickened. Miller pulled to the side and eased down into the ditch, up the other side, and parked between two trees. The SUV was easily visible in the daylight, but might be far enough off the road to avoid being seen once night fell.

Wynn got out, slung the cinch sack over his shoulder, and grabbed the shotgun. Miller met him at the rear of the SUV.

"I'm feeling a little underdressed," she said, looking at Wynn's shotgun, her right hand on her service Glock.

"It's for contingencies only. As long as you've got your phone and Parker's number, that should be all we need."

"Cell service is notoriously spotty out here."

"Check it," he said.

She did. "Two bars."

"Good to go."

He closed the SUV's door and glanced down at his phone, getting his bearings. "This way." He took off walking through the trees.

CHAPTER 37

THE GOING WAS slow as Wynn and Miller hiked through the forest. The late afternoon sun was sinking into early evening, casting long shadows among the trees. The ground was rocky and uneven, littered with fallen trees. Not only did they have to avoid the natural obstacles, but Wynn well remembered his run-in with the biker at the Little Griz campground on Tuesday night. If there were guards on patrol up there, it stood to reason there would be here, also.

When they were due north of the compound, Wynn stopped. "Let's split up. If they do have a lookout, we don't want to make it too easy on them. You wait here and I'll go up another fifty yards. I'll text you. We can both approach with some distance between us."

Miller nodded.

Wynn said, "Go slow, stay hidden, and keep your eyes open. Text me if you see anything."

"Count on it," Miller said.

———

Miller pulled her Glock from its holster and crouched down between two trees to wait.

Five minutes later Wynn texted that he was in position. She started moving slowly south in the direction of the compound, catching an occasional glimpse of Wynn as they moved through the forest.

As she continued, a large barn and horse shed materialized through the trees a hundred yards ahead. Miller got to within fifty yards when her phone vibrated with a text from Wynn: *Hold position. Let's watch a while.*

Miller found a semi-sheltered position in the lee of a large boulder that gave her a good 270-degree view of both Wynn and the compound. Directly in front of her was a medium-sized horse shed with four small windows spaced every eight feet or so.

Twenty-five yards west of the horse shed was a second, much larger barn. She estimated it close to a hundred feet long and sixty feet wide. On one end a set of oversized double doors with a personal entry door faced the horse shed. Other than a small, vertical rectangular window set in the personal door, there were no other windows along either side.

Visible between the two barns and thirty yards south sat a two-story farmhouse. A large porch stretched across the front while two dormers overlooked the driveway as it approached from the east. There was no activity outside and no sign of Nathan Craig or his blue Ford. After a few minutes, her phone buzzed with another text from Wynn: *Anything?*

She typed a quick reply: *No. All quiet.*

Can you see the Ford?

No.

I'm going to circle west. You go east but stay hidden from the driveway.

Ok.

Staying hidden was easier said than done. The sun hung low in the west, largely blocked by the trees, but the occasional beam that did sneak through created an almost spotlight effect when she moved through it. Thirty paces on, she was able to find a shaded position next to a fallen tree that gave her a good view of the house and both barns. She settled in to wait.

————

Wynn had the opposite problem as he moved around the other side of the compound. In those areas where the sun snuck through, he cast a long shadow sure to draw attention each time he moved. Holding the shotgun low, he made his way quickly to the northwest corner of the large barn. He placed his ear to the cement-fiber siding but heard nothing.

He peeked around the end of the building and seeing no one, edged along the side. About twenty feet down he came to a large double door. Getting down on his hands and knees, he put his head to the ground, trying to see under the door, but it extended below the concrete floor, blocking any view inside.

He got to his feet and, remaining low, hustled past the double doors to the personal entry door near the corner. Once again, he put his ear to the door but heard nothing. Slowly, he risked a peek through the window.

Inside, the building was more like an auto service garage than a barn. A long workbench stretched the length of the south wall while the space itself was divided into several service bays. Various vehicles, some parked nose-out, as if ready to go on a moment's notice, occupied most of the bays.

Closest to him was the old red Jeep Cherokee that Davies had been behind when stopped at the construction zone almost a week ago. Further down he saw Nathan's bright blue Ford and next to it sat the white van, the one that used to have *All Season Plumbing* painted on its side. It now read *JT Electrical*. Next to that sat the skeletal remains of what used to be Davies' black Subaru.

Bingo.

Opposite the service bays, what appeared to be a bunkhouse was built inside the barn. A heavy steel door with a padlock was set midway down its length. A betting man would say Davies was in there.

Having seen enough, Wynn backed away and crept to the far corner the barn. From there he darted back into the trees, giving himself some cover from the compound. He looked east to see if he could spot Miller, but she was already gone. He pulled out his phone and sent her a text: *Call Parker. Blue Ford, white van inside. Get FBI here asap.*

Miller's response popped up a moment later: *OK. Johnston or Smitty?*

No. We still don't know if they're involved.

Night rules?

Definitely.

Confident that Parker would soon be on his way, Wynn began to formulate a plan. If he imagined a circle around the compound and put himself in the six o'clock position, that would put Miller at nine and the driveway at ten. If he could make his way counterclockwise to the eleven o'clock spot, he and Miller would have positions on either side of the only way in or out. At that point, there was a good chance they could hold down whoever was in there until Parker and his reinforcements showed up. There was a slight risk that Craig and his crew could make a run for it through the trees in any other direction, but they wouldn't get far on foot. Satisfied, he began to work his way around the compound.

CHAPTER 38

JOHN WORKED LATE at the construction site. There were certain projects you couldn't just abandon because the clock hit five. While Nathan and over half the crew got off early, he and a dozen others were stuck until almost 6:30 getting a culvert secured in place. When he finally got back to his truck in the staging area, he was tired, hungry, and needed a beer. Several, probably. Worst of all, he knew they were going to be moving the "cargo" later, so it was going to be a long night.

He proceeded south out of the staging area for three miles, then turned right onto a gravel road that led off to the west, a more direct route to Tomas's ranch. Ten miles and fifteen minutes later, he came to an intersection with county road 27, where he turned toward the compound. Eight miles later, when he was still a mile away from the long driveway, he noticed a car, a Ford SUV to be exact, parked among the trees, well off the side of the road.

John slowed and pulled over. He looked at the SUV and considered it. Why would someone park here? Maybe an old woman looking for a place to pick berries? Not hardly. A couple of high school kids looking for a private place to romp? He didn't see anyone inside the SUV, or close by. He pulled out his phone and called Tomas.

"Hey. Are you aware we've got a Ford SUV parked in the trees about a mile north of the driveway here on 27?"

"No," said Tomas. "Is there anyone around?"

"I don't see anyone."

"Is the engine warm?"

"Let me check." John got out of his pickup and trudged through the ditch to the front of the SUV. While he walked, he could hear Tomas relaying the situation to someone else in the room. John put his hand on the SUV's hood.

"It's cool. Not ticking or anything. Probably been here a while."

"What's the license number?" Tomas asked.

John backed up a step and read it off.

"Stay there. I'll call you back."

———

Back at the farmhouse, Tomas relayed the number to Craig, who called it in.

"Hey Marjorie," Craig said when he got her on the line. "I need you to run a plate for me."

He gave her the number and heard her tapping on the keyboard.

"That's a Ford Explorer that belongs to a Samantha Miller," Marjorie said. "Hold on, there's more." There was a pause as Marjorie read and connected the dots that Craig already knew. "She's that deputy with Wheaton County that was here on Monday. Which reminds me, that biker that was with her, the one you and the sheriff interviewed yesterday about Lester? He stopped in here a couple of hours ago just after you left asking for you. Did he ever catch up to you?"

"Not yet," said Craig, trying to remain calm, "but I'll find him. Thanks."

He disconnected, then yelled, "Shit! It's Miller and Wynn.

They're probably hiding out in the woods waiting for the feds to get here. We gotta move."

"Calm down," said Tomas. "The closest FBI field office is in Denver. Even if they have people in Sturgis, it's a minimum of two hours for any force to mobilize and get here. We've got time. Besides, I'm not going to let some bitch deputy take us down. You two," he pointed at Tony and Nathan, "Go get the van and the bitches ready to move. Stay with 'em 'til we come over."

Tony and Nathan hustled out the back door while Tomas dialed John.

"It's Wynn and that fucking cop Miller. Get in there, find 'em and take 'em out."

"I'm on it." John ran back to his truck, pulled his Ruger from the glovebox, and set off into the woods.

————

Wynn had only made it a few steps when the back door of the farmhouse burst open. Nathan Craig and another man Wynn hadn't seen before came hustling out and jogged over to the large barn. He ducked down to watch as they crossed the open space between the buildings and disappeared inside. Wynn was torn. On the one hand, he was tempted to creep back to the window to see what they were doing, but knew that would put him out of position should they attempt to leave. His best move was to get around to the southeast side of the house, the eleven o'clock position, to help Miller defend the driveway. Reluctantly, he moved further away into the woods and began tracing a long arc to the south.

————

Miller was anxious as she waited. Parker was still more than ninety minutes away, and it had been almost a half-hour since she'd heard from Wynn and saw the two guys hustle from the house to the large barn. Out on the plains, the sun was dipping onto the horizon, but here in the forest it was all but completely blocked out, creating a dull grayness that made it hard to see. She wished she had something darker to put on. Her khaki uniform top seemed to glow in the withering dusk.

As she'd been doing every few moments, she scanned the forest all around, pausing longer to look south across the driveway, to where she expected Wynn to be showing up any minute.

She still saw nothing.

But she did hear a sound.

Behind her. A branch cracked.

And then she felt something.

A cold steel barrel pushed against the back of her head.

"Don't move," a male voice said.

Miller froze.

"Arms out. Stand up slowly."

Miller did as she was told, still holding the Glock in her right hand.

"Stop. I'll take that." The guy reached from behind and took Miller's gun. "Turn around."

Miller turned. The guy was skinny. Mid-forties. Blond hair turning prematurely gray.

He crouched down and put her gun on the ground behind him, then stood up and motioned to the utility belt at her waist. "Slowly, take those cuffs out and put them on. Behind your back."

Miller reached down and unsnapped the clasp holding her cuffs. She slowly pulled them out. She brought her arms together and used her left hand to snap one of the cuffs onto her right wrist. Then she moved her arms behind her back and balled her left hand into a fist, then used her right hand to secure the remaining cuff.

When she was finished, the man asked, "Where's your boyfriend?"

"Who?"

"The biker. Wynn. Where is he?"

"How would I know? I haven't seen him since I left Sturgis."

"Bullshit. Sit down."

Miller sat on top of the fallen tree she'd been hiding behind moments ago.

The guy pulled out a phone and dialed. "I got the bitch. No sign of the biker. What do you want me to do with her?"

Miller couldn't hear what was being said on the other end of the line.

"She's alive."

More silence as the guy listened, his face turning to a twisted smile. "That she will. Be right there," he said.

The guy disconnected the phone, then reached down to pick up Miller's gun. "How's your Spanish, bitch? Stop in Denver tonight and you'll be in Mexico by this time tomorrow."

Movement from behind caused Miller's eyes to flash to the left. The guy turned to see what she was looking at. His eyes opened wide. Wynn emerged like an apparition from the trees, his arm held high with a softball-sized rock in his hand.

The guy swung the gun in Wynn's direction, but Miller was already moving. She slipped her left hand through the loose cuff and lunged, swinging her right hand with the cuff trailing behind it toward the gun, knocking it from the guy's hand.

Miller's momentum carried her into him as the guy continued to turn toward Wynn. She jumped onto his back and wrapped her arms around his neck, then found the loose end of the cuffs with her left hand and pulled back, tightening the chain against his throat. The hard steel bit into her wrist as she kept the pressure on, the guy suddenly gasping and grabbing at her hands.

As Miller pulled tight, Wynn swung the rock, smashing it against the side of the man's head. The guy dropped to his knees, held up by Miller as she tightened the cuffs around his neck. His arms dropped to his sides, his head rolling to one side. Miller put a knee in the middle of the guy's back, then leaned backward, readjusting her grip as she pulled. She held him up for a long moment until Wynn leaned in beside her.

"I think you got him."

Miller gave one last tug, then released her grip, allowing the body to fall away. She stepped back, breathing heavily, then collapsed onto the log. "Is he dead?"

Wynn knelt and felt for a pulse. "Yeah."

"Good. I hope it fucking hurt. He was going to do the same thing to me they're planning for Davies."

"He had no idea who he was dealing with."

"Thanks to you. How'd you know?"

"I circled around to the south of the driveway. Spotted him when I was looking for you."

"Well," Miller said as she took a key from her belt and removed the cuff. "I'm glad you did. That was way too close."

"It's gonna get closer."

"How so?"

"They're expecting him to bring you out in a few minutes."

"Shit. What should we do?"

"How far away is Parker?"

"At least another hour."

"No choice," Wynn said. "Let's go meet them."

"We have no idea how many there are."

"At least three, probably no more than five or six. If we don't go down there, they're going to get spooked and run. Once they get in a vehicle and get moving, they're going to be hard to stop. Better to keep them locked down here. Hold on."

Wynn walked about ten paces back into the woods. With darkness quickly descending he almost disappeared completely before reappearing with the shotgun in his hand.

Miller looked to the ground and found her gun sitting atop a mound of grass and pine needles. She also found the guy's gun and cell phone, both of which he'd dropped during the struggle. She holstered her Glock and put the Ruger in the back of her jeans, then turned her attention to the guy's phone.

"Maybe we can buy some time and lure them out." She walked over to the guy and held the phone in front of his face. The screen brightened. "Got it."

"Facial recognition?"

"Yep. But he didn't turn on the 'attention aware' feature so he doesn't have to actually look at it."

Miller went to the phone's settings and turned off all the locking features.

"What are you thinking?" Wynn asked.

"He asked where you were, so they already know you're here, but he didn't know where. Let's send them a text saying he's delayed because he's spotted you, too. At least buy us some time."

"Okay."

Miller composed a short message: *Spotted biker. Going after.*

"Looks good," Wynn said.

She hit send.

"Let's move closer," Wynn said. "But keep your eyes peeled. There might be more out here."

"Will do." She pocketed the phone and pulled out her Glock.

———

Inside the farmhouse, Craig had changed out of his uniform and was now dressed in street clothes, peering out the front window. A small handgun, a Sig Sauer P238, was tucked into the back of his pants. For the past thirty minutes, Tomas had been sitting in a chair across the room, quietly contemplating the evening's events. A semi-automatic rifle lay across his knees.

"Where is he?" Craig asked no one in particular.

Tomas's phone pinged with an incoming text message.

"He's delayed. Says he's going after the biker."

"Where? Maybe we can help him," Craig said.

Tomas composed a one-word text: *Where?*

A long minute later his phone pinged again: *S of dr way. 50 yds out. Distract.*

"Wynn's south of the driveway fifty yards out," Tomas said. "John wants us to distract him."

"How are we supposed to do that?" Craig asked.

"Go talk to him."

"What?"

Tomas raised the semi-automatic from his knees and pointed it at Craig. "Go talk to him."

"Don't bullshit me with empty threats, old man," Craig said. "I'm the one keeping the heat off."

"Seems to me you've been outed," said Tomas. "There are only two possibilities. Either they know you're involved, or they don't. If they do know, they might try calling you as a setup. Maybe they would, maybe they wouldn't. But if they don't know, they definitely would have called your Sheriff Johnston right away, who then would have called his most trusted deputy, you. The fact that your phone hasn't rung tells me you've been outed, and therefore have little value. So if you want to stay alive or have any hope of containing this thing," Tomas raised the gun further, "go talk to him."

Craig couldn't argue with the logic.

———

Wynn and Miller were much closer, thirty yards north of the driveway and just inside the tree line, which put them only ten yards from the southeast corner of the horse shed. They had used it as cover as they approached.

"You stay here," Wynn said to Miller. "I'm gonna move closer to the driveway. Let's see what they do."

Holding the shotgun to his shoulder, Wynn slipped through the trees and settled into a position twenty yards further south. Miller ducked down between two pines and alternated her gaze between the house and the barn.

———

Inside the barn, Tony and Nathan had been waiting for the better part of a half-hour. Prepping the van consisted of simply fueling it up, checking the tires, and parking it facing the east doors, ready to go. The women, on the other hand, took a little more effort.

When they first entered, Tony went straight to the bunkhouse, pounded on their door, and yelled, "Ten minutes. Be ready to go!"

When they returned to the bunkhouse, they had taken the women one by one, tied their hands behind their backs, blindfolded them, and put duct tape over their mouths. Then they walked them over to the van where, once inside, they used more zip ties to secure their ankles. Hailey had cooperated fully, but Jessica needed a little persuasion from the stunner They eventually got them both in the van and secured their bindings to metal rings bolted into the van's floor.

Ann, however, was completely useless. Whether it be from the injuries sustained from the lashing last night, or a simple unwillingness to cooperate, she lay unmoving on her bunk. While it was easy enough for Tony to bind her wrists and blindfold her, she couldn't – or wouldn't – walk to the van. With his broken arm, Nathan was little help in carrying her, so Tony hoisted her up to his shoulder and carried her to the van, dumping her alongside the other two.

"Aren't you going to tie her ankles?" Nathan asked as Tony walked away.

"Fuck it. She's not going anywhere," he replied.

Tony went back into the apartment side of the bunkhouse and returned a few minutes later with his own Ruger stuck in the back of his jeans. In his hands he carried a Heckler and Koch MP5 semi-automatic. Over the next half hour, they alternated between keeping an eye on the women, and watching out the window.

"Someone's coming out," Nathan said when the farmhouse's front door opened.

Tony's cell phone pinged with an incoming text from Tomas: *Bitch is down. Wynn in woods south of driveway. Circle north, I'll be south, John east.*

Tony immediately understood. The lady deputy was either dead or captured, while John was approaching Wynn from behind. Tomas was going to circle to the south. He was being told to approach from the north. With Craig facing him head-on from the farmhouse, they'd have him covered from all directions.

"Be ready to move," Tony said to Nathan. He grabbed the MP5 and sprinted out the back door on the west end of the building.

As Tony left the barn, he saw Tomas coming out the back door of the farmhouse thirty yards to his left. They nodded to one another and took off in opposite directions, Tomas south around the farmhouse while Tony went north around the end of the barn. Tony paused at the corner just long enough to grab a quick glimpse down the north side. Seeing nothing, he sprinted east to the corner, where he paused again as he heard Craig's voice calling from the farmhouse porch.

CHAPTER 39

Wʏɴɴ ᴡᴀᴛᴄʜᴇᴅ ғʀᴏᴍ the cover of the trees as deputy Nick Craig, now in civilian clothes but unmistakable due to his bulk, stepped out from the farmhouse door and onto the porch. Craig was facing southeast, in the direction he thought Wynn was hiding.

"Wynn!" Craig called from the porch. "We know you're out there. Come on out. Let's talk about this."

Wynn remained silent. He moved forward a little closer to the clearing, still in front of Craig but widening the angle.

"Come on Wynn, it's over. We've already got Miller. She's going to make us a lot of money down in Mexico. She could make you some, too. Not to mention the brunette bitch. She's a hot little piece. I had a good time with her the other night. No reason you can't, too. Besides, we could use a guy like you. Come on out. Let's talk about it."

Wynn's jaw tightened. *This guy knew all along.*

From the first moment Wynn had seen him in Johnston's office on Monday, he could've stopped it. He could've saved her. Instead, he'd raped her.

This fucker's gonna pay.

"Come on, Wynn," Craig yelled. It was clear he was buying time.

290 KEITH J. WEBER

Wynn scanned the trees to his left and right, looking for any sign of movement. Twenty yards to his right, Miller did the same.

"We're wasting time here." Craig walked down the porch steps into the grass, widening the angle even more. Wynn was now almost a full ninety degrees to his left. "Parker's more than an hour away, Miller's ours and we got more men in the woods than you could possibly see, let alone take out. You've got a choice. Either join us now or die, 'cause we've got to get moving."

Wynn didn't see any movement in the darkness, but on the off chance what Craig said was true, he wanted to focus their attention on him, not risk them finding Miller.

"Where's Miller?" he called out, revealing his general position.

Craig wheeled to his left, peering into the darkness in the direction of Wynn's voice. He swept his eyes through the trees. "You're good, Wynn. Like I said, we could use a guy like you."

"Where's Miller?" Wynn called out again.

"She'll be along shortly. A gal like that isn't going to come easy, so she's either fighting it the whole way, or she's being carried, but she'll be here."

Wynn scanned the forest behind him. For the second time in three days, he wished for a pair of night-vision goggles. He crouched low and moved quickly behind another tree ten feet further back from the clearing.

———

That was all the movement Tony needed.

Moments earlier, when Craig started talking, Tony ran from behind the large barn, across the grass, and into the horse shed. There, he silently opened a window looking directly at Craig and the clearing. Like Craig, he had also been startled when he heard Wynn's voice in the trees just thirty yards away. When Wynn spoke a second time and then shuffled away, Tony spotted him.

He eased the MP5 to his shoulder, sighting down the barrel, its tip extending beyond the window, giving him a clear shot at Wynn.

But also exposing his position to Miller, who sat hidden ten yards away.

Then all hell broke loose.

————

It started with Miller, who put five rounds from her Glock into the side of the shed, two feet behind the exposed tip of the rifle. Three of the rounds hit Tony in the arm, chest, and shoulder. His finger squeezed the trigger of his MP5 as he fell backward, creating a rapid zipper of gunfire that hit the trees above Wynn, and then sailed harmlessly into the night sky.

Wynn dove to the ground. Bullets whistled above his head and small twigs rained down around him. He looked up in time to see Craig running toward the large barn firing the Sig Sauer blindly as he ran. To his right, Miller returned fire.

At the barn, Nathan pushed open the large double doors revealing the white van inside. Craig ran past his brother, jumped behind the wheel, and slammed the transmission into gear.

The hollow click of Miller's Glock reached Wynn's ears when she emptied her magazine toward the barn. He rose to his knees, brought the shotgun to his shoulder, and fired two huge blasts toward Nathan, who fell into the open side door of the van. Tires squealed as the van burst out of the barn, two bodies falling from the cargo area onto the ground.

Wynn was about to open fire on the van's tires when more bullets whistled above his head. They punched into the trees behind him, followed by the unmistakable sound of another MP5.

Tomas had circled the farmhouse and was firing from across the driveway. He appeared at the edge of the trees as the van roared past the farmhouse. Wynn rolled onto his back and fired two quick blasts in Tomas's direction, while Miller slammed her spare magazine into place and returned fire. The van slowed just long enough for Tomas to hop in the open side door and took off down the dirt driveway.

Wynn lay still on his back while Miller crouched thirty feet away as the echoes of the gunfire faded around them. They could hear the van speeding away in the distance but were unsure of their situation. Two bodies lay outside the large barn, illuminated by light spilling from the open double doors. One was squirming slightly while the other was not moving at all. They didn't know the status of the hostile in the horse shed.

"Take cover," he said to Miller.

She made herself as small as possible behind a large tree.

Wynn rose to his knees, found a rock, and tossed it through a window in the shed. The sound of shattering glass was immediately followed by a single shot bursting low through the south wall. He crouched low and ran over to Miller.

"Still alive," she said. "But a pretty weak response."

"Keep an eye on those two." Wynn indicated the bodies by the barn. "I'm gonna go around and take this guy out. When you see me at that corner," he nodded toward the corner of the shed, "count to ten then put a shot through the side. I'll go in and get him, then we can see who those two are."

Miller nodded as Wynn slipped away through the trees. He was no longer concerned about anyone else hiding in the woods, figuring they would have already joined in when the shooting started. The silence now broken only by the sound of crickets resuming their chirping as he jogged around the shed.

He looked around the corner and saw the two figures in front of the barn now both lying still. He thought one of them might be Nathan Craig, the other small by comparison. It could be Davies, but he couldn't tell.

This needs to be over quickly.

Wynn crept down the west wall, past a small door, until he reached the southwest corner. He stepped around the corner and gave Miller a thumbs up, then moved back toward the door while counting slowly. As he hit ten, a shot from Miller's Glock thundered through the night. He yanked the door open and flung himself inside firing three huge blasts in a shallow arc from left to right. Down on one knee, Wynn scanned the dark interior and listened intently for any noise.

As the blasts faded, Wynn's eyes adjusted to the dim light. Twenty feet ahead a skinny figure lay on the ground. It was the Latino guy he'd seen come out of the house with Nathan earlier. It looked like the guy had been sitting, legs out, leaning against a post, but had then slumped to his left, away from Wynn. He wasn't moving.

Keeping his shotgun aimed at the guy's chest, Wynn glanced around the shed looking for other threats. Seeing none, he turned his attention back to the guy, where a large, dark pool was forming beneath the body. The right side of his shirt was tattered and torn, soaked with blood. Miller's initial shots may have incapacitated him, but it was one of Wynn's blasts that finished him off.

The threat now neutralized, Wynn went back outside and signaled for Miller to join him. Together, with guns drawn, they approached the two figures lying in front of the barn.

A cast on the right arm confirmed that the big one was Nathan Craig, his bruised, lifeless eyes stared up to the night sky. Blood pooled into a huge, open cavity where his stomach used to be.

The other was a woman, blindfolded and bound with her hands behind her back. She was breathing but barely moving. Miller rolled her over and removed the blindfold and duct tape. Wynn found a utility knife and cut the zip tie from her wrists. She had fair skin and sandy blond hair cut to just below her shoulders.

Not Jessica Davies.

"See if you can find some water, maybe a washcloth," Miller said.

Wynn hustled back inside and over to the bunkhouse. Past the heavy steel door was a laundry room with a door on either side. The door on the right sat open to a sparse room with four sets of bunk beds and a bathroom. *This is where they were held.* Scanning the bathroom, he found nothing suitable to carry water.

He retraced his steps to the laundry room and crossed through the open door to the studio apartment on the other side. In design, the rooms were mirror images of one another. In furnishings, one was a comfortable living space, the other a prison.

Wynn ran back to the kitchen area and found a large glass and ragged old dish towel. He filled the glass from the sink and wet the towel, then hustled back out to where Miller leaned over the woman. He knelt and handed Miller the wet towel who used it to gently pat the woman's forehead and cheeks.

"It's okay, Ann. You're safe now. We'll take care of you," Miller said softly. Then to Wynn, "Her name's Ann Cowans. She was the first of the two other missing persons I told you about. Been here a week. Davies and the other were taken in the van."

"I'm going after them." Wynn stepped over to Nathan's body and patted down the pockets. He pulled out a large set of car keys, a metallic Ford emblem hanging prominently from the ring.

"Sean, wait. You'll never catch them. Let me call Parker. They're heading to Denver. He can set up a roadblock and catch them before they get there."

"Okay, do it," Wynn agreed. "But make sure they set up south of Cheyenne. From here there are two logical routes, but that's where they merge. We don't know which one they took, but if Parker sets up south of Cheyenne, they'll get them regardless."

"Got it," Miller said. She pulled out her phone and called Parker, giving him all the pertinent details.

In the meantime, Wynn stepped away from Miller into the darkness. He pulled out his own phone and a card from his back pocket. He dialed the number on the card.

When it was answered, he said, "This is Sean Wynn. I need a favor."

CHAPTER 40

WYNN AND MILLER hung up their phones at the same time.

"Parker's a half-hour away," Miller said. "He's coming here but he's got a team from Denver setting up a trap south of Cheyenne. We'll get them."

"That's good, but I'm going anyway. You alright here?" he asked.

"I'll be fine. Who were you talking to?"

"A friend. Calling in a favor. Not sure it'll help, but it can't hurt."

Miller's eyes narrowed. Finally, she said, "Well, be careful."

"You, too."

Wynn jogged through the barn and dragged open the west doors, then ran back and climbed into Nathan's bright blue Ford. He backed it out of the bay, then pulled out of the barn, turning a tight U-turn between the barn and the farmhouse before speeding past Miller down the driveway.

A mile later he faced his first decision. Left, to the north and at least fifteen miles to the nearest highway, or right, to the south, only seven miles to Highway 18.

Easy decision.

He turned right.

Five minutes later, the next decision wasn't so easy. Left to Linert, and then south toward Cheyenne on a two-lane state highway, or right, toward Prairie Junction, and a straight shot south on the fast-moving interstate.

He turned left.

Eight minutes after that, he was driving past the truck stop café when his phone rang.

"Yeah."

"You're in luck. We have a crew in Cheyenne. They're moving," the voice on the other end said.

"Good," Wynn replied. "Remember, they need to cover both routes north of Cheyenne. The target won't want to stop so you may have to make them. And one of them is likely to flash a badge, but ignore it. He's dirty. If you get them, take them someplace remote and sit on them. Text me the coordinates. I'll be there as soon as I can."

"You got it," the voice replied, then disconnected.

Wynn powered the Ford south of Linert on the two-lane highway. Finally, a stretch of road he hadn't been on this week.

———

Craig fought back tears as he drove. The sight of his little brother's chest, blooming red as he tried to jump into the van, had been replaying over and over through his mind for more than an hour. Craig wasn't sure if Nathan fell out of the van on his own, or whether that bitch Ann, who had somehow gotten loose, had pushed him out. Regardless, he'd seen enough gunshot wounds to know Nathan was dead. Whether it happened before he fell out of the van or after didn't matter. He was gone.

He looked over at Tomas, sitting quietly in the front passenger seat, drifting in and out of consciousness. Wynn had gotten off two blasts of his shotgun toward Tomas, and one of them had somehow found its mark. Tomas's upper torso was peppered with small holes, as was his face and forehead. Miraculously, he was still functioning. Rumor was Tomas had an extra thick skull. Something about getting bashed in the head with a baseball bat when he was younger. Maybe it was true. He looked like he should be dead, but he was still talking. At least he was two minutes ago.

The two girls lay behind him in the cargo area, but even that was a problem. They had taken three girls from the Mexican traffickers, but now had only two to deliver in return. They wouldn't like that. Maybe he could stop in Cheyenne or Fort Collins and find a third before reaching Denver. He was forty-five minutes from Cheyenne. Maybe he could come up with a plan before then.

Shit, who am I kidding? he thought. He'd never even participated in an abduction, other than to stop traffic, let alone tried to pull one off by himself. That wasn't his role. His job was information. Tell Tomas what the authorities were doing, and when and where it was safe to move the merchandise.

But he did have a gun.

And a badge.

Maybe grabbing someone wouldn't be that hard after all. He started working through various scenarios. Where would be the most likely place to find someone? How could he get them alone? How would he get them into the van, without them screaming their head off at the sight of Tomas and the two girls? Lots of details, but he could work it out.

Craig was so preoccupied with his planning, he didn't notice the brake lights flare on a couple of motorcycles that passed him in the opposite direction.

But a few minutes later he did see the bright orange glow of several flares lighting up the road almost a mile ahead. He strained to see beyond the headlight's beam, but it was too far away.

"Tomas," he said.

No reply.

"Tomas!" He reached over and pushed roughly on his shoulder.

Still no response. Craig couldn't tell if he was unconscious or dead.

"Shit," he muttered as he checked his rearview mirror.

There were two motorcycles about a hundred yards back. No other vehicles in sight.

Ahead, the scene was becoming clearer. A motorcycle was down in the middle of the road. Several others were parked all around, blocking the entire road. Close to a dozen people milled about in the glow of the flares.

He slowed as he approached, looking for a path through, but the ditch was the only option. He wasn't sure the van would make it. His headlights lit up the first of the bikers, a grey ace of spades on each of their backs.

Craig slowed and turned on his hazard lights and flashed his headlights. He reached into his pocket and pulled out his badge as one of the bikers broke from the group and approached.

Craig rolled down his window and held out his badge. "Guys!" he called out. "I need you to clear a path. Police emergency."

The guy who was approaching was now only a few feet away. "You a cop?" he asked.

"Sheriff's deputy. I've got an injured man here. I need to get to Cheyenne. You need to clear a path."

The biker pulled a gun from behind his back. "I don't think so." He stuck the gun through the open window, into Craig's face.

At the same time, the passenger door flung open and a second biker appeared in the doorway, also pointing a gun.

Craig was stunned. "What the..."

"Shut up!" the first biker yelled as he yanked open Craig's door. "Get out!"

"I'm a cop, asshole," Craig said. "You don't want to do this."

"Makes me want to do it more. Get out."

Craig put the van in park and slid out, holding his hands in the air. A third guy jumped into the now vacant driver's seat as the first marched Craig around the van to the passenger side.

"Shit, man," the second biker said as they came around. He indicated Tomas sitting slumped in the passenger seat, dried blood all over his shirt and face. "This guy looks dead."

"I told you," Craig said. "Police emergency."

The first man used his gun to push Tomas's head to the side. There was no response.

"Too late for this guy. The emergency's passed."

He stepped back and once again faced Craig. "Open it," he ordered, indicating the sliding side door.

"You really don't want to do this," Craig said.

The biker pushed Craig up against the van and jammed his gun into Craig's cheek. "I really do," he said. "Now open it."

The biker stepped back as Craig opened the door, revealing Jessica and Hailey lying bound and blindfolded inside.

"This just gets more and more interesting," the biker said. "Get in. All the way back."

The second biker pointed his gun at Tomas and asked, "What do you want to do with this guy?"

"Take him with us," the first biker responded. "Let the man decide what to do with him."

The second biker closed the passenger door on Tomas, while the first biker climbed into the van and closed the door behind him. He sat facing backward against the passenger seat, back-to-back with Tomas. He kept his gun pointed at Craig, who sat against the rear doors of the van. Jessica and Hailey lay between them. Jessica remained silent, while Hailey whimpered through her gag.

"Let's go."

The driver pulled the transmission lever into gear and accelerated away, a string of bikers both ahead and behind. The flares had been extinguished, leaving small burn marks on the pavement as the only sign they were ever there.

CHAPTER 41

WYNN HAD BEEN driving south for more than an hour when his phone finally rang. He picked it up on the first ring.

"Yeah?"

"We got them," the voice on the other end said. "Sending you the location now."

Wynn waited for the ping of an incoming text before remembering he'd put his phone on silent mode back in the woods. He looked at the screen and saw the text with the location coordinates. "Got it. Hold on."

He tapped on the coordinates link and a map app opened.

"I'm close. Let them know I'll be there in ten minutes. And thanks."

Wynn clicked the "Start Route" button and then slowed as the electronic voice told him to prepare to turn. He turned left onto a dirt road, and followed it more than a mile back into the dark prairie. About a half-mile from where he expected to find the Dead Aces crew, a pair of bikers stood in the middle of the road, their bikes parked along the side.

He coasted to a stop and buzzed down the window as one of the bikers approached.

"Name?" the biker asked.

"Sean Wynn."

"Your contact with the Aces?

"Damon Styre."

The biker nodded and stepped back. Wynn rolled slowly past.

As he rounded a turn, a faint glow appeared on the road ahead. Where the map told him Damon's crew should be waiting, but there was nothing visible. No bikers, no van. Nothing.

He tensed as he approached, pulling the Glock from his vest.

But then relaxed.

The Dead Aces weren't dumb.

They'd stopped in a bowl where the road dipped down into another dry creek bed, the wide arroyo providing the perfect cover below the flat prairie. To the left, ten Harleys formed a wide circle around the van, a pair of Harley headlights crisscrossing the open space and dimly illuminating the scene. The side door of the van was open, the interior shrouded in darkness. Craig was on his knees near the back of the van with his thick fingers laced behind his head. A biker stood beside him with a gun.

Wynn eased the Ford down into the sandy arroyo and parked off to the right. A big man wearing a skull cap and leather vest approached.

"You Wynn?" he asked.

"That's me."

"I'm Max. Damon said we owed you."

Wynn glanced across at Craig. "Not anymore you don't. Anyone else in the van?"

"Two girls tied up in the back, and a dead guy in front."

"Dead?"

"Looks like he was hit by a shotgun. Messed up pretty good."

Wynn nodded, not at all sure he was satisfied with that answer.

"The girls?" he asked.

"They're alive."

He nodded again. "Let's go take a look."

Wynn ignored Craig as they walked through a break in the bikes and over to the van. Their long shadows cast the area into near-total darkness as they passed in front of the headlight beams. Max stood back as Wynn approached the passenger door. An older Latino man, with dried blood covering his shirt and face, slumped against the window.

Wynn opened the door.

Tomas swung his right arm up and jammed a Ruger beneath Wynn's chin.

"Not yet, fucker," Tomas said.

The sound of guns being drawn and slapped into ready position filled the air. Ten guns from around the circle pointed at Wynn and Tomas.

"Here's what we're going to do," Tomas said as he slid out of the van and leaned back against the doorframe. His voice was raspy and weak, his breathing labored. But still, it didn't take much to pull a trigger.

"They're going to let my friend go," Tomas wheezed. "You and I are going to get in the back, and we're going to drive out of here."

"Not gonna happen," Wynn said. "These guys just met me. I'm not one of them. They could give a shit if you blow my head off. Ain't that right, Max?"

Max nodded. "Take the shot," he said.

"See? I told you."

Tomas stared hard at Max, then darted his eyes around the circle, his expression transforming from confident to confused.

"Take. The shot," Max said again.

A thunderous gunshot exploded as Tomas's head erupted into a bright red mess. Bone, blood, and brain matter splattered across Wynn's face as the gun that had been held to his chin fell harmlessly, along with Tomas's now nearly decapitated body, slowly to the ground.

As the initial blast faded, Wynn looked to his left and saw one of the bikers sighting down the smoking barrel of an MP5.

Max hadn't been talking to Tomas.

Wynn nodded a quick thanks to the shooter when a commotion came from behind. He glanced back to see the biker who had been covering Craig sprawled on the ground. Craig was gone.

Wynn rushed over, blood covering the downed biker's face.

"Fucker broke my nose!"

"You're lucky it's no worse." Wynn glanced around the ground after seeing the guy's hands were empty. "Where's your piece?"

Max arrived just in time to hear the guy say, "He took it."

Wynn and Max exchanged a look. Max turned around and took charge. "The big asshole's our target! He's armed and desperate. Bear! You and Mick get back out to the main road. Make sure he doesn't pick up a ride. Tell Shack and Collins to spread out and watch the dirt road. The rest of you, if you've got a light, grab it, then form up right here, twenty feet apart. We're gonna flush him out! You've got thirty seconds!"

As the bikers burst into a hive of activity, Wynn and Max exchanged a look. Max nodded toward the van. Wynn used his shirt-tail to wipe Tomas's blood off his face as he crawled inside next to the girls. He removed the blindfold and duct tape from the mouth of the brunette.

"Jessica?" he asked.

She blinked to adjust her vision, then looked at him with frightened but hopeful eyes.

"Jessica Davies?"

She paused, then nodded tentatively.

"Hang tight. It's almost over."

Jessica closed her eyes and trembled as tears streamed down her face.

Wynn jumped out of the van and got a knife from a passing biker then climbed back in and cut them free. "Stay down and sit tight. This is the safest place for you right now."

He crawled forward and pulled the keys from the ignition, then stuffed them in his pocket as he climbed out the side door. Max had the Aces lined up and already moving into the tall grass.

Wynn walked a few steps from the van, pulled out his phone, and called Miller. She picked up on the second ring.

"Sean! Where are you? Are you okay?"

"I got them," he said, relief heavy in his voice. "Davies and another girl. They're safe. I'm gonna send you their location. Have Parker send his guys to pick them up."

"Oh my God! That's great! How did you find them?"

"Luck and favors. Hold on."

Wynn sent Miller a text with their location.

"Where is that?" she asked.

"Thirty or forty miles north of Cheyenne. Have Parker get his men moving. These girls have had a rough night."

"What about Craig?"

Wynn turned and scanned the clearing. Only he and Max remained. "Yet to be determined." He punched the button, ending the call.

He put the phone back in his pocket and walked over to Max. "The FBI will be here within the hour."

"We can't be here when they show up."

Wynn nodded. Stayed silent while he thought. "Call 'em back. Leave me one guy and the rest of you can leave."

"You sure?"

"I'm sure."

Max walked to the edge of the arroyo, fired his gun three times into the air, then whistled loudly. "Bring it in!"

A few minutes later the bikers emerged from the dark.

"We're done here!" Max called out. "Feds are coming. Load 'em up!"

The Aces fired up their bikes and rumbled away, taking the little bit of light that came from their headlamps with them.

Max stayed behind. "What's the plan?"

"He needs wheels," Wynn said. "He can hide in the dark but in five hours the sun will come up and he'll be a sitting duck. My guess is a big guy like that never bothered with cardio, so at best he'll get no more than twenty miles away. Probably half that. Nowhere to hide and he knows it. He heard your guys leave, which means he's sneaking back to us right now."

"What do you need me to do?"

Wynn glanced back at the van. Jessica and the other girl stood in the open side door, watching. "Just sit in the van, protect those two."

"Decoy?"

Wynn shrugged in the moonlight. "And protection."

"He'll know it's a trap."

"With just two of us, he'll like his chances."

"Where will you be?"

"Close."

Max nodded. "Then get to it."

They walked over to the van. "Jessica, this is Max. The FBI is on their way. He's going to stay with you until I get back."

"Where are you going?" Jessica asked.

"Don't worry. I won't be far."

Max settled into the open side door as Wynn jogged over to Nathan's pickup and grabbed the shotgun and cinch sack. He rolled the windows down and left the keys sitting on the dash, then scrambled up the embankment and disappeared in the tall grass. He kept low as he circled to the left, finally settling in just off the dirt road.

From his vantage point, Wynn had a good view of Max and the van, parked eighty feet away and slightly to his right. The pickup sat a mere forty feet to his left. Max's Harley was parked ten feet in front of the van and the other Harley was parked—

There shouldn't be another Harley.

A sense of impending dread welled up as he waited patiently, hidden in the tall grass.

Within ten minutes his patience was rewarded, exactly as he feared.

Craig emerged from the tall grass on the other side of the arroyo, his arm wrapped around the neck of one of the Aces, using him as a human shield as he pushed him along.

"Hey, fat boy," Craig called out to Max. "Toss your gun into the grass and get out here where I can keep an eye on you."

Max tossed his gun and stepped away from the van.

"Over here," Craig said.

Max walked over and stood in front of Craig.

"Turn around. On your knees."

When Max did as instructed, Craig said. "Wynn! I know you're out there! I'm getting tired of this shit. You've got five seconds to show yourself or I'm blowing this bastard away."

Wynn stuffed the Glock in the back of his jeans, slipped off the holster and called out, "If I show myself, you're going to kill us all anyway, so what's the point?"

"If you don't, he dies right now."

Wynn racked the shotgun, the sound loud and unmistakable.

"And so will you."

Wynn paused, waiting for some response. When none came, he said, "Looks like we've got a stalemate. The problem for you is that Parker and the FBI are on their way. I'm willing to let them sort it out. Are you?"

Craig remained silent.

Gotta get Max and the girls out of here. "Tell you what." Wynn stood up and sighted down the barrel as he walked down the embankment, coming to a stop sixty feet away on the opposite side of the wash. "Why don't you let Max and his friend drive the van out of here, then you and I can settle this man-to-man."

"A Ruger against a shotgun? I don't think so."

Wynn stepped forward, readjusted his grip to steady the shotgun with one hand, then reached behind his back and pulled out the Glock. In a flash, he dropped the shotgun and pulled the Glock into a two-handed grip.

"Is this better?"

Craig hesitated, then nodded to Max, who stood up.

Wynn kept the Glock trained on Craig while he reached into his pocket, retrieved the keys, and tossed them to Max.

While Max walked around the van and climbed in behind the wheel, Craig shuffled slowly to his left, keeping the biker in front of him until they were both standing behind Max's Harley.

Max pulled the van forward until the rear bumper was even with Craig. He rolled down the window. "You scratch my bike, I'll come back and kill you."

The corners of Craig's lips curled as he shoved the biker away and unloaded three shots toward Wynn, then ducked behind the bike. Wynn dropped and rolled, hesitating to return fire until he saw the biker jump in the side door. Max hit the gas and spun out, sending a cloud of sand and pebbles flying toward Craig.

Wynn got to his feet and raced up the embankment, dropping to his stomach as Craig sent three more bullets speeding in his direction. Wynn returned fire, sending sparks flying off the Harley as the nine-millimeter rounds ricocheted off the chrome engine.

The van's taillights sped away down the dirt road as Wynn and Craig blasted shots back and forth. Rock chips flew into Wynn's face as a shot bounced off a boulder next to him. He rolled and returned fire.

Once.

Twice.

He pulled the trigger a third time, but nothing happened. The trigger stuck, no longer able to move either forward or back. Wynn rolled onto his back, ejected the magazine, and tapped the gun against a rock. Pulled the trigger again. *Jammed.*

He rolled onto his stomach and saw Craig leap up and run toward Nathan's pickup, firing wildly as he ran.

Within a few steps, Craig's gun clicked instead of fired. He dropped it and continued sprinting for the truck.

Wynn jumped up and raced down the embankment, catching up to Craig just as he reached the truck. Wynn shoved him hard, sending the bigger man headfirst into the tailgate as Wynn sailed past.

Craig dropped to the ground and crawled to his knees. Wynn skidded to a stop and came back, launching a huge roundhouse kick that caught Craig square in the jaw and sent him spiraling into the dirt.

Wynn stepped back, not wanting to get into a brawl with this guy. With their difference in size, Wynn couldn't afford to let Craig grab him.

To his credit, Craig kept trying to get up, but every time he got to his knees, Wynn darted in and tagged him with a jab or a kick that sent him back to the ground. Again and again, Craig tried to rise, only to have Wynn strike him down.

After what felt like the twentieth time, Craig finally stayed down, face in the dirt, moaning, moving slowly. Wynn looked around for the shotgun, then realized with a sudden cold terror, that Craig was lying on top of it, rolling over, bringing it around, pointing it straight at him.

Wynn's mind raced. Could he get to Craig before he pulled the trigger? *Doubtful.* Jump behind the truck? *Maybe.*

Three blasts in quick succession came from Wynn's left.

Craig stopped. The shotgun fell from his hands. He looked past Wynn, then flopped backward.

Jessica stood twenty feet away, a smoking Glock in her hand.

Wynn glanced back at Craig. Two dark stains were growing on his chest, another on his cheek.

"Is he dead?" Jessica asked.

Wynn stepped over to Craig's body. His eyes stared blankly at the sky. "Yeah. He's dead. It's over."

Jessica lowered the gun. Wynn walked over and took it from her hand, her body trembling uncontrollably. Her knees buckled and he eased her to the ground.

Wynn settled in beside her as they both lay back, exhausted.

"Where'd you get the gun?" Wynn asked.

"Max gave it to me when we were waiting in the van."

"I saw you drive away."

"I jumped out."

Wynn paused for several beats. "Why?"

Jessica laughed, releasing some tension. "I don't really know."

Wynn let out a heavy breath. "Well, I'm sure glad you did."

They lay in silence for a few minutes until Wynn heard a car coming up the road. He sat up as Max pulled the van down into the wash, its headlights stopping on Wynn and Jessica. Max and the biker who'd been Craig's hostage got out. Hailey also jumped out and ran to Jessica.

"You guys all right?" Max asked.

Wynn nodded toward Jessica. "Thanks to her."

The biker had continued past Wynn and stood over Craig's body. "Better than this guy."

Max looked around. "Damon's gonna want to know. Are we all square?"

"All square," Wynn said.

"In that case, we'll get out of here. Before the FBI shows up."

"You were never here."

Max shook Wynn's hand, then went over to his bike and fired it up. It was loud. Real loud. He pulled up beside Wynn as the other biker rode away. "There's a bullet hole in the pipe."

"My bad. Bill me," Wynn said.

"Count on it." Max smiled, eased out the clutch and rumbled off.

Wynn lay back and looked up at the night sky. The sound of Max's pipes faded in the distance. The stars were brilliant and bright and endless. A cool breeze swayed through the tall grass.

Jessica and Hailey held each other.

Eventually, Jessica asked, "What now?"

"The FBI should be here any minute."

As if on cue, sirens sounded in the distance.

CHAPTER 42

Sunday

Two days later, Wynn was once again sitting at the bar at The Gilded Queen in Sturgis.

Alone.

Parker hadn't been the first agent to arrive as he sat in the sandy arroyo with Jessica, Hailey, and the two dead bodies. The ones who did took one look at him, and promptly cuffed him and sat him in the back of their cruiser. When Parker finally showed up, they removed the cuffs, but he was a long way from free. After more than an hour of questioning, and a solemn promise to come in to Cheyenne the next day, Parker had one of his agents give Wynn a ride back to Linert, where he picked up his bike from the lot behind the diner.

From there, Wynn turned off his phone and rode three hours north back to Sturgis. The eastern sky was beginning to lighten by the time he made it back to the Boulder Canyon Motel Inn. The room had been cleaned but his duffle appeared untouched, exactly where he'd left it. He put the "Do Not Disturb" sign outside the door, stripped off his clothes and took a quick shower, then crawled naked into bed. He slept until late afternoon.

When he woke, he was famished. He took another hot shower to make sure there were no more of Tomas's remnants in his hair, then dressed in clean clothes from his duffle.

Pulling the leather vest from the back of the chair, he noticed a large patch of dried blood and dozens of tiny specks of other material he'd prefer not to think about. He grabbed the liner from one of the trash cans and stuffed the vest and all the other clothes he'd been wearing into the bag, then dropped the whole thing into the motel trash bin as he walked out to his bike.

He rode into town, and wandered back to the booth where he and Miller had gotten their vests on Tuesday night. It was the last weekend of the rally. The whole downtown area was packed with bikers and partiers reveling in their last hurrah. It also meant the vendors were running low on stock. They didn't have the same vest he'd bought with Miller, but he was able to find a suitable alternative. He bought it, tore off the tags right there in the booth, and put it on before heading back out to the street in search of a meal and a beer.

He picked up an event schedule along the way and leafed through it while sipping a Corona at a bar overlooking Main Street. The concert lineup at the Grizzly Butte looked interesting. Maybe he'd go out there.

The servers apparently also knew it was the last weekend of the rally and responded by minimizing their clothing in hopes of maximizing their tips. The same bartender who wore the black leather corset and cat-ears earlier in the week, had ditched the corset in favor of a flesh-colored string bikini. She still wore the cat ears and added a tail, but beyond that, she looked naked. Luckily, she had the body to pull it off, as proven by the lewd stares from around the bar. When she brought him his order, a ten-ounce Ribeye, she asked if he needed anything else, with a look and a tone that suggested much more than steak sauce.

Forty-five minutes later he put two twenties down on a thirty-dollar tab and headed out to the Grizzly Butte. As he passed Fort Meade, he wondered if Graciela and the two other girls were still there, or if they'd been moved somewhere else. He hoped they'd be reunited with their families soon.

It was still early, so he rode past the Grizzly Butte, the familiar melancholy of a post-operation letdown driving him on. He wanted to get a look at the house where the raid went down Tuesday night, so he rode past the grass parking lot and open fields, up into the wooded hills. As before, the long, straight road turned to twisty curves as lengthy driveways appeared every quarter mile or so.

The makeshift campground was still there on the east, although now with a few empty spaces. Wynn rode up the long driveway, through the tents, just as he had on Tuesday. Yellow police tape blocked access as it rose up the small hillside into the thicket of trees. A cop decked out in full battle attire, including a bulletproof vest and automatic rifle, stood in the middle of the road at the top of the hill.

Wynn could practically hear Parker's voice in his head. *Move along folks, nothing to see here.*

He turned around and rode back to the Grizzly Butte, this time pulling into the grass lot and walking across the street. He bought a wrist band and went in.

Once again, rather than go straight into the amphitheater, Wynn circled to the left and came up to the central intersection where he and Miller had waited four nights earlier. He walked through the intersection to where the rows of RVs were parked and went down the fourth row.

The fifth wheel was gone. A thirty-six-foot RV was in its place with eight or ten people gathered around a portable barbeque outside. They seemed to be enjoying themselves.

Wynn walked past the group, cut up between two RVs, and went back to the amphitheater. Inside, he passed a beer stand where two Dead Aces were next in line. He strolled over and pulled out his wallet as they stepped up.

"Hey guys. This round's on me," he said.

They looked at him, suspiciously.

"Why?" one of them asked.

"Is Damon here?"

"Who's asking?"

"Tell him Sean Wynn says thanks."

"You're Wynn?" Clearly, they'd heard what happened.

Wynn shrugged as he handed the cashier a twenty.

"You should come join us," the nameless Ace said.

"Maybe later. Just tell him thanks."

"Will do. And thanks." The guy saluted with his beer, then both Aces turned and walked away.

Wynn walked to the end of the line and waited to buy his own beer, then found a relatively quiet place to stand back and watch the band. Within moments, his eyes instinctively scanned the crowd. While there were lots of people, nothing struck him as out of the ordinary. No pairs of men, furtively checking out the ladies; no young women approaching groups of strange men.

Parker's voice once again sounded in his head. *Move along folks, nothing to see.*

As the band was finishing its last song, Wynn sensed a large presence appear beside him.

"My guys tell me you handled yourself well last night," Damon said.

Wynn shrugged, "Couldn't have happened without your help."

"Glad to even the score. Did you get back what they took from you?"

"Yeah. We got it back. But it was never really mine."

"It seldom is." Damon paused. "You still not riding with anyone?"

"Nope."

"The offer's still open. Why don't you hang out with us tonight, get to know a couple of the guys, then decide?"

"Won't matter," Wynn said. "You could all be saints or sinners or just my kind of guys, but I'm not the club type."

"Ha," Damon laughed softly. "We don't have any saints. Plenty of sinners and a few assholes, but I hear you. Why don't you hang with us anyway? You might rub off on a few of the guys. It'd be good for them."

So Wynn did. He hung with the Dead Aces throughout the concert, and then was coerced to tag along as they went back to their cabins to continue the party until almost dawn. They swapped stories about various misadventures they'd had while riding, and he made up stories of his adventures during his time with MARSOC. His real stories were classified.

Regardless, it was a chance to normalize. Socialize. Build camaraderie and hear stories about other people's lives. It was the reason he came to Sturgis in the first place.

But by 4:00 a.m., it was time to call it a night. He said his goodbyes and shook hands all around, then rode back to his motel and again slept until early afternoon.

He'd showered and dressed and went into town to take in a few of the last races and stunt riding exhibitions, but by Sunday evening, the rally was winding down, and he once again found himself sitting alone at the bar in The Gilded Queen.

A woman sat down next to him.

"You turned off your phone," Miller said. She was wearing the deep V-neck t-shirt with the lace sleeves. She looked good.

"Needed a little downtime," Wynn said.

Miller nodded. "That's what I told Parker. Figured you'd need it. But he was pissed you didn't come in as promised. He wants to see you tomorrow. Fill in a few gaps."

"Won't be here," Wynn said.

"That's disappointing," Miller said, not referring to the meeting with Parker.

"What gaps?"

"Little things," she said with mild sarcasm. "Like who were those bikers that rescued Jessica and the other gal, Hailey? How'd they know to stop the van? Who actually shot Craig and that other guy? Where are the weapons? Just little things."

"Can't help with any of that," Wynn lied. "I saw some headlights off in the distance, followed the dirt road and found the van. That's when I called you."

"That's it? That's your story?"

Wynn looked her in the eye. "As far as Parker is concerned, that's all I know."

Miller paused. "Fair enough," she said. "I'll let him know you don't have anything new to add."

"Thanks."

They sat in silence for a few moments. Miller looked over her shoulder, then turned back to Wynn.

"There's someone here who wants to see you," she said.

"Who's that?"

Instead of responding, Miller waved someone over. Wynn turned in his seat as two women approached.

One was Jessica Davies. The other, Wynn assumed, was Davies' sister.

Jessica was wearing jeans, a t-shirt, and a baggy jean jacket. She was cleaned up, but not wearing any makeup. As she approached, her demeanor was cautious. When she saw Wynn, she visibly relaxed and recognition spread across her face.

"You," she said as she stopped in front of him. Miller arched a knowing eyebrow.

"I don't believe we've formally met." Wynn extended his hand. "I'm Sean Wynn."

"Jessica Davies," she said, taking his hand.

"I wanted to thank you," Jessica said. "Deputy Miller here says you were key in rescuing me. Not just the other night, but all week."

"Glad to see you're all right."

"If half of what she says is true, I owe you my life."

"I think we're even. Besides, don't believe everything you hear," Wynn said. "I'm just happy you're okay."

"Well, I will be," she said quietly. She paused a moment then continued, "Everything's kind of jumbled. I... I have a lot of questions." She glanced at Miller, then back to Wynn. "Some things are coming back to me, but others aren't. I understand some of the things that happened, but not everything."

She paused again, then, "Would it be alright if I could get your phone number? I mean, if things don't come back and I have questions. Would it be okay if I called you?"

Wynn gave her his number.

"Thank you," she said.

There was an awkward pause as no one knew what else to say.

"Well, thanks again," Jessica finally said.

"You're very welcome."

Her sister tugged gently on Jessica's jacket as she turned to leave, but Jessica shrugged her hand away and stepped forward, wrapping her arms around Wynn's shoulders in a huge embrace.

"Thank you," she whispered tearfully as she kissed his cheek.

"It's okay," he whispered back.

They held each other for a long moment before Jessica finally stepped back, turned, and followed her sister toward the street.

"Another fan," Miller said.

"A guy gets lucky every now and then."

"So, you're leaving tomorrow?"

"Yup," Wynn replied. "You?"

"Don't have to be back at work 'til Tuesday," Miller said. "I kind of like this biker scene. Thought I'd stick around tonight." She looked him in the eyes. "Maybe a gal can get lucky, too."

--- THE END ---

For more Sean Wynn thrillers, including a free short story, visit
www.keithjweber.com.

Dear Reader,

If you enjoyed *Night Rules*, please let your fellow action/adventure/thriller readers know by telling your friends about it and/or leaving a review at Amazon.com or wherever you downloaded the book. Your review will help other readers discover Sean Wynn and allow me, a grateful author, to continue to tell his story. Select reviewers may also be part of the Sean Wynn "Advance Team," with early access to unreleased novels as well as special content and events. As always, I too, would love to hear from you. If you have comments, ideas, or would just like to talk about books, writing, or motorcycles, feel free to reach out. You can reach me via my website at:

www.keithjweber.com

With Gratitude,

Keith

ALSO CURRENTLY AVAILABLE

Intentional, the 2023 Grandmaster Award Finalist in the Clive Cussler Adventure Writer's Competition, follows Sean Wynn as he discovers his wife's death may not have been an accident, and seeks answers—and vengeance—from those responsible.

The Interviews, a Sean Wynn short story. Special Agent Mark Ruiz needs help with a case—a bad one. Is Sean Wynn the right guy to help? Maybe talking with the people who know him best will shed some light on just who is Sean Wynn.

Sean Wynn returns in late 2024!

A woman's been murdered, a man's been kidnapped, and pieces of him are being mailed to his parents. But the kidnappers don't want money; they want a boy. The problem? The boy's been dead for seven years. Can Sean Wynn find the man while there's still something left to save?

ACKNOWLEDGMENTS

Writing is a solitary activity, but creating a book cannot be done without the help of countless others. In this case, that includes Lynne Bulmer, Veronica Falk, Josie Grey, Mary-Theresa Hussey, Laura Ingle, Bette Kosmolak, Carrie Lange, William Nuessle, Dave Pasquantonio, Juan Rangel, James Snell, Carly Stephens, and Stacey Sweeney. Many, many thanks to all of you.

ABOUT THE AUTHOR

Keith J. Weber is a long-time writer, short-time author. After spending decades writing everything from advertising copy to magazine articles and financial education, his debut fiction novel *Night Rules,* along with its sequel, *Intentional,* were both released in 2024. An avid motorcyclist, Keith enjoys riding the majestic mountains of Colorado as well as the magical Black Hills of South Dakota. On a Friday or Saturday night, you may even find him strumming a guitar with his band at a local brewery.

www.ingramcontent.com/pod-product-compliance
Lightning Source LLC
Chambersburg PA
CBHW020905200626
46814CB00001BA/181